PENGUIN

FRAGMENTS

OF THE

LOST

FRAGMENTS
OF THE
LOST

MEGAN
MIRANDA

PENGUIN BOOKS

PENGUIN BOOKS

UK I USA I Canada I Ireland I Australia
India I New Zealand I South Africa

Penguin Books is part of the Penguin Random House group of companies
whose addresses can be found at global.penguinrandomhouse.com.

www.penguin.co.uk
www.puffin.co.uk
www.ladybird.co.uk

First published in the USA by Crown Books for Young Readers, an imprint of
Random House Children's Books, a division of Penguin Random House LLC, 2017
First published in Great Britain by Penguin Books 2018

001

Set 10.67/16 pt in Berling
Printed in Great Britain by Clays Ltd, St Ives

A CIP catalogue record for this book is available from the British Library

ISBN: 978–0–241–34442–2
International paperback (Australia) ISBN: 978–0–241–34444–6

All correspondence to:
Penguin Books
Penguin Random House Children's
80 Strand, London WC2R 0RL

For A & J

PART ONE

The Fragments

A Blue Door

There's no light in the narrow stairway to the third floor. There's no handrail, either. Just wooden steps and plaster walls that were probably added in an attic renovation long ago. The door above remains shut, but there's a sliver of light that escapes through the bottom, coming from inside. He must've left the window uncovered.

The door looks darker than the walls of the stairway, but it's hard to tell from this angle, without light, that it's blue. We painted it during the summer from a half-empty can he'd found in the garage, a color called Rustic Sea.

"A complicated color for a complicated door," he joked. But it turned out to look more like denim than anything else.

He stepped back after applying the first stroke, wrinkled his nose, wiped the back of his hand against his forehead. "My feelings on this color are also very complicated."

There was a smudge of Rustic Sea over his left eye. "I love it," I said.

I reach for the door now, and I can almost smell the fresh paint, feel the summer breeze coming in from the open window to help air it out. We painted it all the way around—

front and back and sides—and sometimes, the door still sticks when you pull it open. Like the paint dried too thick, too slowly.

There's a speck of paint on the silver doorknob that I've never noticed before, and it makes me pause. I run my thumb over the roughness of the spot, wondering how I missed this.

I take a slow breath, trying to remember the room before I see it, to prepare.

It's got four walls, a closet, slanting ceilings before they meet at a flat strip overtop. There's a fan hanging from the middle of that strip, the kind that rattles when it's set to the highest speed. Shelves built into the walls on both sides, giving way to a sliding closet door on my left. A single window, on the far wall.

There's a bed, with a green comforter.

A desk to my right, with a computer monitor on the surface, the tower hidden below.

The walls are gray and the carpet is ... the carpet is brown. I think. I'm no longer sure. The color blurs and shifts in my mind.

It's just a room. Any room. Four walls and a ceiling and a fan.

This is what I tell myself before I step inside. This is the whisper I hear in my head as I stand with my hand on the knob, waiting on the top step.

For a moment, I think I hear his footsteps on the other side of the door, but I know this isn't possible. I picture us sitting across from each other on the floor. My legs, angled between his.

He leans closer. He's smiling.

Then I remember: the carpet is beige. The door will squeak as I push it open. The air will be hotter or colder than the rest of the house, depending on the time of year.

All these things I know by heart.

None of this prepares me.

SATURDAY MORNING

▶ ◀ ▲

His mother asked me to do this, because she said it wasn't something a mother should ever have to do. I don't think it's really something an ex-girlfriend should have to do either, but mother trumps ex any day of the week.

"The room is full of you, Jessa," she explained, by which she means the pictures. They're taped around the room, directly to the gray slanting walls, and in all of them I have my arms looped around his neck, or his arms draped over my shoulders from behind me. I can't even look directly at the photos, but his mother is right. I'm everywhere.

Sometimes I wonder if his mother knows about the ex part. If he told her, if she overheard, if she could tell all on her own. Though something about the way she stands at the base of the stairway watching me linger at the entrance to the attic room, something about the way she asked me to do this in the first place, makes me think that she does.

There's a chill up here, but I know it's nothing more than the poor insulation of a converted attic, heat escaping through the cracks of the window frame, the November air seeping in from the outside.

His clothes are still on the floor, however they fell when he last kicked them off, on that rainy day in mid-September. His bed is unmade. His computer monitor sits black on the desk, my distorted reflection looking back. His desk is stuffed full with ticket stubs and old homework, and more, I know, and so is the closet. Caleb wouldn't want his mother doing this, either. Under the bed, between the mattresses, there are things a mother shouldn't see. My stomach rebels, but I can feel her still watching, so I step inside.

I don't know where to start.

I don't know how to start.

If Caleb were here, he'd say, *Just start.*

I hated that, the way he'd brush aside everything else, forcing the point, or the issue, or this moment.

Just forget about it—

Just leave it—

Just say it—

Just pick up the shirt at the foot of the bed, the one he wore the last time you touched him.

Just start.

Dragonfly Necklace

The shirt still smells of him. Dove soap. The cologne that always let me know when he was behind me, a smile starting even before he'd place his hand on my waist, his lips on my cheek. I don't bring it to my face. I don't dare bring it any closer. I throw it into the corner—the beginning of a pile.

See, Caleb? I'm starting. I've started.

Underneath the shirt, there's also the jeans. Knees worn thin, hem slightly fraying, soft and familiar. I'm holding my breath by the time I get to the pockets, except I already know what's there, so it should prepare me. But it doesn't. The chain crackles, cold on my fingers. And then I feel something else: the memory of his warm skin as I placed it into his open palm.

I said: *Please hold this for me.*

I said: *Please be careful.*

He put it in his pocket, no big thing. He did it like that because of everyone watching. To show me he didn't have to be careful anymore. Not with me.

The clasp of the necklace in my hand is broken, had already broken when I gave it to him, but the gold chain is now kinked and knotted too, from sitting buried in his pocket. I wore it every race, even though we weren't supposed to, taping the dragonfly charm to the inside of my jersey to keep it in place while I ran. I wore it because it was good luck, because it was a ritual, because I had a hard time doing things any other way than how I'd always done them.

It broke on the starting line as I raised my hands over my head in a stretch. The pop against my skin, sickening. My body already wound tight, waiting for the gun. I scanned the crowd, and there he was—familiar. It didn't occur to me right then that he had no reason to be there anymore. It didn't even register. There was no mystery, just the momentary panic of a broken necklace and a race about to start.

Wait, I begged, leaving my place on the field. I jogged over to him, standing near the starting line, as everyone else took their places.

Please hold this for me.

Please be careful.

He frowned at the dragonfly in the crease of his palm, closed his fist, slid his hand into the right front pocket of his favorite jeans. Shrugged.

I wish I had known that this would be it—the last time I saw him. I would've made sure the last image I had of him was not like this: this apathy; his blue eyes skimming over me, settling to the side; and then the breeze, blowing his light brown hair across his eyes, shuttering everything. The image I see constantly, now burned into memory.

He left before the race was over, probably remembering he didn't have to be there for me anymore. Or maybe it was something else. The rain. A word spoken. A thing remembered. Either way, he left. Came back home. Tossed his jeans on the floor of his room, my necklace still inside. Left them there. Changed.

Changed everything.

Caleb. Be careful.

The attic is too quiet without him, and the angled walls too narrowed, and I want to be *out of this room*, but then I hear his mother arguing below. She's arguing with someone very particular. She's arguing with Max. Sometimes his voice reminds me of Caleb's. Sometimes, when I hear him, it takes me a second to remember Caleb's gone.

"She shouldn't be here," he's saying. "I told you I'd do it."

"She will do it," his mother says.

And this is how I'm sure that this is my penance.

Broken-In Baseball Cap

I slide the necklace into my pocket, leaving his jeans on the floor—the outline of his ghost. I look over at the pile of flattened boxes leaning against the wall just inside the door, left there by his mother. His baseball cap hangs from the doorknob, wedged between the boxes and the open door. The room is untouched otherwise, frozen at the exact moment Caleb last left the room.

I can picture it so clearly, see it happening as if I were in this room that afternoon, beside him. The rain pelting the single window, the whir of the ceiling fan overhead. He throws his clothes on the floor as he changes. He must've been in a rush, because the clothes are just lying here, and he was usually pretty good about getting his laundry the three steps from his bed to the hamper in his closet. And then: he leaves. He braces his hands against the narrow walls on the sides of the stairs as he catapults himself two, three steps down at a time.

There was this feeling, with Caleb, that he was always late for something.

I imagine this room would've stayed like this forever—

the door shut, everything frozen in time, his mother sealing off the entrance, preventing anyone from touching it. Except they're leaving. Leaving this town, leaving it all behind. It's been one month since the memorial service, one and a half months since the flood, nearly two months since we broke up.

But as I stand in his room, all that time disappears, and I have to remind myself he's not about to walk in and ask what I'm doing here. I swing the door slightly closed to prop open the first box, and his broken-in baseball cap sways faintly side to side. It's solid blue with a white swoosh symbol, the brim arched, the edges worn and off-color, bleached from the summers of salt and sun.

And suddenly I can see him turning his face to me on the beach, as he did that first time, the summer before last.

Hailey and I sitting on our towels, side by side, sipping the last of our cold sodas from the cooler, all the ice melted, the afternoon sun baking my exposed skin. Sophie Bartow's shadow falling over Hailey—they'd been in some class together the year before, but I didn't know her well—staking out a spot beside her, calling back to someone over her shoulder.

I saw Max first, who I'd heard had started seeing Sophie earlier that summer. He was weaving around towels with Caleb beside him, midconversation, when Max looked up to where Sophie waited, caught my eye, and waved. I waved back.

Caleb tilted his head to the side, said something to Max. To hear Caleb tell it, it was the first time he saw me. He asked

Max who I was. And Max said, "Her? That's Jessa Whitworth. Julian's sister." I'd known Max for years, a permanent fixture from the years of Julian's Little League teams. He knew me as the younger sister of their star player, scorekeeper, stat recorder, occasional Gatorade provider, until I was old enough to grow sick of it all.

"Hey, Jessa," Max said as he took up his spot beside Sophie. But Caleb stopped in front of me, his shadow blocking the heat of the sun for a moment.

"Hi, I'm Caleb," he said.

I knew who Caleb was, knew vaguely in the way that you know most people in your year and above, in the way that hearing the stories and rumors about them made you feel like you already knew them. And how the years below kind of faded into the background—like I did for Caleb.

He sat beside me on my beach towel, like he'd known me forever, and took a sip of my soda. I was kind of horrified and said, "I'm not that kind of girl, you know."

Which made him laugh. "We need to be friends first, don't we?" he said.

I nodded.

He leaned close and whispered, "I can't stand Max's new girlfriend."

I pulled back, shaken. "What are you doing?"

"I just told you something I haven't even told my best friend. And I'm trusting you not to tell. Friends, right?"

I rolled my eyes. "You really, really want my soda, don't you?"

"Oh God, you have no idea. Please. I'm dying here."

I squinted against the glare. "I'll trade you for some sunscreen. My nose is burning. I can feel it."

"Not a fan of the sun?" he asked.

"On the contrary. I love the sun. But in a cruel twist of fate, the sun and I can't be in contact for more than thirty minutes at a time without SPF 50. And I'm all out."

He laughed, and the sound caught me by surprise. He took the hat from his head, lowered it over my own, readjusted the brim, and tapped it once, as I tucked my shoulder-length hair behind my ears. He reached his fingers for a wisp of blond hair that blew across my face, brushing it aside.

"Better?" he asked.

I peered up at him from under the brim, his hair moving with the breeze, the side of his mouth turned up in a grin as he watched me back. Caleb looked like he and the sun were made for each other. His light brown hair streaked nearly blond in sections, his tan golden.

I took a long sip before handing the soda to him, and there it was: we were friends. Our circles blending together— Hailey to Sophie, Sophie to Max, Max to Caleb. A month of hanging out that summer before we got together, but he had me right then. He had me with his ease, hooked me with the secret.

SATURDAY AFTERNOON

▶ ◀ ▲

Max's voice breaks me from the memory.

"Jessa?" It's a whisper-yell, like he's not supposed to do it. He must be standing at the bottom of the steps, his voice funneling up the narrow halls and crooked stairs, spanning the distance between us.

I hear water running through the pipes and imagine Caleb's mother is in the bathroom or rinsing the dishes.

"You doing okay?" he whisper-yells.

Okay? Whatever it is I'm doing, it's not okay on any level. My hand is on the ball cap, scared to move it from its spot on the door, as if I am the great disturbance of this room. The air changes. The room changes. The meaning behind Max's words changes.

"Tell her I need some tape," I call. This is the only thing I can think of to say. I can picture Caleb on his bed, trying not to smile. The way he thought it was cute when I said the wrong thing.

I prop open the first box, scoop up the clothes, the ball cap, all of these things that Caleb once loved, and I pile them into the bottom of the box with a knot in my throat.

I look around the room, expecting that something will have changed, but everything remains the same.

We're here. Caleb's gone.

I hear Max talking low downstairs again, Caleb's mother's voice in response, and he's the one who brings the tape. I hear his slow steps on the wooden stairs, the creak that Caleb used to leap over on the way down. Max shuffles his sneakers against the rug at the entrance, and I can almost hear the zing that would always come after, when Caleb touched the light switch—how he always seemed to accidentally charge himself on the rug, shocking himself on the way in.

But Max doesn't touch the light switch. He doesn't move any closer. "I told her I'd do it," he says. He doesn't look at me when he says it. Max and Caleb aren't related, but they told me they once had the whole sixth grade convinced they were. They don't even look that much alike—Max is tall and thin, with pitch-dark hair, where Caleb was more broad-shouldered, his light brown hair even lighter in the summer. But there's a similar cadence to the way they speak, a lilt, like a script they both tend to follow. A habit of people who've known each other for years, who've spent so much time together.

I ignore him, emptying an entire drawer into a new box in one fell swoop. A summer wardrobe. An entire season. Months and months of a life. Just gone.

He leans against the wall behind me. I see his sneakers, notice him rock back on his heels, like he isn't sure whether to stay or go. "We missed you at the meet," he says.

That's when I notice his hair is still wet from a shower,

his school track pants and jacket still on. He must have come straight from the meet. Today was the last race of the season. I've missed this one, and every one, since September.

And for a moment, I can hear the cheers of an early Saturday-morning race, smell the dew on the grass, feel the adrenaline surging to my toes. I reach for the necklace at my collar on instinct, then remember it's no longer there. I finally have it back in my possession, but I know I'll never wear it again.

Like everything else in this room, the necklace belongs to another time. Even the weather has turned. Caleb's summer wardrobe will never be needed again.

"Jessa—" Max says, reaching for the box. "Here, let me help."

"She wants me to do it," I snap, folding over the top of the box, holding out my hand for the tape. I position the box between my legs and peel the tape across it, the noise cutting through the room. I slice it off, stick another strip across in the opposite direction, a crooked X. I pick up the box and thrust it at Max. "Here. So tell her. Tell her I'm doing it."

I push him with the box, and he backs away, and he keeps going, as if he cannot stop the momentum. I hold tight to the feeling, and I keep moving.

I'm doing the clothes. I've done the hard part, the ones on the floor, the ones I can picture him still in. These will all be donated, I assume, belonging to someone else soon enough. I do this every year, cleaning out my closet, making room for the next size, or the next style, or finding the ones that had accidentally been shrunken in the dryer by my dad. The emptiness of the closet only temporary, a gap that would ultimately be filled. A sign of change—with the seasons and me.

The clothes in the drawers are the easy part, indistinguishable in their current form, folded into tight squares. They smell like laundry detergent and dryer sheets, the pine scent from the inside of the dresser. I leave them folded and try not to look too closely. The drawers are mostly jeans, khaki shorts, gym shorts. The T-shirts with band names and brand names. Socks and undershirts and boxers. I don't differentiate. I don't care. She said pack, and I'm packing. It all goes into the same place, before it can register. I'm taping boxes, I'm stacking them on the floor, on to the next, and the next, and the next.

At some point I hear the back door open and close, and I know that Max has left. I know because I go to the window and watch as he walks across the backyard, his head tucked down—how he pushes the latch at the back of the fence and looks up once before slipping to the other side, where he lives. I duck myself behind the window curtain, but it's too late.

And then I see her reflection in the window, filling up the doorway. I spin around, my back pressed to the wall beside Caleb's bed. Her eyes are red-rimmed and she's staring at the boxes, and then she's staring at me, standing beside the window. I think she's going to tell me it's okay, that I should go home, because she always had a soft spot for me—

inviting me to stay for dinner, asking about my plans—but instead I see she has a black Sharpie in her hand. "You need to label them," she says, her voice cool and flat.

And what can I do except take the marker from her hand and nod?

His clock on the wall above me keeps ticking. A cruel, even tempo. On and on, a tally of moments in which Caleb remains further and further behind.

I want to tell her that I haven't had lunch yet; that my brother is home from college this weekend; that I'm sorry.

"I'm almost done with the clothes," I say, because she's still standing there, and I don't really know what to say to her, this woman I believe secretly blames me for the death of her son.

It's not until I turn to the closet that I hear her footsteps retreating on the stairs.

Sign for the Bunker

The hamper in the corner is empty, and I fold the wooden stand, flattening the fabric to a square on the floor. But underneath, right side up, is a slab of wood with words carved in and a rope attached by nails to the edges. I run my fingers over the letters—this must've once hung from his doorknob when he was younger.

The Bunker, it says, and even here, even now, I can't stop the smile from spreading.

Last year, Labor Day weekend, my first time seeing his house. The first official day of us. I had just turned sixteen, the day before.

School would be starting on Tuesday, and the group of us were enjoying the last days of summer. Hailey had to leave early for back-to-school shopping, and her mom was picking us up, but Caleb offered to drive me home later. Hailey smiled at me then, like she knew.

On the way home later, Max and Sophie rode in the back. Max was in a rush—he had to get to work—and Sophie's car was at his place. So we hit Max's house first. This was the first time I had seen either of their homes. They both went to my school, which was private and not exactly inexpensive, and I didn't want to judge too much, but their neighborhood didn't seem to scream *I can afford to send my kids to private school.*

The town itself was considered affluent, but their homes were narrow and older, small yards crammed back to back, in a track. Max, I knew, had an unofficial baseball scholarship (*unofficial* because the school did not officially give athletic scholarships, but a rose by any other name and all)—my brother was the one who convinced him to apply to our school in the first place. But I didn't know much about Caleb's family situation.

"I live right behind them," Caleb said as Max and Sophie piled out of the car, dragging their beach gear behind them. "Do you want to stop for a sec? Get something to eat first?"

He drummed his hands on the steering wheel, didn't look at me when he asked.

"Okay," I said, and my heart beat faster.

He drove around the block and parked in front of a small brick house, in a parallel spot, zipping into the space in a way that seemed like it was second nature to him. I followed him up the concrete steps, the iron railing wobbling under my hand. He used his key, one of several on a chain that held the letters of his favorite football team, and called, "Mom?" as he swung open the door.

His words echoed through the narrow halls. The floor was wooden, as was the staircase directly across from the front door. He dropped his bag at the entrance, led me through two small, partitioned rooms—a living room with an oversized couch across from the television; a dining room with a wooden table with red placemats and family pictures hanging on the walls—until we reached the kitchen.

He opened the pantry, then the fridge. "Okay, confession, really slim pickings here." He squeezed his eyes shut, held out his hands. "I have food in my room, and I swear this isn't a line."

I laughed, and he opened his eyes, grinning sheepishly.

"After you, then."

I followed him up one narrow flight of steps, and then the second, until I stepped across the threshold, looked at the built-in shelves along both side walls, which did hold bottles of sports drinks and assorted snacks.

"Welcome to the bunker," he said, gesturing his arms around the room.

"May I?" I asked, grabbing a bag of M&M's, which had been leaning against a stack of books on the bottom shelf.

"By all means," he said, smiling. I ripped into the bag, surprised by how bright the room was with the sunlight pouring in through the single window behind his bed. "It's not very bunkerish," I said, "if I'm being totally honest."

He put his hand on his heart, feigning shock. "Exhibit A, the shelves."

I looked again. "The bookcases?"

"No, not *bookcases*. Pretty sure the people who lived here before us were end-of-the-world believers."

The candy was slightly melted from the direct sunlight,

and it stained my fingers red and green and brown. "You don't believe in an eventual end of the world?" I asked.

"Oh, I do. I mean, eventually the sun will explode, or some supervirus will wipe us all out, but nothing that an attic full of food would save us from. I'm not *that* type of believer."

"Or it was just a library," I said.

"Oh," he said, and he narrowed his eyes at the space. "I mean, I guess that's possible. Except I found a box of cereal left behind the day we moved in. Just a single box of unopened cereal in the middle of the shelf. Like it wasn't worth packing up."

I looked again, tried to see this room filled with food, but it didn't take. "I'm trying here, Caleb. But all I see is a library."

"It doesn't sound as cool to call it the library. Don't go messing with my street cred, Jessa Whitworth."

And then he took a step closer, like I knew he would, and he put a hand on my waist, like I knew he would. "Okay, I lied," he said, "it was kind of a line."

"I *know*," I said, which made him laugh. And then his expression turned serious, his hand moved to the side of my face, and he stepped even closer, so his body brushed up against mine. I could feel his breath, the tremble of his hand, smell the salt and sunscreen and summer air as he leaned in to kiss me.

I kissed him back, my hands sliding around his waist, thinking that everything about him reminded me of the ocean, and that was perfect. His skin was still hot from the sun, and the salt water had dried in his hair, and I lost myself in the feeling of floating, of drifting. Then I heard a pitter-patter of steps echo from below, like an animal was loose.

Caleb pulled back, stepped away. "My mom is home," he said. The four words every girl is dying to hear.

He launched himself down the steps, in that Caleb fashion I would come to know so well, but at the moment, I was just trying to orient myself, think up an excuse—*Oh, hi, I was hungry and the M&M's were upstairs;* oh God, really? *Really?* I was practically tripping over myself to keep up.

"Hi, Mom," he said, standing at the base of the stairs.

His mom was carrying a paper bag of groceries, lettuce peeking out the top. She had long, dark hair, the color of ink, and green eyes lined expertly with makeup, her lips a pale rose. Her eyes shifted from Caleb to me, currently standing behind him and trying not to die of embarrassment. A little girl darted in and out of view, a carbon copy of her mother, not paying any of us much attention.

"This is Jessa," he said. And he left it at that. So many things he could've said, to clarify. For all of us.

This is Jessa, the girl I just kissed.

My friend, Jessa.

Julian's sister, Jessa.

"Jessamyn Whitworth," I said, stepping out from behind Caleb and sticking out my hand, as if I were here to sell her something.

I felt Caleb cut his eyes to me and grin, shaking his head.

She shifted the bag to her hip, took my hand in hers. "Ah, Jessa," she said, like she'd heard my name before.

Caleb blushed. I blushed.

"Well, stay," she said. "We just picked up way too much food. Sean won't be home until later."

I looked to Caleb, questioning. *Stay*, he mouthed.

"Okay," I said. "Thanks, Mrs. . . . ." And then I blanked. Caleb's last name was Evers. But his mom had remarried. I had no idea what to call her.

"Eve," she said. "My name is Eve. And this"—she tipped her head to the girl, now hanging off Caleb's waist—"is Mia."

This house feels so much larger with just me and his mother right now. I think of the two of them—Mia and Eve—alone here now. Caleb's stepfather Sean left them first, and now Caleb is gone. The house was built for four. The master bedroom on the first floor, with the kitchen and living room and dining room. The second floor, with Mia's room, another bedroom (which was probably supposed to be Caleb's), and a bathroom. A set of narrow wooden steps of exposed wood to the attic, which was probably not supposed to be a bedroom at all. *The bunker*, I whisper to myself.

I try to picture it as the room it had been when Caleb moved in. Bare walls, empty floor, a single box of cereal on the shelves, like a pantry. Except there's a closet. Pantries don't have closets. I'd told Caleb this.

Bunkers do, he said.

I'm trying to latch on to the sound of his voice, hold his words tight in my head, because I can feel them fading away. Drifting into the fog of memory.

This house always felt so alive, with Caleb up here, his sister below, music playing from his speakers, the television blaring from downstairs.

I want to tell him about silence now. How silence can fill a room, seep into the corners, take a place over. How it feels heavy, heavy enough to drown out the memory of his voice. I want to tell him how I spent that first week calling his phone before it was disconnected, just to hear the sound of his voicemail recording, because I felt the silence pressing down. Everything about him, slipping through the cracks, taking me with him.

Gray Pinstripes

I drop the sign into a new box for his personal things while I finish the clothes, because it was his hand that made this, and it seems like something someone might want to keep. His mother wants a different box for his personal things, so I keep this separate, before going back to the clothes.

His polos are hanging in the closet, rugby-striped, his go-to school uniform. We have to wear collared shirts at school, though that unifying thread is taken in many different directions: button-downs; fitted preppy polos; relaxed rugby-style; sweater vests over white oxfords. Girls can also opt for dresses, skirts, or capris, in addition to the rule for the boys of pants in khaki, black, or navy.

Everything about our school is a few degrees fancier than the norm.

This closet is *School-Caleb*. The drawers hold the relaxed version, the one he would become at three p.m.—a spare pair of jeans and a T-shirt always in his locker for after hours.

Hanging in the corner of the closet is a black zipped-up bag, the suit he wore last October for Homecoming inside.

I place my fingers at the cold zipper, but leave it closed. It had been his dad's, he told me that night, when I ran my hands down his sleeves appreciatively. I remember seeing it as something new, how he filled it up, growing into the absence, a person with the same dimensions. My heart had ached for him when he told me—his father had died when he was younger, but his stepfather, Sean, had been in the picture for as long as I knew him, so that sometimes it was easy to forget that, to overlook what was missing.

Still, it was a simple statement that bonded us closer. A piece of his past that he was letting me see.

I toss the bag on the bed—it's almost person-sized, and it does something to my head, making me believe I will uncover something different inside. My fingers itch. I unzip the bag. The scent of starch escapes first, and I know it's been dry-cleaned.

I don't take it out, because it's pressed perfectly and neatly and exactly as Caleb meant to leave it. And it has its own history, like a family heirloom. I run my hand against the fabric inside. I close my eyes and feel him spread out his arms at my front door, letting me do the same that night. It's gray pin-striped; an older style.

"Wow, look at you," I said, and whatever Caleb was about to say as he looked me over halted, with my brother in the background, waiting for his teammates who would all be heading over together with their dates.

My mom snapped a picture of us, his arm tucked around me, his tie matching the sky blue of my dress, and his eyes. He and Julian did this awkward handshake in the front parlor while I introduced them, though I was sure they already knew each other—knew *of* each other, at least.

"Bye, Mom, bye," I called as I pulled him by the hand, both of us smiling, everything so new we couldn't wait to be alone.

When Julian called after me, "See you there, Jessa," it sounded like a warning.

While every other guy at the dance wore plain black or dark gray, jackets optional, Caleb stood out. The suit made his eyes look bluer, his body leaner. I remember the feel of the fabric as I leaned into him, his hands on my back, the music beating in time to our movement. The whole night, a blur of laughter and color.

The school cafeteria was transformed into a dance hall, the full moon visible through the big windows spanning the entire wall, everyone dressed up like this was a different place than the one where we spent every lunch hour, and we were different people.

I try not to think of his jacket thrown haphazardly in the backseat of his car after. His tie that matched my strapless dress, undone. My fingers on the buttons of his white button-down shirt. His hands on my bare shoulders when he kissed me. The way he said, "Lo, Jessa Whitworth, I think I like you," after.

The way he said things like *lo* and *hark now* like he was tempering everything in case he needed it to be a joke.

The next morning, at breakfast, Julian told me, "Be careful with that kid, Jessa. He's older than you."

"Just a year," I'd said. And Julian looked at me like he

had missed the fact that I was no longer the kid in middle school playing dress-up and singing karaoke in my bedroom. "Besides," I said, "he's friends with Max."

I'd known Max since elementary school, in the same way I knew most of my brother's baseball acquaintances: they were just *there*. Same as I was to them. And then I went to school, and an entire team of people already knew me as *Julian's sister, Jessa*.

Caleb was an exception.

Max and Caleb were a year older than me, and Julian one year older than them. Unlike me, who ran cross-country and track all year round, since freshman year, Max only started running this year, as a way to stay in shape for baseball season. By the time I met Caleb, Julian was about to start his senior year, Max and Caleb were juniors, and I was a sophomore.

Julian grunted. "I wouldn't pick Max for you, either."

"Good thing you're not picking, then."

Julian had eventually warmed, in the only way it seemed he could manage. Distantly, and with a look of surprise whenever Caleb showed up—as if this detail of my life managed to slip his mind, every time.

I zip the bag back up and place it carefully inside the box, folding it in half, covering the polos. I look away as I close the lid. My blue dress from last year still hangs in my closet, in the plastic dry-cleaning bag, untouched. I missed Homecoming this year. It was last month, on a clear and crisp

Saturday night. The dress I bought for it at the end of the summer (Hailey, pulling it off the rack, holding it up to me, her eyes shining. *You have to get this, Jessa. It's perfect. It's perfectly you.*) still has the tags.

I bought the dress because it was on sale, and because I was an optimist.

But even then, it felt like a lie. Like I was trying to re-capture something between us that was already gone.

Out-of-Tune Guitar

I'm pulling down the rest of Caleb's clothes from the closet when I feel something bump against the back wall—a faint hum, a flat twang. I push the hangers aside, and in the middle of the space is his guitar, leaning against the wall. It's propped up precariously between a deflated football and a spare blanket, folded up and gathering dust. I grab the neck of the guitar, and my fingers brush the strings—letting loose a tense, sharp cry in the empty room. The moment like muscle memory, as I run my fingers against the untuned strings.

It was November, and we'd just finished morning finals. Everyone was heading to the school library if they had an afternoon final, or to lunch and study groups if they didn't. We opted for studying at Caleb's house. "Everyone should be out," he said. Mia was in third grade, Eve worked pretty regular hours at a real estate office, and Sean's job alternated between days and nights, depending on the project.

Music was playing from Caleb's computer speakers, which seemed to be focusing him, but it had the opposite effect on me. I sat at his desk with my math notes out on my lap, swiveling back and forth in his chair. I was mostly watching his reflection in the computer screen as he was reading over the physics notes to himself on the bed, when his body suddenly stiffened. He leaned from his bed to his desk, reaching beyond me. He turned down the volume on the speakers, and frowned.

"What?" I asked, but by then I heard it, too. Slow footsteps on the stairs. Caleb's eyes went wide, and he took me by the shoulders, gently pushing me toward the closet.

"Shh," he said as the darkness engulfed me, his shirts closing in around me, his face a pale sliver in the gap of light before he slid the door shut entirely.

I tried to slow my breathing, to mask the sound of my existence.

"Caleb?" The door to his room creaked open and someone stepped into the room. "I thought I heard someone up here." Sean's voice, low and gravelly. I imagined a lifetime of smoking cigarettes, though I never smelled any smoke in the house.

"Yep. It's just me."

"Thought you were supposed to be at school." An accusatory edge.

"It's finals week. I'm studying," Caleb said. His voice had risen to the same level, matching Sean's. "What are you doing home?"

I heard something move—an object picked up and placed back down. "We finished up early. Physics, huh?" Sean said. He must've picked up Caleb's textbook. I heard a slight jangle as he stepped closer, the chain of his pocket watch, always connected from his pocket to a belt loop whenever I saw him. "You sticking around? I could use your help carting some junk from the garage to the recycling center."

The silence lingered, the tension radiating all around the room. I held my breath, so sure he could sense me, in the silence. The way you can feel the presence of another, without seeing them. I was a rustling in the walls, a shadow in the closet. I wondered if Sean was staring at the gap under the closet door right now.

Finally, Caleb spoke. "On second thought, think I'll head to the library."

Sean made a noise that could've been a laugh. Hard to tell, behind the door, without perspective, with no body language or facial expression to accompany the moment.

Something pressed against my back, and I jumped, thinking it was an arm, or a hand, until I reached behind me to grab it. The strings brushed against my fingers, but my hand held them silent and still, the shape of the neck gaining context in the dark. I had no idea Caleb could play an instrument.

I stayed where I was, holding the guitar, listening to Sean's steps descend. Caleb didn't move until he heard a door close somewhere below us. Then he opened the closet door, and I pushed him with my free arm, annoyed. He laughed, fake-rubbing the shoulder I'd just shoved.

"I didn't know I needed to be hidden," I said.

"Trust me, it was the quickest way to deal with him."

I rolled my eyes. "So many secrets, Caleb. You play the guitar?"

He saw what I had in my hand and laughed. "Hardly. It was a gift from my grandparents when I was younger. I don't know how to play."

"At all?"

"Nope."

The guitar, I then saw, had a fine layer of dust covering the sides. Remnants of a spider web clung to one of the tuning keys at the top. I brushed away the dust and debris, swung it in front of my body, looping the strap onto my shoulder. I placed my fingers in the position of the single chord I knew the best, which my father had taught me years earlier.

"Wait, you can play the guitar?" His face contorted, stuck somewhere between confusion and delight.

"I wouldn't say I can *play* exactly, but apparently I can play better than you." I strummed another chord, smiled, tried to remember the few basic bars from the handful of lessons I took back in middle school. The guitar was out of tune, but the notes still sounded familiar.

"What else don't I know about you, Jessa Whitworth?" he whispered, leaning closer. We were at that stage where we thought we already knew all the important things, but then something like this would come along, and we'd realize how much more there was still left to discover.

"Well, for one," I said, placing my hand over the strings, to still them. The room fell silent. "I don't like being hidden in closets."

He tipped his head back, laughed—laughed louder than he expected. He cut himself off, cut his eyes to the stairway.

"Point taken," he said. "But we should go before Sean comes back inside, unless you want to end up back in there."

I slid the guitar strap off my shoulder, handed it to him, and watched as he restored it to its original position, in the back of the closet.

"Who owns a guitar and doesn't know how to play?" I mumbled.

"I'll let you teach me if you want," he said. He threw me a look over his shoulder, then motioned for me to follow him silently. We snuck down the steps, peering around corners, until we were down the front porch steps, in the open air, then in his car, driving to a place I can no longer remember.

Now I hold the guitar to my hip. He never asked me to teach him. I never did. It sat in the same spot, apparently for nearly a year, unmoved, untouched. The strings remain intact—I strum them once, then place my hand over the top, to stifle the sound.

I lean the guitar gently against the wall at the door—it won't fit in a box. Still, it has value, if his mom decides to sell it. I figure that's the point of all this packing: an ordering of what needs keeping and what can be donated or sold.

I've filled boxes, labeled them *Shirts, Pants, Shorts, Socks.* They tower along the wall, but the room is still full. He's still everywhere. It's Saturday afternoon, and there are six boxes of Caleb on the staircase, and I'm wondering how much longer it will take before the room becomes something else. Before I stop seeing him in every corner, every heartbeat, every tick of the godforsaken clock. Before I can breathe deeply without this suffocating feeling.

It's the pictures, I decide. His eyes. They're everywhere.

I think of the last time I walked up these steps, peering into this room, when he was still here. The way he stood in the entrance, his arm outstretched, bracing himself against the doorjamb. His body said everything: *You are not welcome.*

And now here I am, precisely where he let me know that I am *not welcome*, and I feel him watching me. Watching as I go through his things, tossing pieces of his life aside.

His words from that day, his expression flat as he said, "What are you doing here, Jessa?"

I hear the words again. Coming from the walls. Coming from everywhere.

Pictures of Us

I lunge for the window and push it open. The cold air rushes in, seizes my lungs midbreath. The room flutters all around me, coming to life. Pictures flap against the wall in a wave; a paper on his desk turns over, as if Caleb himself were circling the room. I hang my body out the window, resting my waist on the ledge, and I know I must look like I'm trying to escape, that there's a fire, or thick smoke, when really there is only me.

There used to be a screen here. I'm not sure what happened to it.

I listen to the birds, to the wind through the tree branches, to a car engine turning over down the street. I close the window, and the cold lingers. It will take a moment for the heat to rise again.

The pictures come down next. One by one. Because I can't stand him looking at me. I can't stand *me* looking at me. The way we used to be, taunting me.

I'm somewhat surprised to find the pictures are still up. Maybe he was keeping up appearances; maybe he hadn't had the time or the energy to eradicate me completely from his life yet. Maybe he had grown so accustomed to the images, like background music, that he didn't really notice them anymore. Or maybe—and this is more painful—he was an optimist underneath everything, too.

As I take them down, I notice he's written on the backs of them, in pencil, and something in my chest squeezes closed. Who prints pictures anymore? It's sweet. This is too much.

There's one from when we were still just friends, sitting at the beach. I have my cover-up on, my hair is wild, my nose is sunburnt, I can feel the sand gritty beneath my toes. August, that first summer, which the date on the back confirms. Caleb held the camera away from us and leaned in close, telling me to smile, but in the photo I'm mostly squinting against the glare.

I knew that day, he'd said, pointing to this picture on his wall.

I smiled to myself.

I knew before. The first day he sat beside me and took my soda, the flip of my stomach, the way he made me feel like I was someone worth knowing.

Next there's the shot my mom took before the Homecoming dance, the first picture of us as a couple. We were practically glowing, smiles so wide I could still remember the feeling—how I couldn't wait to get out of the house, how I was just about bursting, something fighting its way to the surface.

Caleb is—was—a collector. Which was basically about half a step from a scrapbooker. He kept everything. Ticket stubs from our dates, old graded assignments, notes passed back and forth. So it shouldn't surprise me to find the months and years written on the backs of the pictures. Still, there's something almost desperate about it as the dates progress, the way they're faint, written in the corners, as if he knew he would one day look through them as memories. As if he could feel, even back then, the gradual unraveling of us. Trying to hold on to the moment, even as he could feel it slipping. A date scribbled on the back, a piece of sticky tack, Caleb pushing the photo onto the gray wall, standing back to look it over.

Next to come down is the photo from Halloween, where Hailey and I kept up our yearly tradition of dressing as a famous set of twins, even though we looked nothing alike (per the school rules, we had to remain in dress code, so we had to get creative). We had gone as the twins from *The Shining*, since Hailey was in the midst of a Stephen King kick. Never mind that Hailey was at least four inches taller than me, or that her eyes were brown to my blue, or that she took after her father's side of the family, from Puerto Rico, her skin a deeper shade of olive, while I was incapable of tanning. Hailey curled her long dark hair to make it look shorter, and I tucked my blond hair into a brown wig, and we'd both slipped a barrette into the side. We'd found the matching dresses at a thrift shop and tied a bow around each. In the photo, Caleb stands between us in a cape, his button-down shirt open up top to reveal the letter *S*, the blue of his Superman uniform. (There was nothing in the dress code about capes, he claimed.)

Then the one at a Christmas party, our eyes sparkling like the lights around us. Next, the ones of us sitting in this room, when I started to spend more time here than at my own house. There's one including Max. One with Caleb's little sister, Mia, on my lap. I freeze, thinking I should leave this for her instead, but no. I keep going. Keep moving. They all go facedown on the carpeted floor, the dates a timeline that I could order, piecing together our relationship, like a bell curve.

I watch as my hair grows longer, my smile more comfortable, how we slide together, our arms entwined, a second nature. I pull them all off the wall, one by one, flip them facedown in a pile. These don't need to be boxed up, but I can't bring myself to throw them out, either.

His mother wants his personal items in a separate box. But this isn't something I'd want her to sort through on her own. These, I decide, are mine.

This room is full of me. She said it herself. I can't cut these down the middle, an arm on my side, a hand on his. There's no easy way to untangle the images.

The pictures stop long before the end. We go to a baseball game, we take a picture in this room, sitting on this bed, with him kissing my cheek, holding the camera, me scrunching up my nose while laughing. We go on a hike. And then they stop. I wonder if there was a moment up here where he knew. Just like the beginning. Whether he knew first. Whether I did. If it was a moment for him, where he could see it clearly. Or whether, like for me, it was a feeling I didn't recognize at first, sitting in the pit of my stomach, waking me up at night—gently gnawing, a slight unease. Not a bang, not a fight, but a slow and inevitable slide.

I flip over the last picture, the one from the hike, and

there's the date again. June of this year. Five months ago. My name below. *Jessa Whitworth, Delaware Water Gap.* As if this were merely a file already, a piece for a museum archive. As if he knew someday, somewhere, these would belong to someone else.

Once they're all down, I flip over the stack as I go to slide them into my bag, and there we are again—at the beach.

Now I want to ask him, *What did you know, Caleb?* That a year later, you'd be gone and I'd be peeling all evidence of you and me off the wall? That your mother would hate me, and Max wouldn't look me in the eye, and your baby sister wouldn't say a word to me, no matter how many times I said hello?

Salt water helps you float, you said that first day we met at the beach, when I told you I couldn't swim well. That I didn't like the feeling of the current in the ocean. That I had this irrational fear of being swept out to sea, and that nobody would ever find me.

You laughed.

Caleb, you *laughed*.

His Glasses

After the pictures come down, the walls are bare, except for a few pieces of sticky tack, and the ticking clock above his desk, which was more a piece of football memorabilia than a functioning clock, since you couldn't really make out the numbers. The room looks like it did that first day, when I came up here and he told me it was the bunker. It feels like forever ago. It feels like a moment ago. One year together, a bell curve in photos.

There's a version of me and Caleb that fell apart. There's a version of him that braced his arm against the doorjamb, banning me from his life from then on. There's a version of me who walked away. There's a version of him who changed, grabbed his keys, left this room for the last time—

But right now I want this part of him. I want to find him here, see him at the moment when everything was right.

I know what I'm looking for. A navy blue, hard case, usually kept in the top drawer of his desk. But it's not where I thought it would be. It's not where it's always been.

It's almost desperate, the way I'm ignoring everything,

wasting time in search of this one item: it's a case for these generic black glasses that he's had forever.

They had smudged lenses that he'd have to rub against the hem of his shirt constantly. He'd only wear them at home, even though he would sometimes complain about his contacts bothering him. Sometimes I wondered if some days he wasn't wearing his contacts either, if that accounted for the faraway look, the things he didn't notice about me, that he ignored. I like to think it was that, at first: that he just couldn't see it.

But he hated these glasses. Hated wearing them, and hated being seen in them.

I caught him in them the first time I came up to the bunker unannounced. It was just before Christmas break, I remember, because he was working on a history paper due the last day of class, which he claimed was ruining the holiday spirit. He had his headphones on when I knocked, and he hadn't heard me. I cracked open the door, careful to inch it open, call his name—give him time to react. But he was sitting at his computer and had a textbook out in front of him. He had a thick pair of glasses on, and they turned his expression solemn, his face more boyish. The music drifted faintly across the room.

It took a moment for him to register my presence, and then he spun his chair toward me, swiped the glasses off his face in one quick motion, as if I'd caught him doing something embarrassing, like I had stumbled upon him writing in a diary.

It was the moment I fell. When I knew it was more than

a crush—that I was drawn by more than the charisma, the smile, the way he made me feel like I was someone worth desiring. No, it was this. This moment. I almost said it right then, was sure he could see it in my stunned expression, but his gaze had gone watery, and he said, "I'm pretending that I can see you right now, but I totally can't."

"At all?" I asked.

"I mean, I can see like the shape of you," and he ran his hand in the air, tracing my outline. A shiver ran through me. "But I can't tell if you're, like, smiling or laughing or totally appalled right now."

I took one step closer. "How about now?"

He scrunched up his nose. "Still nothing."

"Why don't you put your hot glasses back on then?"

He lunged off his seat for me, missed as I sidestepped, and I was laughing. He caught me around the waist, pulled my body flush with his. "Got you," he said, and his eyes searched my face, his smile stretching wider.

"My contacts were bothering me. Those are emergency only," he explained.

"So put them back on."

"Oh no, no no no, you do not get to see me in my glasses until you definitely, one hundred percent, have fallen in love with me."

I froze in his arms, and he seemed to sense something then. If only he had understood it was that moment itself. That moment, that insight, that vulnerability that did me in. I felt his breath on my face. His lips gently pressed to mine. He didn't make me say it, and didn't say anything back. He stepped away, put the thick-rimmed glasses back over his nose, so his eyes looked so large, so freaking blue, and went back to his work.

It was later that night, when he told me. When he was dropping me back off at home, and the sky was dark, and the heat in the car was running, and I was bundled in my jacket with a hat pulled down over my ears. "I love you too, you know," he said, like he'd been thinking about it. His voice was low, and his words hung in the space between us.

"Too?" I asked.

"Yeah, too," he said.

"You're doing it all out of order," I said, but I was smiling, my whole body thrumming.

"Doesn't mean it's not true," he said, unbuckling his seatbelt and leaning toward me.

I whispered it to him then, like I was the first one to say it, in the moment before his lips met mine.

"I knew it," he said, and the memory of his smile warmed me as I walked to my front door in the cold winter night.

I shift the contents of his top drawer around, checking again—nothing. Next I check the surfaces of his dressers, the backpack in the corner, still filled with a few notebooks from the last day at school. The glasses are a part of him that only I had been allowed to see.

And now they're gone. Missing.

I didn't hear Eve coming up the steps. Didn't feel her standing at the top of the steps. Didn't notice until I spun around and saw her standing there, watching.

"What are you looking for, Jessa?" she asks, not unkindly, but not gently, either. She has no need to be gentle with me any longer.

I tell his mother. "I can't find his glasses." But she doesn't seem to get the implication. She does not understand the significance for me. Because there's always this hope, some-where in my mind, that this is all some huge misunderstand-ing. And the glasses seem to support this fact. That there's something we are all missing, that is so obvious, that I am bound to uncover.

She ignores my comment about the glasses. "You've only just started," she says, and I nod. They could be anywhere, she's implying. Keep working, she's implying.

But it's dinnertime on Saturday, and my parents expect me home, and I tell her this.

She considers, nods once, relieving me of my penance.

"When should I expect you tomorrow?" she asks.

Tomorrow, Sunday, there's still so much to do. "In the morning," I say. "As soon as I'm up." And when I leave his room, she pulls the door shut behind me.

There's a mystery, if you can call it that, at the heart of Caleb's last day. It's why his mother blames me. It's why I come here, letting her blame me, in the hope that I will find out the truth. It's why people don't quite know what to say to me—whether to feel sympathy or something else. It's a mystery that keeps me tethered to this room, this hope that if I keep at it, I will finally and completely understand.

Because I don't. And it grates at me. This is the first thing, and it's a *big* thing, for which I cannot get a clear answer. And I worry that the moment will always sit incomplete. There will be no resolution that will let me move on. I can see it, even now, as if I am ten years older, looking back.

And that is the question of where Caleb was going, and why he was at my cross-country meet to begin with.

Part of me thinks it was just habit.

Part of me thinks he'd forgotten he didn't need to be there anymore.

Part of me thinks it was Max, who he came for.

But the fact remains that he told his mother he couldn't watch his sister Mia because I had a race. He always used to come to my meets. I wonder if it was a slip of his tongue, a mistake, that the breakup hadn't quite registered yet. Or if he hadn't told his mother and didn't want to. If he was thinking, even then, that we might mend things. If he'd come because he wanted to—and then, for some reason, decided he didn't want to be there after all.

Or if he just didn't want to watch Mia. He was good with her, and Mia idolized him, but he also wouldn't rearrange his own schedule just to accommodate his mother's, or Sean's. *She already has two parents*, I'd once heard him say to his mother as an excuse. I'd watched her flinch, turn away, and wondered if she could hear the longing for the same thing in his voice, underneath the bitterness.

So he said he couldn't watch Mia, and then he came to my meet. I saw him there, not quite registering the surprise of it. I asked him to hold my necklace. The gun sounded. The rain started, but it began as a steady drizzle. It wasn't until the end of the race that it started falling fast, and hard. We kept running anyway, as we always do—the winner of the boys' race was probably already finished by then anyway.

The rain kept coming. By the time I crossed the finish line, mud-streaked and dripping wet, Caleb was gone.

I wonder if maybe it was that—the rain picking up, and not me—that made him leave early. He came home first, we know that. From the neighbor who saw his car, to the clothes on the floor, to the timing.

Meanwhile, we waited out the rain after the race, the coaches and spectators all dripping inside the athletic center after, the floors slick with muddy water, the lobby humid and sweaty. I remember pressing my hands to the glass doors, watching the way the rain came down in a sheet. "It's like standing inside a waterfall," Hailey said. Her hands pressed to the glass beside mine, her nails painted alternating green and black, our school colors.

We stayed there, sitting cross-legged on the linoleum, playing with a stack of cards from Oliver's bag, while others spent the time on their phones, leaning back on their gym bags. Max tapped out a rhythm on the floor with two pencils—taken from Skyler, who was doing her homework. One hour passed. Two. Before the school deemed it safe to drive, and the flash-flood warnings were over.

And while we sat there—deliberating over our hand of playing cards; counting out a frantic beat; trying to remember how to find the inverse tangent; taking a nap—what were you doing, Caleb? Where were you going?

No one is sure. But the last thing you said to your mom

was about me. The last place you said you'd be, with me. Had something else driven you to this sequence of events? To convince you to go home, and to leave again?

It's a mystery that has me complicit, in this room. Because I want to know. And I have this painful hope that I will pull open that drawer, or find a note in your handwriting hidden under that book, or see something on a calendar I didn't know existed, and everything will become clear. The mystery solved. And I will be absolved.

Caleb, please, I need to know.

SATURDAY NIGHT

▶ ◀ ▲

It's impossible not to notice that Julian's home. My father is making chicken potpie, his favorite. My mother has the laundry basket on the coffee table, and there's a pile of Julian's folded shirts on the couch while she watches television.

Even if they hadn't given me fair warning (a verbal countdown, each morning), it would be obvious. So much of our family life revolved around Julian's ball games and his schedule these last few years, it's like we don't know what to do with each other now that he's gone. So my parents take it upon themselves to make his return visits as welcoming as possible, to entice him to want to return.

They do his laundry. They cook his favorite meals. They leave him be. There's a calm in the house when he's home, like I know my place again in our family unit. Without him here, I feel my parents' focus too strongly, like they're surprised by the person I have become.

"Where've you been?" my mother says, her substitution for a greeting because I'm supposed to be engaging in family time, now that Julian's home.

"Helping Eve with the packing," I say.

"Oh," my mother says, and her voice falls, her face falls. She moves around the couch, places her hand on the side of my head, and I look away, too aware of her gaze. "How is she? I can't believe they're really doing it. Really moving."

I don't answer any of it, because really, what is there to say? Sean's gone and Caleb's gone and soon they'll be gone, too. Nothing more to remind us.

"I need to go back tomorrow."

I feel the tension through her arm before she trails her fingers through my hair, and she shifts her focus. "But you're going to miss seeing your brother. He leaves tomorrow evening."

"I'm seeing him now," I say.

She shakes her head. "He's going out after dinner. Some baseball thing. Oh, you should go." Then, she calls louder, "Julian! Do you think you could bring Jessa with you?"

"Ugh, Mom, stop." The last thing I want is to be dragged around as an appendage to Julian. It'll be a bunch of people I've known for what feels like my whole life, mixed with my classmates who know me with Caleb. A blending of worlds, and I won't know which person to be.

"It's fine," he says, stepping out of the kitchen, where he was undoubtedly helping my father, because Julian can also cook, of course. "I'm going back to talk to the team at the coach's place."

It's fine, he says, like I am the chore.

"God, don't do me any favors, Julian. What if *I* don't want to go?"

My mother mumbles at the television, picking up another shirt to fold. Julian grins and tilts his head. "Would you rather . . . ," he says, letting the thought trail off. He raises his hands in a balance of scales, as if to say: *Pick, Jessa.* A night home with your parents asking you questions, trapped in this house? Or an escape.

"Ugh, fine," I say. I roll my eyes at him, and he laughs. I hate that I like my brother as much as I do.

I've sort of inherited Julian's car, in that the car is here, and Julian's usually gone. But when he's home, I'm reminded that it belonged to him first. He takes the keys from their familiar spot hanging in the kitchen. He sits in the driver's seat. I stew silently, wondering if he's noticed the keychain with my name (well, it's really a *Jesse*, the *e* turned into an *a* with red permanent marker, the closest name Caleb could ever find on the store display; I was always searching for my name, everywhere), or the seat that's been adjusted to my height, the mirrors angled to my field of vision.

He adjusts things smoothly as I make a show of sliding into the passenger side, but he leaves the radio on my station at least.

The coach's house isn't far from campus—an older colonial that makes me suddenly wonder how much history teachers–slash–high school baseball coaches are paid.

Julian, as if reading my thoughts, says, "Mrs. Peters works in banking."

There are cars already filling the driveway, a few parked

along the curb. "So," I say, "you're giving, like, an insight-to-college talk or something?"

He shrugs. "They do this yearly alumni-family gathering thing. Like a chance for the kids to ask questions about applying, or scouts, or whatever." He fidgets with the controls on the car, turning the lights off. "We don't have to stay long. Maybe we can catch a movie on the way home. Or get some ice cream. Or whatever."

He stares out the front window as he says this, and I groan. "Oh my God, did Mom put you up to this?"

"No, I just thought—"

"I'm fine, Julian."

"I know, I know, it's just—"

"We broke up," I say, and he sits straighter. "Caleb and I had broken up." I did not lose my boyfriend. That, at least, was a role I could figure out how to fill. The tragic figure left behind. A future full of never-haves and what-might-have-beens.

"Yeah, I heard that. Still . . ." *Still. You missed a week of school. You stopped showing up to cross-country. You don't see your friends. You go to school and back, stuck in a lifeless cycle, like a ghost.*

"Still, what?" I'm going to make him say it, sharing in the discomfort of the moment.

But before he can answer, someone knocks on the window; another alumnus, a year older than Julian. Terrance Bilson. He smiles widely, and Julian launches himself out of the car, laughing, embracing his old teammate. I trail behind as they walk together toward the house, and then Julian gestures toward me, saying, "You remember my sister, Jessa?"

Terrance's smile fractures for the slightest moment. If the outside porch light hadn't been trained directly on him, I wouldn't have noticed. But I did. I do. Then the smile is back, and he says, "Right, hi, Jessa. Nice to see you."

Inside, there's a spread of finger food on the long dining room table. There are kids I recognize from school who nod their hellos after they fawn over Julian. Sometimes there's a benefit to being Julian's sister, to fading into the background, to being generally ignored. I let the conversation hum around me. I check out.

I sit on a hard-backed chair with a plastic cup of soda in my hand, and I take out my phone, pretending to look busy. Pretending like anyone has texted me in the last month.

Someone's knee nudges mine, and I ignore it at first, assuming it's an accident. I shift my legs farther to the side. But then they're bumped again, and I look up, catching Max's eye briefly before I look back at my phone. "Oh, hi," I say. "My brother's in the kitchen. Though I see you've picked your seating strategically."

But he ignores me. His leg is bouncing beside mine. "How long were you over there today? I left for work, and your car was still there."

"Yeah, till dinnertime." And then, in the silence, I tell him. Hoping it will mean something to him as well. That he will sit a little straighter, lean a little nearer, drop his voice in surprise. "I can't find his glasses," I say.

His leg stops bouncing. "You mean the ones from middle school? Thick rimmed, black?"

I nod.

"I haven't seen those in years. He still had them?"

"Yes, he still wore them."

He laughs, and the sound makes me mournful. It was a piece shared only with me, then.

"Maybe he finally tossed them," he says.

Nothing. No spark. No meaning.

"I'll check again tomorrow," I say.

I feel him looking at the side of my face. "You're going back?"

Of course I'm going back. It's all that's left of him, whether his mother is punishing me or not. It's the first time I've been invited back into the house since before that day. It's my last chance for answers, for some sort of absolution, to see if I can uncover what he was doing, where he was going. The cause and effect that led us all here. "It'll probably take me at least a week," I say.

"You don't have to do that. I'll do it. Don't show up, and I'll just do it, okay?"

"Max," I say, and I am so serious, so deadly serious I grasp onto his arm so he will understand how serious I am. "Do not touch that room."

It's mine. My grief, my guilt, all of it—it belongs to me, and it's mine to go through. I had no idea how possessive I felt over Caleb, even now. Even though Max probably has more claim to that room, if he wants to make the argument. But he doesn't.

Instead Max seems to remember that he doesn't look at me anymore, and I remember that I don't touch him, and we quickly disentangle and look away. I find Julian, sit beside him on the couch, listen to him tell the stories about college, poised and filtered because of the fact his coach is listening, and so is the coach's wife.

And then he says, "I need to get Jessa home," and I roll my eyes. He says a thousand goodbyes, all perfect smiles and perfect handshakes. Even his hair, which is the same color and texture as my own, obeys him, while mine inevitably succumbs to chaos by the end of the day, with either static or humidity, depending on the time of year.

On the walk back to his car, he says, "Thanks for the excuse. That was totally painful, right?"

"Totally," I say.

We go to a movie. We get ice cream after. It's midnight when we arrive back home, and our parents are asleep, and I sit in the car beside Julian in the driveway as he drums his fingers softly on the steering wheel, like he's working himself up to something.

"I'm sorry, Jessa," he says.

I want to tell him to stop, but it's too late. He's already said it, and everything comes back in a rush, like a flood. I feel my eyes burn, the hot tears on my face, as I look away.

He sits beside me with the engine off, until the cold from the outside seeps through the steel door, my jacket, the layers of clothing, my skin.

I wipe the side of my face before opening the car door, and he hands me a tissue without saying a word. I take it, ball it up, say, "Of course you have a tissue. Of course."

"I should've come home," he says. "I'm sorry."

"Don't. Mom was right. You needed to stay, get used to college. Acclimate."

The corner of his mouth twitches. "Did she really say 'acclimate'?"

"She really did. I overheard her talking to Dad about it." I look straight at my brother then. Give him the absolution I so desperately want myself. "There was nothing you could've done. Really." And then I push the door open, step out into the November night.

"No," he says as he exits the car. "I should've been here. She was wrong."

I turn around, grinning. "Oh my God, don't tell her that. Never tell her that."

He smiles as we walk to the front door.

It's my key that lets us back in, where my parents have left the entryway lights on. I head up the steps, and he lingers near the kitchen. We don't say goodbye, even though I know I won't see him tomorrow.

Everyone says I'm *so lucky* to have Julian as my brother, and I roll my eyes. But I know this. I know I am.

SUNDAY MORNING

▶ ◀ ▲

It's easier to leave before everyone else is up. Before the questions begin. Before the chaos of Julian leaving and the inevitable silence that follows—where we're all trying to figure out how to be with each other, without ball games to schedule and booster clubs to run, and the fact that it's always my turn to clear the table.

There are two possible routes between Caleb's house, in Old Stone Pointe, and my own, in East Arbor. The first is a loop outside the town centers, hooking back in through the other side, closer to the shore. It avoids the traffic lights, but also takes a little longer—closer to twenty minutes instead of fifteen. The other cuts clear across the county, a direct path through the town centers, separated by residential streets, strip malls, and the river.

I decide on coffee. I decide on the river. I haven't been this way since. But there's something about being in his room that shakes everything loose.

First come the strip of stores, the gas station, the ice cream place, and the dress shop. The sky is light, but there's a sense of fog, a blurriness as I approach the sign.

Coats Memorial Bridge. The road narrowing and the trees thickening, and my hands gripping the wheel, my lungs burning with the breath I'm holding.

It never occurred to us to question what this bridge was a memorial for.

The sunlight catches on a new stretch of guardrail in the corner of my vision. And then I'm past it, and my breath releases. The trees thin out again, the stores begin picking up, and I pull into the lot of the coffee shop I used to meet Hailey at on Saturday mornings, setting up in the corner booth with our schoolwork and a chocolate scone and coffee (for me) and hot chocolate (for her).

The clerk doesn't look up after handing me the cup, steaming hot against my cold hands. It's not until I have it in my grip that I realize there's a tremor in my fingers. The guy looks up and smiles. "Sure you haven't had enough already?"

I take a sip, and it burns the roof of my mouth. "I'm sure."

On the way back to my car, I see her: Hailey, in the car with her parents, eating something with a paper wrapper. She's in a dress, like usual, but more modest than her typical flared style, this one with a higher collar and in a shade of navy. Even through the window, I can tell her makeup is toned down. They're on the way to or from church, I decide.

I don't knock or wave or anything, but I can tell the moment she sees me. She stops chewing, the food still positioned between her teeth. I raise my hand to her, and she slowly raises hers back, her eyes wide, like she hasn't seen me in ages. And maybe she hasn't. I've built a nice, dark cocoon for myself these last few months, the sheen of everything around me dulled and filtered. I've been to school. I've been home. I've kept moving.

But I've quit the team. And I've quit my friends. Or my friends have quit me. I can't really remember which way it went—my lack of response, or their lack of attempt. All I know is that it felt like relief. Nothing is expected or required of me; there's nothing to mess up, no actions to undo or words to unsay. My presence or absence affects no one. I am blameless.

I think the last time I spoke to Hailey might've been at Caleb's service, but I can't remember what she said, or what I said. I do remember her shoes: silver, with straps. I remember wondering if she had anything more appropriate, then thought: probably not. I don't remember if I voiced that out loud. I probably did. That's probably part of the problem.

I couldn't tell you what happened there, because it still struck me as such a ridiculous concept: the service. Up front, there was a montage of pictures of him—some including me. And more: Caleb in his lacrosse uniform, with his team-mates. Caleb giving his sister a piggyback ride. Younger versions of Caleb and Max smiling up at the camera, a pile of wood between them, a hammer in Caleb's hand.

The pictures would have to do, because there was nothing else remaining. A crooked license plate, stuck between river rocks the next town over; a section of the bumper, trapped in an eddy near the inlet; a single tire, washed up on a nearby beach.

The engine exhaust lingers in the parking spot as Hailey's car pulls away. I can't catch my breath. I picture Caleb running down the front steps, his head ducked low because of the rain, his wipers squealing as they cut through the torrent while he drives.

I wonder if he could see through the rain.

It's just rain, our coach said. *Just rain.*

My mom used to say the car was the safest place to be in a storm, with rubber wheels that ground you in the event of a lightning strike. It's a piece of metal, two tons, designed for our protection. There are airbags. Safety protocols. Antilock brakes. All to keep us safe.

The surge came later. A flash-flood warning on the radio, lighting up all our phones after the race, but we get those all the time. *Turn around, don't drown*, says the alert, but nobody takes it too seriously.

The Old Stone River snakes through town, under Coats Memorial Bridge, and then continues on. That day, the river kept rising, with nowhere else to go; it breached the guardrail of the bridge. *In six inches of water, you lose control. In twelve inches, the car will float. The current will take you.*

The river curves through another town on its way to the coast, where it empties out into the Atlantic. A whole ocean, where he might be.

There was nothing to bury. Nothing to reduce to ash. Nothing to feel in the second-row pew of the church other than the fact that nothing was there.

I shiver, holding tighter to the coffee cup. I scroll through my phone until I reach Hailey's name, see her photo: an up-close shot of the two of us with our eyes squeezed shut and our faces pressed together.

I don't know what to say. I don't know how to start.

Hi, I write.

I'm halfway to Caleb's when I hear the *ding* in response.

The last few miles of the drive pass in a blur—the larger suburban homes giving way to narrow brick homes wedged closer together in a grid of streets. But you couldn't beat the location. Caleb's home was effortlessly close to the shore, and we could walk to the shops on the outskirts of town, with no highway or major roads cutting through the path.

I parallel park in the spot in front of his house that once belonged to him instead. I see the curtain shift in the front window, the profile of a little girl with dark hair. I wave, and the curtain falls shut. The little girl disappears.

I check my phone and see Hailey's response. *Hi*, she says.

The front door opens, and Eve is waiting for me. Her mouth is set in a grim line, like she disapproves of the fact that the phone is in my hand.

"Who was that?" she says as I walk up the porch steps. Her gaze shifts to the phone still in my grip.

"Hailey Martinez," I say. And then I show her the display, as if she has forced it from me. As if I have to prove that I have not taken up with some other boy who is not her son, to be granted access to this house. That I am loyal, even now, to his memory.

Eve is still looking at the phone, at the meaningless text, when she asks, "Do you have my number, Jessa?"

"No," I say.

"Next time, call when you're on the way, so I make sure I'm here in case anything comes up." She holds out her hand for my phone, and I place it in her palm. *If anything comes up.* It's an empty room. What could possibly *come up*?

She adds her number as a new contact, and I'm startled by the sound of footsteps behind me.

I turn just in time to see Mia disappear up the steps. Upstairs, I hear her door slam closed. Eve says nothing when she hands back my phone, so I make my way up the steps. I decide to make a visual dent this time. So it seems less and less like Caleb's room, as if that might make it easier.

The Birds

The door is closed, like yesterday, but I know Eve has been in here, because she has moved the boxes I finished. Most of what I packed was inside drawers, so the room doesn't look much different, other than the walls.

Except it's darker in here. The window curtain has been pulled shut, shadows dancing along the wall. The switch on the surge protector under his desk glows an eerie red, which you only notice when the lights are off and the shades pulled closed.

It's not really a window shade but a shower curtain that hangs in front of his window. It's white, with black birds. But, like, Alfred Hitchcock–level birds. Horror-movie-level birds. You don't realize they're birds at first: at first, it just looks like a bunch of thick black lines intersecting on a white background. A pattern you can't quite figure out. You have to step back, see it from the entrance, look closer. Find one bird, the rest come alive.

Caleb put it up for Halloween last year to get into the spirit, he said—but he never took it down. When the light hits in the morning, they cast shadows across his bed, the walls, the floor. Us.

"And my soul from out that shadow . . . ," he said, my head resting on his chest. The words vibrated through his ribs, into my skull. We were lying across his bed. He ran his fingers through my hair, absently.

"Wow, so romantic," I said.

The clock ticked above us. Just minutes after nine a.m.; I had woken him up. Or, I was still waking him. I'd walked right in the front door, up the steps, and let myself in his room. It was the first day of summer break, after we'd spent the whole school year together, and he was supposed to be babysitting Mia, who was watching television downstairs by herself when I arrived.

"You're coming to the party this weekend, right?" I asked.

"Hmm?"

"Julian's graduation party? It's this Saturday."

Caleb's arm tensed under my head. "I don't think he'd want me there. I don't think I'm his favorite person."

It was true. Julian had never quite fully warmed up to him, maybe because Caleb was my first serious boyfriend, maybe because our circles were overlapping in a way he wasn't comfortable with. Either way, I knew Caleb could sense the discomfort, just as I could. "*I* want you there."

"Maybe call me after, Jessa. I'm supposed to help my mom with something."

"Right," I said, pushing myself onto my elbows. Lately it felt like our days revolved around his schedule, his plans, his family.

"Wait, don't get up," he said, his fingers circling my arm.

"Your sister needs breakfast," I said.

"Yeah," he said, and suddenly he was up, out of bed, searching his floor for a pair of pants to slip over his boxers. He looked over his shoulder, catching me watching. "But that's not your job."

He shut the door behind him, but said, before it latched, "Don't move, I'll be right back."

It is a truth universally acknowledged that a guy who cares for his much younger sibling somehow has an unprecedented appeal. Listen, it's just biology. Many other things are forgiven in its place. Like: the way I'd sometimes catch him staring out the window when I was talking; these vague excuses he'd started giving me more and more often; how *college* was a topic that had recently become off-limits, as if I was a distraction from the decision.

I pushed myself to sitting when I heard his steps on the stairs again, saw the envelope on top of his desk. The top slit open, rough and ragged. He opened the door just as I reached for it.

"Don't," he said.

But I did. Of course I did.

He reached for it too, grabbing it out of my hands before the handwritten words could slip into focus. I felt the sting of a paper cut on my index finger. "What the hell?" I said.

"Just leave it, Jessa," he said, dropping it into the bottom desk drawer, leaning back against it. Creating secrets, instead of giving them away—the opposite end of the bell curve.

Just say it, just say it, just say it—

The sound of Mia's scream cut through the moment, cut through the tension. Caleb's eyes went wide, and he launched himself down the stairs, with me scrambling to keep up. Mia stood beside the kitchen table, staring at the overturned cereal bowl, the shattered glass beside it, the juice seeping across the floor. Her toe was bleeding from where she'd stepped in glass.

"Oh," he said, scooping her up. "It's okay, Mia."

Her green eyes were wide and overflowing with tears. "I just wanted more juice," she said, and she let out another wail.

I cleaned the floor, carefully picking up the pieces of glass, while Caleb tended to Mia's foot. Everything that had just happened upstairs, forgotten. Until my paper cut made contact with the orange juice, and I sucked in a quick gulp of air, from the sting.

My hands shook as I finished cleaning, and all the while I heard Caleb's low, soothing voice across the room, in words that were too far away to hear clearly.

Caleb took the plastic trash bag with the pieces of glass out to the garbage around back, and Mia looked up from the chair across the room. "He's supposed to be watching me," she said, the corners of her mouth tipping down, a shadow of Eve. An echo of a grown-up, those same words probably spoken in this very room.

It wasn't my fault. The excuse on the tip of my tongue. *He was sleeping when I arrived.*

"I have to go," I told Caleb when he came back inside. "Feel better, Mia."

I hear her words again, standing in the entrance of his

room now, watching the shadows of the birds lighten and darken on the walls, the bedspread, the desk, from a cloud moving across the sun.

He was supposed to be watching me.

The course of events would be different had he done what his mother asked of him. I wonder if Mia still feels those words, understands that there is an alternate outcome, if only he had done what he was supposed to do. Caleb in this house, instead of driving through the rain. *It's not my fault*, I want to tell her. Pointless words now. I barely believe them myself. I stride across the room, my steps angry.

The curtain comes down first. I have to stand on the desk chair, which swivels, to reach the curtain rod. The metal bar tilts when I lift it off its bracket, and the birds slide off in a heap to the floor. The light is too bright, and my eyelids slam shut on instinct. The room is bathed in light, and I think: *There will never again be the shadow of a bird on the wall. On the bed. On us.*

The curtain feels much lighter and ethereal in my arms, as I fold it over, fabric billowing up again as I push it down, deeper into the box.

The surface of his desk is now bare, other than the computer screen. I haven't touched the desk drawers yet.

I picture him leaning against it, hiding the envelope, the words that wouldn't slip into focus.

Next, I drag the box over to the desk. I drop to my knees. I need his secrets to be mine again, hear him whisper them into my ear as he sits beside me on the beach. As if I could save us, even now.

College Letters

I am captured by this version of Caleb, the one who cannot exist. Wondering where he would've gone to school, what he would've done. What schools were scouting for him, sending him letters, asking him to come visit?

By the start of Julian's senior year, things were already firmly in motion. The letters arrived during junior year, and I remember my parents spreading them out on the kitchen table, Julian sitting between them, making a plan.

I go for the bottom drawer first. It's deeper, and used less. Inside are the things he doesn't reach for often: computer wires, an old speaker, a tangle of cords, a spare mouse. I dump them all into a box, label them *Electronics*.

The letter isn't here. None of them are.

I try the middle drawer, and here's where the college letters are. He played lacrosse, but he wasn't going to be recruited for it. That's what he told me, anyway, explaining why he was so diligent about his grades.

It was something I understood all too well, being related to Julian, who had been naturally gifted at something so definitive from a young age. Meanwhile, I was an above-average runner, but I had to really work for it. Nobody was going to come looking for me.

Still, Caleb had offers to come visit schools. To stay with other students, see how things work. He was a good student. A decent athlete. His test scores were high. He would've gotten into a good school.

The college pamphlets are from state schools. There are letters, folded up in envelopes with his name and address typed on the front, all touting their schools' benefits and inviting him to consider applying. There are thick packets with applications inside, still untouched.

I don't see the hand-printed envelope that gave me the paper cut. He probably threw it out. I don't see anything in these papers that would make him want to hide it from me. These are all for in-state schools. What was there for me to be so worried about?

But in some ways, it was the beginning of the end.

He made it a thing, by hiding it. Manifested the worry out of thin air. So at any mention of *college*, my stomach would knot, and my shoulders would tighten, and I'd picture a different Caleb, in a different place, with a different girl, while I stayed here, finishing out my last year of high school.

He went on his first school visit in early September of this year, not even thirty miles away. *I won't be far,* he'd said, not looking at me as he packed.

His duffel bag was in the middle of his bed. I was standing near the entrance, watching his back. "Jessa," he said, "you're making me nervous, just standing there."

What I wanted to tell him was that *he* was making *me*

nervous. There was something off in his energy, in the way he was moving, like he wasn't focused on any one thing.

I couldn't watch anymore. Couldn't put words to the feeling growing between us. "I have to go," I said, "I'm meeting Hailey to study."

"See you in a few days," he called after me, when I was already halfway down the steps.

But his phone, the entire trip, went straight to voicemail. He said he forgot his charger. He said he was just really busy. But not too busy to return home with a school T-shirt and a hangover.

Just leave it, Jessa. I hear him again.

What's the point? He's gone.

I decide these college letters will go in the box of his personal things. So his mother can see the Caleb who might've lived. All the potential paths he could've taken. All the men he could've become.

Letter Opener

Underneath the college letters are a collection of notebooks with spiral bindings that I recognize from school. They say MATH and ENGLISH and SCIENCE on the fronts, in black marker. He never got rid of them, even after the semester was over, saying they might be useful one day, which made me laugh. But he was serious.

All this planning, Caleb. All these things you kept.

And then there's the letter opener, buried below. The light from the uncovered window hits the sharp point, and I grab it in my hand, the metal colder than I expected.

The first time I saw this, one Saturday in early July, it was on his bedside table. I'd thought it was a knife. He thought that was hilarious.

I'd been sitting on the edge of his bed, waiting for him to finish his shower. I'd used the hose in his backyard to wash away the sand and the salt. We'd just come in from the beach, the one place where everything felt normal, and I'd tell myself it was all in my head; the silence and the distractions, the distance I felt growing between us.

He'd stood in the doorway, rubbing a towel over his drying hair, grinning. "Badass with a letter opener," he said.

"A what?" I looked again. It looked like a miniature sword, fashioned into a point.

"An opener. For letters." He walked across the room, took it from my hand, demonstrated on a folded-over piece of paper on his desk. A sharp tear of paper, the sound like nails on a chalkboard.

"I'm sorry, we need a tool for that?"

He smiled, flipped it around, showing me the base. "It was my grandfather's. Then my father's. Now it's mine."

The initials *DE* were engraved into the silver handle. The letter opener became something else in his hand. Pieces of his family, passed down.

Now I wonder who this would go to next. Mia has a different father. Maybe his mother knew of some other descendants of his grandfather. Maybe there were cousins. He never mentioned them, if he had them.

There was something serious about the moment I'd held it in my hand that first day, as if I were holding generations and history and blood and weight.

But I'd made light of it instead, desperate for these moments when we were laughing, and everything felt fresh and surface-new. I took it back from him and held it in my hand like a miniature sword, keeping light on my toes, backpedaling as if defending myself. He sidestepped behind me, wrapped me up in his arms so I lost my concentration, kissed me on the neck and disarmed me in the same breath. Smiled with the letter opener in his hand as he spun me around.

"Cheater," I said.

"Practice," he said, smiling wide. Then he turned and

flung the letter opener at the wall, like we'd seen in a hundred different action movies. But it ricocheted off the wall at the base instead, landing on the carpeted floor with a faint thud.

I'd burst out laughing, from the impulsiveness, from the ridiculousness. Anything to fill the silence, where the gap between us grew.

The spot on the wall where the letter opener hit has a faint chip in the paint, and I find my eyes drifting there now. I can see it, in the light. But there are several scratches. I stand, as if compelled by the wall across the way, and I walk around the bed, my fingers raised in front of me, until they touch the wall, the chips and dents in the gray paint. I run my fingers through the grooves, unable to decipher the dent he had made that day from all the others.

Because it seems like he must've sat on his bed, practicing that throw, over and over, afterward. Seeing if he could get the point to stick in the plaster. Driven by the idea of it. *Practice*, he'd said.

I bring the letter opener closer to my face, turning the blade over. There's a streak of gray along one of the edges, like it had been embedded in the wall. And suddenly it's not my hand, but his, clenched in a fist around the base. For a second, I catch the faintest scent of the river, and my grip loosens, the blade drops, and Caleb is gone again.

Hiking Boots

Bending down to pick up the letter opener, I see a shadow in the shape of feet under the gray bed skirt that skims the floor. Almost as if someone is standing at the other side of the bed, watching me. But lifting the bed skirt, everything slips into focus: they're just shoes. I pull out the boots, which turn from shadowed shapes to a muddy brown in the sunlight. The rubber soles still have pebbles lodged in the grooves. The laces are undone and stiff from dirt and dried water. I put them aside, thinking *trash*—because really, they're kind of gross—but they're also pretty good hiking boots, or so he informed me.

When we went hiking in the beginning of June, I wore sneakers. My running shoes. They'd gotten me through all sorts of terrain, up and down hills during cross-country practice, through wind and rain and the occasional snow day.

Caleb picked me up that Saturday morning before dawn, and I was the only one awake in my house. It felt like the world was ours. He raised an eyebrow at my gray and purple bag. My backpack, really. And my choice of footwear. My sneakers. It felt like he was criticizing me with his look, when all he'd said the day before was, *Will you come on a hike with me tomorrow?*

"Sorry, I didn't have time to go shopping for camo-style hiking gear," I said. "But it gets the job done."

We left at six a.m. and drove for just about two hours, past signs for the Delaware Water Gap.

I slept on and off most of the way there. The crunch of loose gravel under the tires was what woke me, as we pulled off the main road. My head was leaning against the window. I caught Caleb staring out the front window, looking up.

"We're here?" I asked.

We pulled off the road at a sign with an arrow, a hiking trail name, an icon for picnic tables. Caleb eased slowly into a small circular lot made of dirt, where another pair of hikers were loading up supplies from their trunk.

He shifted into park. Twisted in his seat for his hiking boots, changed out of his sneakers.

This was my second indication that hiking was not going to be what I thought it was. My first indication being the six a.m. start time.

It didn't take me long to realize that the sneakers were a mistake. The rocks were slippery with morning dew, nearby moisture from the stream trickling down beside us. I stayed on the dirt path, feeling blisters forming at my heels, even though I'd run in these shoes up and down hills and dirt tracks before. There was something to the motion that was different, and at one point I threw my backpack to the ground and let out a huff.

"Come on," Caleb said, unamused.

"Maybe I should leave the bag and just try running."

He checked his watch, looked up the trail again, tapped his heel against a rock while I adjusted my socks. "Anything that will make you go faster," he mumbled.

I swatted him with my bag as I hooked it back on my shoulders, and he grinned, relenting.

I kept my eyes on his boots while we moved, trying to step in his steps, breathe when he breathed. Within minutes, I was in perfect sync with Caleb, and I felt close to him, even as he was facing away, looking away, in silence.

Eventually his steps sped up, and he was scrambling up the rocks, and I fell out of sync, silently cursing both the lack of traction on my shoes and Caleb for not waiting. Then, abruptly, he stopped. I almost ran smack into his back. He was frozen in a clearing made of boulders, and we were on the top of the mountain. There was a drop-off beyond, and the valley and the river stretched below us, in endless green and blue.

"Oh," I said as I came to rest beside him.

Caleb's mouth was slightly open, and his eyes had this faraway look, and I thought, in that moment, that he was heartbreakingly beautiful. Without looking, he reached a hand over for mine, lacing our fingers together—both of our hands pulsing hot from the hike, a sharp contrast against the cold of the breeze on the exposed overlook.

He didn't take a picture, and neither did I, because I understood. You couldn't really capture it. Anything we did, forcing the look and feel into a flat two dimensions, would strip the moment for the both of us.

I sat on the rock behind us, and Caleb looked down at me. "We're not done," he said.

I scrunched up my face. Thought about the length we'd already walked, and would most likely have to walk back. "You were right," I said. "About the sneakers."

He reached a hand down and pulled me up, pulled me close, so it was just us and the trees and the sky. "It'll be worth it. I promise."

The trail snaked downward this time, down off the mountain, into the trees, the path turning back to roots and dirt. The sound of birds calling, insects crying, and the hint of something more, in the distance.

We were making our way toward something—what had started as a faint hum was slowly becoming a roar. Eventually we reached a clearing, which gave way to a wide river trailing between large, flat rocks, and a waterfall streaming down from the rocks behind us. Close to the shore, the mist rose up off the water, coating everything.

On the other side of the river, there was a group of people having lunch, and a few others swimming. In the distance, through the trees, there were a scattering of tents, a make-shift campground. Caleb sat on a stone at the water's edge, used a stick to try prying a rock from the sole of his boots.

"This is the end," he said.

"Of the hike?"

He grinned. "That. And New Jersey."

"Ohh," I said, raising my hand to my forehead, as if surveying a foreign territory. "The fabled land of Pennsylvania? I've heard stories of such a place."

He laughed, extracted a larger section of mud from his shoe, and tossed it into the river. Then he fell silent. He was watching the group on the other side of the river—a father, a mother, children. There were other adults, presumably relatives. A few people were swimming, independently, closer to the waterfall. I wondered if he yearned for something, if he saw what was lacking in his own life. Or if he was just hungry for their food.

"We should've done the picnic thing," I said.

He seemed startled by me standing there beside him. The sound of the water was hypnotic, making the nearby voices fade away.

"Oh, and who would've carried that?" He shook his head and pulled out his camera. "Come on," he said, unlacing his shoes.

I did the same, glad track season was over, because my feet were pretty beat-up looking from the hike, and my coach would have a fit if I came to practice complaining about blisters.

Caleb waded out a little into the river, holding my hand, and I was unprepared for the shock of cold. But he kept moving, until we were as deep as I wanted to go, in clothes. The water was up past our knees, touching the base of his shorts, and mine.

We stood in the river, on the border, rocks and dirt under our toes. "We're not in New Jersey anymore. But we're not in Pennsylvania, either," he said.

"We're nowhere," I said, and the current ran over my bare feet, up my bare legs, numbing and enticing all at once.

I hopped onto his back, made him carry me out, laughing as my toes tapped the surface of the water when he pretended to drop me.

We tried to get a picture when we were back on the shore, the two of us in a frame, the waterfall behind us. But our faces were too close, blocking everything. One of the men who'd been swimming was now wading up to his knees, and he offered to take the photo for us. "You guys look like you could use some help."

Caleb passed him the camera, and the man shook off his hands to dry them first before taking it. He didn't count us down, or say *ready* or anything; he just took the shot and handed the camera back. In the photo, I'm half wincing from the cold on my feet, and Caleb seems distracted, looking somewhere beyond the camera. Neither of us is truly smiling, but there's something beautiful about it, still. Maybe it's the waterfall. Maybe it's the way we were both caught unprepared. Or maybe it's everything surrounding us. The mist coming up off the water. The scattering of people at the end of the frame, caught midmotion, hands scooping water, an arc of water droplets, a child with his hand on the way up to block his face.

It was worth it later, he was right. If only for the drive back, and the stop at the drugstore, and the way he set me in the backseat, holding my bare foot in his hand, wrapping the Band-Aid around.

And because, when he dropped me off, my legs sore, my body sweaty and gross, he said, "Thanks for today, Jessa."

It was the last time he thanked me for anything and meant it.

I throw the hiking boots in an empty box and the sound echoes through the room. I remember that waterfall photo—the last photo of us that had been on the wall. The beginning of the end. I make my way back to his desk, needing more.

Ticket Stubs for Bleacher Seats

After emptying the rest of the middle drawer, I move on to the last.

The top drawer is in disarray, as I had expected. There's the calculator to the side, a heap of papers, ticket stubs, receipts. All thrown in, one on top of the other. You can work your way down to the bottom, like moving back in time.

Except there's something wrong with the chaos. The receipt on top is from a year ago, covering the concert tickets from last spring. I piece through them gently, so as not to disturb the balance.

Near the bottom, completely out of order, I find two ticket stubs from a Yankees game, his and mine, a secret my parents still didn't know about. I wasn't supposed to be in New York City at all. I wasn't even supposed to be off the school grounds.

Late April. Max and Hailey and Sophie. A guy named Stan who lived in the city, who Max knew. Hailey's brief failed date with Craig Keegan. All of us bursting with energy on the train station platform, skipping out on school.

Max had gotten bleacher seats through his friend Stan, twelve bucks apiece, a perfect outing on a sunny April afternoon. It was unofficially senior skip day, so half the school would be missing anyway. Julian was visiting the UPenn campus for the long weekend, and my parents were driving him up and spending the day. Skipping school was not something I did often (or ever, really), and the day buzzed with the added adrenaline.

We took the train into the city, switched to the subway, riding it out to the Bronx. Holding on to the bars overhead in the packed subway car, holding on to each other. Taking the stadium ramp up and up and up until we emerged to the sunlit arena, the green and brown of the field, the players moving like miniature figurines in the distance.

I don't remember much about the game itself. I do remember the hot dogs, the pretzels, the ice cream. How far away we were, in the bleachers. The players indistinguishable below. Three hours laughing with Caleb and Hailey, and Hailey giving me a look about Craig Keegan, like, *This is so not happening.* Craig had spent most of the time asking Stan what other tickets he could get. Max was the only one who seemed to be paying attention to the game. The rest of us were just there for the thrill of it.

On the way home, we got caught in the exit rush, streams of people funneling back down the ramps, out into the street, down into the subway station. Caleb and I had calculated how much it would cost for four subway rides, and put the money on a card together—not realizing the card itself had a purchase fee.

Not realizing until that moment when Caleb handed me the card to use after him, as he slipped through the turnstile, that the card wouldn't work. Me left on the other side, with a huge crowd waiting behind me, pushing up against me.

"You need to put more money on the card," the man behind me said, shoving me aside as he went through. I turned around. There was a swarm of people in the station, surrounding the card machines and the turnstiles. My friends were on the platform, running toward the arriving train, pushed along by the chaos.

We had been a trail of people connected hand to hand, dragging each other through the crowd. And then I wasn't. I stepped aside, the sickening knot back in my stomach. The line for the card machine was endless. I didn't have cash to add onto it, and I felt a lump in my throat, thinking *This was all a mistake, such a mistake.*

I'd have to use my credit card, stand on the line for the one working credit-card machine, miss a train or two, and hope they waited for me at Penn Station before heading back to New Jersey. I took a deep breath, realizing there was a good chance I'd be alone the whole way to Penn Station—and maybe all the way home. I felt a flash of anger and resentment as I stepped away from the turnstile.

It was Max who appeared, pushing back through the crowd. Calling my name. Shoving a five-dollar bill at the woman behind me, begging her to take it and let me through with her card. She didn't smile, but she took it. Swiped her card once, and Max pulled me through, hands linked together so we wouldn't lose each other. We were practically sprinting, weaving around clusters of people, and I was so sure we would make it—like a race we would win.

But by the time we made it to the platform, it was empty. I heard the rumble of a train fading into the distance. Everyone else was gone. My calls to Caleb and Hailey went straight to voicemail, and I figured they didn't have service between stations. I sat on the bench, closed my eyes, rested my head on the wall behind, and let out a shaky sigh.

Max sat beside me on the bench, tensely put an arm around my back, and let me rest my head against his shoulder. "We'll catch up at Penn Station," he said.

"I just thought we would make it," I said, hoping he understood. I wasn't upset or sad; it was more a disappointment, a hope cresting and then falling—a bell curve.

I had felt, in the span of a day, the freedom of adulthood—the freeing feeling that I was independent—and then the crushing other side, the alienation of being left on my own. The big, big world moving on without me. My friends not waiting for me here, not in the hustle of the city.

"At least the game was good," he said.

"I'll have to take your word for it," I said. "I think I missed it."

I felt his shoulders shake in laughter. "You didn't watch any of it?"

I laughed. "I really didn't."

"Travesty, really. Not even the double play down the third-base line to end the game?"

I looked up at him. "Not even that. I'm scared to admit this around you, but I'm kind of sick of baseball." I'd been subjected to the world of Julian's games my whole life, listening to game prep the night before and then rehashing it in the days after. Julian's a pitcher, so it wasn't just the outcome that had to be discussed, but the choices, the game strategy. God forbid he lost, and then I'd also have to listen to the intentions and errors and never-ending second-guessing. I had only been there today because Caleb was going, because Hailey was going, because I wanted to say *I skipped school, took the train into the city, caught a ball game, no big deal*.

"I figured you liked baseball. I mean, I've seen you at hundreds of games." It was true, we were a baseball family to the core—but it wasn't because I loved it; I'd come into it by default. Julian was a great baseball player. My parents were great baseball parents. My mom, unofficial team parent; my dad, cooking for team get-togethers; both of them, driving Julian all over the place for years, to tournaments, clinics, and games. And I would accompany them everywhere. There was always a role for me too—scorekeeper, stat keeper, burger flipper, navigator. But it was Julian's world, and I was just a part of it.

"Yes, turns out at this point I know too much. I've seen it all."

Max opened his mouth in feigned shock. "Jessamyn Whitworth, you have never been so wrong. There are infinite possibilities, with infinite outcomes. An infinite number of potential variables in every game. It's *always* exciting."

I rolled my eyes, laughing at his unrestrained excitement. But while we waited for the next train, I listened as Max recounted the game. I saw it play out in my head, thinking that maybe I would've enjoyed watching it. I didn't notice the change in scenery as we boarded the next train, changed lines, or as I let him drag me through the crowd. All the while leaning closer to hear him over the voices in the car. I didn't notice the missed call that came through. Not until we got off at Penn Station, and found Caleb and Hailey, Stan and Craig, all gathered in a circle, staring at their phones.

Caleb gave Max a look when we returned. Max gave one right back, a small shake of his head. I didn't hear what Caleb said. But I did hear Max. "You just left her there," he said.

I feel those words again. Feel them even stronger.

The birthday card I gave him is below the tickets, even though it was in the summer, months after our trip to the city.

None of this is in the right order. It usually looks like chaos, but it's really an organized chaos. It took a little while to understand that about Caleb—the system in the disorder. And unless he was looking for something frantically, I know: I am not the first person in this room.

The ticking of the clock grows louder in the silence.

Everything changes.

A shadow passes underneath the closed door behind me, but then it's gone, and I'm not sure whether I imagined it.

I look over my shoulder again, staring at the darkness underneath the blue door, holding my breath. As if I am not alone after all.

SUNDAY AFTERNOON

▶ ◀ ▲

I hear Caleb's clock ticking on the wall beside the window, and I'm frozen, staring at the closed door. It's noon, and I'm starving, and the hunger is doing something to my mind, making me imagine things that do not matter. That are not true.

The room, then and now, was always stocked with some sort of food. As if descending two flights of steps was too great a trek to undertake for a quick snack. I check those shelves now and find a bag of peanuts, like from a ball game, and a box of Chex Mix, which is mostly empty.

Both go into the garbage can under his desk.

There, behind a stack of books, I see his familiar stash: mini-boxes from a cereal variety pack, still in the plastic, that he would tip into his mouth like a one-bite snack. Three of eight boxes remain.

My fingers tremble, maybe from the hunger. I pick up the Pops, my favorite. He used to save me this one from the variety pack, even though it was his favorite, too.

The Pops were always mine, and my heart breaks, seeing the box here, still waiting. I open the top, tip the box over and pour the cereal into my mouth. The coating is syrupy sweet; the resulting thirst, endless. I can see the bottom of the bag inside. There will never be enough. Never another of these left behind.

Caleb also used to bring extra snacks to school on test days, saying he needed it for his brain, to focus. He convinced his teachers that a bag of chips was the difference between success and failure, and somehow got away with it. The only place they didn't let it slide was the library, so he had to get a little more creative there.

The gap under the doorway is dark, and I hear no footsteps below. I pull the door open, and the creak catches me off guard. A warmer gust of air filters in from below. Keeping my hands on the walls, like Caleb would do, I make my way down the steps, pausing at the closed bedroom door on the second floor. I place my ear to Mia's door, but hear no one inside. I knock faintly and call, "Mia?" but get no response.

My hand grabs the knob, and I turn it just slightly, just so I can feel that it isn't locked, that I could open it if I wanted to.

"Eve?" I call.

I hear only the ticking clock, from below this time. The grandfather clock in the living room, an old narrow tower that no longer chimes, just makes a dull buzzing that you only hear if you're standing right beside it, like the sound mechanism is broken.

It's Mia, I think, who's been through Caleb's things. It's Mia who doesn't think I should be here trespassing, who deserves to keep pieces of her brother for herself. It's Mia who wants to know who he was, this brother she can now never have growing up.

I push her door open, holding my breath. I only open it wide enough to see inside, to stick my face in the gap and confirm that she isn't there. I'm not sure what I expected to see: Caleb's things scattered around the floor maybe, in a tribute to him; her own room slowly being packed away. But it's exactly as I remember it: the walls are a pale lavender and there are more stuffed unicorns than I can count, and her floor is scattered with toys, a beanbag chair, paperback books, a necklace-making kit.

I guess I expected the grief to seep into everything, turning her as morose and sullen as I am. To cause her to give up her friends and activities and focus only on this thing that is missing.

There are no boxes leaning against her walls yet. I think they're mostly leaving things as-is while the house is on the market, so prospective buyers can imagine their own children in these very rooms, taking up the spaces, growing and thriving.

Only Caleb's room must go. Back to an attic storage area. A library. A bunker. Nobody wants to see a room that belongs to a ghost.

I close her door, creep down the remaining steps, and call, "Hello?"

The ticking is louder, and I jump when the ice maker kicks in, dropping fresh cubes into a compartment in the freezer.

I've never been in the kitchen alone, I realize. I've been

here with Caleb. I've been here with Mia. I've been here with Eve, with Sean. The room looks barren and older without them. The laminate more yellowed and chipping at the edges, everything showing its age. I run my finger along the seam of the counter edge as I circle the room, debating lunch. The pantry door squeaks when I pull it open, but I remember Caleb's words: *Really slim pickings here.*

There's bread and peanut butter, but I hate peanut butter. There's cereal, but it's unopened so far, and I think this must belong to Mia, and she wouldn't want me having it. Anyway, I'm no longer sure if I'm entitled to their food. No, I'm sure that I'm not.

I peer out the side window, and see Eve's car is still there, in the long, narrow driveway that leads to their garage around back. Which means she and Mia are probably out nearby. I pull open the drawer beside the fridge, looking for a pen and paper, so I can leave a note. But it's empty. I check the rest. There's the familiar jangle of utensils, some cooking supplies, some spare batteries. But at least half of the drawers are already cleaned out. As if Eve, like me, has started with the parts hidden from the naked eye first. Carving it out from the inside, until all that remains is the shell.

I decide to just go. There's a sandwich shop about a mile away, off the exit ramp. I can be there and back within thirty minutes. I can even eat on the way here. The front door is unlocked, so I figure they must've just stepped out for a moment.

When I step outside, Mia freezes at the base of the steps. She's crouched over with a piece of chalk, her hands stained pink and green. In front of her are a series of boxes she's drawn, all outlined in chalk, like for hopscotch.

I take a single step toward her down the steps, and she looks back at the sidewalk, dragging the chalk in a new line.

"Hi, Mia," I try, but get nothing. Her face is hidden by the long hair hanging over her shoulder, blocking her face.

"I'm going for lunch. Are you here alone?"

She stops then, looks over her shoulder, and makes eye contact firmly and briefly. "I'm not allowed to talk to you," she says quietly, then goes back to the drawing.

Like a punch to the gut. When I recover, I step carefully around her. "Where's your mom?" I ask.

After a pause, she answers, "In the garage," without looking up.

"Okay," I say, pausing beside her, my shadow falling over her game. "If she asks, I went to get lunch. I'll be right back."

There's silence as I walk to my car, but I don't hear the sound of chalk on the sidewalk anymore. I can feel Mia's eyes on me as I walk away.

When I return, the front yard is empty, and all that's remaining from my ham sandwich is the wrapper and excess lettuce. The car is still in the driveway, and I decide to throw the wrapper out in the garbage around back before coming inside. It seems somehow offensive to return with trash, evidence that I must eat to stay alive, all reminders that I am here and Caleb is not.

I have to walk down the driveway between their house

and the neighbor's to get to the garbage cans in the enclosed area, pressed to the siding around back. I pull out the recycling, cringing at the sound of the wheels on concrete, before I can reach the regular trash. I raise the lid, tossing my trash, but catch sight of a pile of red placemats, cookbooks, and magnets—the guts of the kitchen, dumped and forgotten. I leave my trash on top, then ease the lid closed, stepping off the concrete square at the back corner of their house.

The garage door opens behind the house, and Mia darts out, Eve following behind with a machine hooked up to a hose and wired to an outlet inside the garage. We had our house pressure-washed over the summer, so I know this is what Eve is about to do. Getting the house ready to show, to put on the market. I slip around the corner before she notices me standing there.

I let myself back in their front door, which is still unlocked, when I hear the pressure washer start up, the stream of water hitting the siding.

But I feel someone inside, even before I can hear it. Or maybe one sense gives way to the other. Either way, I just *know*.

And then I hear something upstairs. Nothing distinct, just movement. I ascend the first flight and pause at the landing, listening, thinking Mia made it back inside before me. But then I hear it again, a thud, footsteps, but they're not coming from Mia's room. They're up the last flight, behind the blue door, which isn't latched but mostly closed, so I can't see who's behind it.

I assume it's Mia, that she's going through his things now

that I'm gone, but I don't want to spook her. I want her to look at me. I want to tell her I'm sorry about Caleb. So I tiptoe up the steps, avoiding the creak, and angle my face in the open doorway.

A body moves by in a blur—too big, too fast—and I jump back, surprised.

I must've made a noise, or a gasp, because whoever's on the other side of the door pauses as well.

"Mia?" a deep voice calls. Two syllables, and I already know who it is, and my fear turns to anger as I'm throwing open the door, stomping inside.

Max steps back, his eyes widening, and he starts to speak. But not before I see what he's done. The books are all knocked over on the shelves. The drawers are half open. The backpack is tipped over, contents strewn across the carpet. He's rummaged through the open box; half the items are back out on the floor.

"What the hell are you doing!" I yell. I don't even care if Mia or Eve hears me. I'm so furious I can't stop it.

Max hold out his hands and winces. "Please, Jessa," he's saying, but I don't understand what he's asking.

A hiccup gets caught in my throat, and I feel tears burning my eyes as I look at the shelves. "What did you *do*?"

He runs a hand down his face. "I'm looking for something," he says, and he looks at me, really looks at me, his eyes locking with mine for the first time in forever. In months. "Please keep your voice down." He looks over my shoulder, down the hallway. The noise of the pressure washer below continues.

But then my eyes go blurry, Max goes blurry, and I feel the hot tears overflow, and I look away, so angry that I'm crying. "This isn't yours. Nothing here belongs to you. Get. Out."

And I must be pushing him, pushing him out, back to the steps, because his hands are on my upper arms, and he's pleading with me again, even as he's backing out of the room. "It's mine," he says, the words finally registering.

"What's yours?" Certainly not this room. Certainly not these things. Certainly not the memories.

"What I'm looking for. It's not Caleb's. It's mine."

I stop moving, wondering what it is: shirts that I didn't look at closely enough; notes from school that I dumped in a box. "What are you looking for, Max?"

He doesn't answer at first. He looks over his shoulder. Over mine. I see his throat move as he swallows, but he won't look me in the eye. "Money," he says. And it's so faint that I'm leaning closer without meaning to, just to check whether I've heard him correctly.

I shake my head. "There's no money here." I've been through the desk drawers, the pockets of his pants that he left on the floor. His wallet is gone, along with the rest of him. "If you lent him money, he probably had it on him. I think you're going to have to forgive that debt. Seeing as he can't possibly pay you back." I think of salt water and ocean currents, sand and sea—an endless expanse, an immeasurable depth.

"I didn't lend it to him," he says.

I blink slowly, try to understand what he's saying, though he doesn't seem to want to spell it out.

"How much money?" I ask quietly, in case the question wants to disappear. In case he'd prefer not to answer, and I can pretend not to notice.

"Six hundred," he says. "And nine."

"You think he took six hundred dollars from you?" I say what he's implying, since he won't.

"I don't know."

"When?"

"A while ago." He shakes his head. "A few weeks before."

"You think he took six hundred dollars—"

"—And nine."

"Six hundred and nine dollars, and you didn't ask him?"

"I wasn't sure. I mean, I'm pretty sure. He was the only one in there. He's the only one who knows where I keep it."

There are so many reasons why this is impractical. First, Caleb didn't need the money. The reason he could afford private school, I learned, was because his father had set up a trust in his name, in his will. A lawyer was in charge of the account, but the money was his, and he received a monthly stipend on top of bigger items he'd sometimes get approval for, like school tuition. He didn't have to worry about affording college, like Max. He didn't need the scholarship, or a job. But none of those things mattered as much as what I said. "Caleb wouldn't steal from you. You're his best friend."

He narrows his eyes. "And best friends never take each other's things, right?"

The heat rises to my face, I can't stop it.

He brushes past me, his anger focused on me instead of Caleb.

He searches the shelves, the boxes. Kicks the garbage can,

reaches his hand into the empty boxes of food. Moves the leftover hangers. It's a vortex. A storm. I picture a structure being torn metal from metal, limb from limb.

"Stop," I yell, looking at what he's doing to the room.

But he doesn't hear me. Or he doesn't want to. He runs his fingers between the mattress and box spring. Pushes it completely off, with a great thud.

He stops and slowly turns around.

I must've yelled again.

My hands are over my ears, and I slam my eyes shut from the roaring in my head.

He pries my hands off, gently. His mouth is saying he's sorry, and he is, and so am I. He pulls me to his chest and I wrap my arms around his rib cage. I pull him so close it hurts.

"I'm sorry, Jessa," he says once more. I feel the shudder in his chest, and I know he's crying.

He leaves me there, frozen in this room. He doesn't look up as he walks across the lawn, right past Eve and Mia, who don't even notice him. He doesn't even bother opening the gate. He launches himself over the fence, and he runs. He doesn't stop.

Hollow Fan

It takes me a moment to realize that the noise from outside has stopped. And that something's off in the room. Something more than the chaos and the anger and the lingering adrenaline. It feels colder in here, despite the fact that my heart rate has picked up and I'm breathing heavily. And then I realize what it is—as if a ghost is watching and wants to make himself known: the lights are out, the fan is off, there's no red glow of light under his desk from the power supply. The sounds of the house, the ticking of the clock, above and below, echo and reverberate in the silence.

I'm standing beside the window, and feel the cold air seeping through the cracks at the base. I hold my palm to the sill, in the place where the wood gaps against the wall, a fine spider web of cracks running through. It feels like tiny tendrils of smoke, making their way into the room, taking over the house.

I've been inside the room like this once before, when all the noises were elevated, more focused, closer. And this feeling comes right back, an unsettling, like everything has been displaced, even myself. Like the walls lean too far, and the

99

carpet bubbles up, and there's a scent—debris and dust and things once buried, brought to the surface.

I close my eyes and imagine Caleb standing beside me in this room, with no light, no heat, no electricity. I hear the echo of his sigh. Feel the chill of the cold, seeping under the window seal. Feel him brush up against me when I shut my eyes, and me reaching out a hand for the shape of him in the darkness, coming up empty.

It was the end of November, nearly a year ago. A Friday night. We had been out at the movies with Max and Sophie, Hailey and a short-term boyfriend named Charles who was so short-lived I had almost forgotten about him. He may have only lasted this single date. There was nothing impressionable about him; he was no match for Hailey. I imagined, briefly upon meeting him, that he would become devoured by her, merely by standing too close.

I was telling Caleb this as we walked up the front steps of his house. "Devoured?" he asked, sliding his key into the lock.

"Or, like, absorbed into her aura," I said.

"Hailey has an aura now?" he asked, his hand flat on the door.

"Yes," I said, rubbing my upper arms. To make him laugh, I added, "It's orange. Now hurry up." I was shivering and bundled under several layers, aching for the heat inside the house. My curfew wasn't for another hour and a half, and we were in the habit of utilizing every spare minute. We were at that stage where we couldn't see enough of each other.

Meeting for the two minutes between classes; him pulling me onto his lap in the cafeteria, until a teacher gave a curt shake of the head and I'd slide to the chair beside him; hanging out the ten minutes before practice, leaning close and talking until the very last possible moment.

It was the phase that Hailey made a face about, sticking out her tongue, mock-gagging. *Give me my friend back*, she joked, waving her arm in front of me like she was wielding an imaginary wand. *Undo this curse. She smiles too much; it's embarrassing.*

Caleb paused as he pushed through the front door, as if he could sense something slightly off, even then.

"Hello?" he called into the empty space. His mom and Sean were supposed to be out, and his sister was at a sleepover.

He flicked a light switch, but nothing happened. I tripped over something I couldn't see—a leg of the entryway table, maybe. But in the dark, everything felt slightly out of place.

Caleb tried another switch, cursed to himself. "You've got to be kidding me," he said.

I felt, in the pitch dark, the shock of his skin against mine, unexpected, from nowhere. His fingers lacing through my own. "Wait here," he said. And then he left me.

I heard him exit a door in the back of the house, presumably into the garage. The seconds ticked down, a wisp of cold brushed over my exposed skin, like something was alive inside this house.

"Jessa?" Caleb called.

"I'm here," I called back. He seemed infinitely far away, though he was maybe one room, one wall beyond my sight.

"I tried resetting. The wiring is crappy, so sometimes that happens when the system is overloaded. But it's out."

Then I saw a light heading my way, his phone shining in the dark.

He grabbed my hand, pulled me up the stairs, the beam of light illuminating the steps in front of us. When we reached his room, he held the phone to his ear, and I could hear the ringing in the silence. The cold, from the lack of heat, seemed to grow as time moved on, and a shiver worked its way up my spine and over my arms.

I heard his mother's voicemail pick up, no response from her. He said, "Electricity was shut off. In case you didn't know." And then he hung up the phone, and all I heard was his breathing, thick with something else—anger, I guessed.

And yet, I moved closer.

"Should you try the electric company?" I said.

He was silent for a moment, and I pushed open the curtains so that the moonlight shone through, a light spot on the rug, on him.

He sat on the edge of his bed, and he told me, with his head in his hands, "It won't make a difference. They cut the power, because my mom and Sean didn't pay the bill."

I was trying to find a place for this information in my mind. Caleb, at our private school. Caleb, with his new lacrosse gear. Planning for a ski trip this winter. Everyone I knew may not have had money, but they weren't lacking it in any substantial way—not in a way that would lead to something like this.

"But . . . ," I said. Anything I might say seemed both not enough and also too much. "You go to our school. . . ."

He sighed. His arms reached for my waist, pulling me closer, so his forehead rested against my stomach. "My dad died when I was a kid," he said. "There's a trust in my name. I get a monthly stipend, in addition to using it for school tuition—but I don't control it yet. I can't just go get the money whenever I want."

"Oh," I said. So he had money, and his mom and stepdad didn't.

"It's not like I'm rich and they're not," he said. "It's not going to last forever. But it will get me through college, maybe help with my first house. . . ."

Then he pushed me back, abruptly, and stood on top of his bed, reaching up for the ceiling fan. The base was a metallic semicircle, and when he unscrewed the bottom, there seemed to be nothing there but the exposed wiring, tucked inside.

But he reached inside the metal compartment and pulled out an envelope.

He opened the top of the envelope, and I saw the thick stack of money. My eyes went wide. "You keep it there? What you get each month?" *Banks are safer,* I was thinking; *there's a reason for them, so our money is safe and insured.*

He set his jaw, as if debating what to say. "You can't be the only signature on a bank account until you're eighteen. Some of the money already gets put toward the house bills, to keep me living in the lifestyle to which I am accustomed." He said it in an official capacity, like he was repeating the words his mother or a lawyer had once used. "I'm trying to keep an eye on the rest."

It took me a moment to understand what he was saying.

That whoever else might sign the account with him could also take the money. I couldn't imagine a parent doing that, and it made me angry on his behalf.

Though we were separated by the expanse of his bed, I thought we couldn't get any closer than this. This sharing of secrets. The bond tightening between us. He counted off a stack of bills, replaced the money, and motioned for me to follow down the steps.

When we reached the kitchen, he left the money on the table and exhaled. "I have to get out of here."

I pulled his hand, leading him back toward the front door, thinking *Then let's go*. He followed me out to his car.

Sitting in his car, he turned the ignition, rested his head back, and said, "I can't wait until I'm eighteen. And then college."

And I realized he meant more than leaving his room, his house, in that moment. And that I too would eventually be left behind.

I think, now, of the things kept just out of sight in this room. Max has uncovered the hidden space between the mattress and box spring. The only thing there is the sealed strip of condoms, now on display. This was the point at which Max had stopped. When he'd frozen, and remembered I was standing here, watching. When he realized that he was un-earthing not just Caleb but me.

I throw them into my purse—the things a mother shouldn't see—and right the bed again.

I stand on the mattress like Caleb had once done, and unscrew the bottom of his ceiling fan. It falls off quickly in my hands, before I've had a chance to turn it. It's empty. And inside, the wires are pulled lower, torn apart, as if someone has already been through here, and did not like what they found.

The Lost Book

There's nothing here. Nothing left. I wonder if maybe Caleb found a new hiding spot. I can still hear the blood pulsing inside my skull. Trying to understand Max's words. Money, taken. Money stolen. It makes no sense, because Caleb had access to money, if he needed it.

But still, the thought lingers: money that maybe Caleb had used for something else that day, something that has nothing to do with me. Somewhere else to shift the guilt. Another possibility.

And yet: It was money that Max needs. And he took this room apart, in his fury.

I'm still standing on the mattress in the middle of the mess when I hear Eve and Mia come in from the backyard.

"Try the lights up there," Eve says.

Someone walks up the steps, and I panic.

The shelves are a mess. The floor is a mess. The room is nothing like it should be, and I give up on trying to maintain an ordered chaos.

I jump down onto the carpet and start stacking all the books on the floor into a box.

But the footsteps stop at the bottom, at Mia's room. "They're not working," Mia yells.

"Jessa?" his mother calls from down below. "Are you up there?"

"Yes," I call. "The power's off."

"Just a short," she says. "Hold on."

I get back to work, and eventually the house reboots. A door closes below, and I know Eve has been out to the garage, to reset the power. The power source under his desk glows red. The light in the corner clicks on, the gust of heat from the vent lifting the hair off my neck, like a breath.

I keep stacking, trying to put the room back in some sort of order, in case Eve comes upstairs. One of the books, a paperback purchased *Used* (so says the yellow sticker on the back that he never peeled off), has tears in the edges of the back cover. When I flip to the front cover, it catches me around the throat in a heartbeat, remembering the last time I saw this. I found it for him near the end of the school year. Under the seat of his car.

We were driving to one of Julian and Max's ball games in late May, some big playoff game, and I had my phone out, directing Caleb. The windows were rolled down, and the air smelled of spring and exhaust.

"Oh, crap," Caleb said, craning his head at the sign overhead. "Toll."

"How much?" I asked, scrambling.

I opened the glove compartment, but only found the car manual, a mini-flashlight, his insurance and registration cards. I ran my fingers through the cup holders, the side compartments in the doors.

"Check under the seat," he said.

I pulled out a candy wrapper, three quarters—"I knew it," he declared when I raised them in victory—and a book, facedown, spine broken down the middle.

"Some light reading?" I asked, holding it up to him. "What, can't possibly get enough of *The Grapes of Wrath*?"

He grabbed it from me with one hand, his eyes drifting from the road momentarily. "You've got to be kidding me. I've been looking for that forever. I had to go sit at the school library for thirty minutes until I finished, because Mrs. Laverne wouldn't let me check it out, since there was a wait list. Not that anyone actually came to check it out that week, I might add."

"And how exactly did it end up under your seat?"

He shrugged, slipping it into the gap beside his seat. He paid the toll, took the exit. "Guess it fell out of my bag. You must've kicked it under the seat." But he was smiling when he said it.

I gasped. "Me?"

"Yeah. You can never sit still." He put a hand on my leg for emphasis. The leg that I'd just tucked under the other, unbuckling for a moment to get more comfortable.

Then we passed a small sign with a town's name on it and his fingers tightened slightly, kind of in play, kind of not. "Hey, I want to check something out first. Okay?"

"What?"

But he didn't answer, and he ignored the directions I gave him. "Just, hold on."

We drove for miles, past cornfields, into a more densely wooded area, down curvier roads. Eventually, he swung the car onto an unmarked drive down an unpaved road.

"There," he said, nodding out the front window.

He eased the car to a slow stop, but left the engine running.

"Whoa." We had pulled up alongside what looked like an old barn, blackened in sections and caved in, with boarded-up windows. "What is this place?"

He turned off the engine and grabbed the flashlight from the glove compartment. "Come on, want to check it out?"

I didn't, really. But I didn't want to sit in the car alone while Caleb did, either.

"Caleb, my parents will be worried if I don't show up." They would already be there by now, arriving with the team. And the game was set to start in ten minutes. Julian was pitching, and I should be there.

"Five minutes," he said, brushing the comment aside.

The grass was overgrown and dry, dead around the perimeter, a scorched earth. The door was thin, and gave with the slightest shove. Inside smelled of exposed wood, singed plastic, mold. Caleb had his flashlight in his hand and shone it across the floor, because the windows were boarded up. The floorboards were angled haphazardly, and seemed to give way underneath, to a blackened hole below. I heard birds flying by from outside the boarded-up windows.

Caleb laughed at my expression. "It's just a house, Jessa," he said.

"It's about to collapse," I said. "Caleb, don't." But he was already heading for the stairs.

"I'll be right back," he said, and I held my breath, listening to his steps, the door creaking open, more steps, a pause. Eventually, he made his way back downstairs, looked around the remains of the kitchen, and returned to the front door, where I had never left.

"Satisfied?" I asked.

He pursed his lips, his eyes taking in the rooms again. "I was born here," he said.

"Oh." I looked around again, placing the furniture from his house into these hollowed rooms instead, trying to see it as a home.

"I don't remember it. I just wanted to see."

And then my body stiffened. "Is this where . . . your dad . . ." But I let the thought trail. I felt the ghosts circling, smelled the fire, heard a baby cry.

"No," he said. He brushed the hair from my face, stepping closer. "That was a car accident. I was five. I don't remember this place at all. I don't know what happened to it."

Now I turn the book over in my hands. I don't remember what happened after, with the book. I just know I found it in his car, and then forgot about it. We left the dilapidated home. Went to Julian and Max's game. Had dinner with the team at a diner after to celebrate, the parents all sitting in half the restaurant, Caleb and I tucked in a booth with Max and a few of his friends on the other side. I left with my parents, after. He must've brought the book inside when he got back home, adding it to the collection on his shelf.

It looked like there was still a bookmark inside, which there hadn't been that day. That day, it had been folded open, stuck at the place he'd left off. I thought of him coming back up here, rereading sections of the book. Putting it down, forgetting about it. I opened the book, to see where he'd given up.

He was in the middle of a chapter, no rhyme or reason. Except it isn't a bookmark, but an envelope folded in half. I unfold it, see the jagged top, the black script that had once been out of focus, that he didn't want me to see. His name is written on the front. Just his name.

I pull the notebook paper from inside, read the words he wanted to keep hidden:

C—I miss you. I miss you so much. But I'm scared that if I send you this and you don't show up, it will be even worse.

There's nothing else. This big envelope for three sentences. Three sentences, to break my heart.

I'm holding a secret. Something I don't understand. Someone he was talking to months before we broke up. Someone who missed him, whom he cared for enough to hide from me.

It was no secret that Kylie Vann once had a crush on Caleb. It was no secret that she asked him to help her with homework in the back room of the school library, and then kissed him when he wasn't expecting it. He told me right away. That's how we operated. That's how I thought we operated.

I feel dizzy with the words. With the truth. With the memories. While I had been so frantic trying to hold together the pieces of us, had he already let us go, and just neglected to tell me?

Red Ski Goggles

Secrets. He knew how to reel them out, how to hook you with them. And so he must have known how to hold them.

What I thought I knew about Caleb: the books he read and loved. The things he didn't want me to see, and why he didn't want me to see them (college letters, an uncertain future between us). What he really didn't want me to see: something deeper, darker, more personal. The simmering of a betrayal.

Max had already uncovered the spot between the mattress and the box spring. I'd gone through his drawers, his closet, the books knocked off the shelves. But now I find myself on my hands and knees, my face pressed close to the carpet, the manufactured fibers scratching at my cheek, looking for more. Looking for what else Caleb wanted to keep hidden.

There's an indentation in the carpet, about ten inches from the foot of the bed, as if the entire bed has been shifted just slightly to the left recently. It could be from Max tearing through Caleb's things, or before. Impossible to tell now, with the room out of order, the perspective shifted.

The first thing I do is check for any other place he might have stashed money, thinking this might be where he'd hidden Max's, if he'd truly taken it. My hands brush against the base of the box spring, the metal bed frame, but there's nothing else. No taped envelope, no packet of cash. Now that he was eighteen, maybe he finally opened that bank account after all.

There's a duffel bag, big and bulky, taking up most of the floor beneath his bed. I angle it out, dragging the bag across the carpet, and it snags on a metal foot of the bed. This is his gym bag, for his lacrosse gear; he'd swing it up and over his back, wearing the strap across his chest.

But unzipping the bag, the first thing I see are the long, slender ski poles, the goggles, the hard immobile boots that he'd attach to his skis. As if he stored all his off-season gear in one location. Anything worth something, all stashed under the bed until winter.

I leave the ski poles inside, as they span the length of the bag, giving it shape, along with his lacrosse stick. The goggles, I hold up to the window, though, watch as they color everything red, dulling the glare.

I slip them over my eyes and stare at my hands. They look like they belong to someone else, in another time and place.

Caleb let me borrow these once, during a group outing back in January, seasons before our hiking trip. There had been a picture of this day on the wall as well. A snowy background, the group of us bundled up, all smiles.

My parents made Julian come with us. Not that I'd asked if I could go. Not that I thought I needed to. I'd told them about the trip, and they'd said, "Who else will be there?"

I said, "Hailey, Sophie, Max, Caleb."

I know now I should've led with Caleb. By listing him last, it made it seem like I had something to hide. Something that I was keeping from them, that they should not trust.

"If your brother goes," was their response. A freaking double standard if I'd ever heard one. Julian had gone skiing with his friends the year before. But Julian, of course, was trustworthy. And I'd just been caught with Caleb in my room when Caleb was not supposed to be in my room. We were only doing *homework*. And okay, his hand was on the small of my back, under my shirt, but still. Homework. The mortification still burned. The lack of trust burned even more. Apparently, I was the only one who required a chaperone.

Julian had had *plenty* of girlfriends, I had learned from being at the same school. I assumed he had just not been bold enough to sneak them into his room. Or to tell our parents about them.

Julian acted like being required to accompany us on our ski trip wasn't a big deal. He even drove. Pretended he'd been meaning to hit the slopes that weekend anyway, and if he knew I was interested, he would've gone sooner with me. We picked up Hailey on the way, but Caleb drove Max and Sophie. The whole thing felt like a chaperoned date, one that cut both ways. Hailey's crush on my brother had only grown over the years, and there were few thoughts that weirded me out more than the idea of Hailey and my brother together.

I had not banned her from her attempts, though I did beg her not to share any details. Ever. Ever, ever, ever.

Thankfully, Julian didn't seem super interested. But I think it weirded him out even more, to realize that Hailey was my age, and I was dating someone he knew, was friends with some of his friends too, and suddenly our worlds were interlocked, overlapping, with no defined borders or protocols.

Later, at the resort, Max, Julian, and I picked up our rentals, and met up with Caleb, Hailey, and Sophie, who had their own gear, in the locker area. Caleb took one look at the goggles I was adjusting and frowned. "Those are crap. You're going to break your nose if you can't get them fitted right."

"Unfortunate, since I can't get them fitted right," I said.

He slid his off his head, swapped with me. He used my crappy rentals, which fit to his head just fine.

"Thank you," I said, kissing his cheek. I lowered his goggles over my eyes, and the world filtered to a duller red.

He grinned. "I happen to like your nose."

Hailey and I were testing out the easier slopes first. Me, because I liked to work my way up, out of habit. Her, because she was terrible. But she was terrible in an adorable way. Sliding down on her butt while yelling a string of *ohcrapohcrapohcrap*. Getting up, making her way slowly over to the lift again. Her skis interlocking on the next try, sending her skidding. I thought she was beyond lucky that she had never seriously injured herself. I wished I could fail as spectacularly.

Even Julian seemed to watch quizzically. Captivated by the mess, and the wonder, that was Hailey Martinez.

I was waiting for Hailey at the bottom of a run, because she'd gotten knocked over near the start, and was currently working through the slow process of righting herself. Julian was watching her and not me; he had been accompanying us on our runs, like he'd been put in charge as babysitter by our parents.

I caught sight of Caleb making his way toward the lift from the other direction, and I raised my hand, about to shout his name—and then froze. A girl had pulled up beside him, and I could tell from his body language, even from the distance, that he knew her. That he *liked* her. And what wasn't to like? She had a long blond braid trailing down her back, fitted white and red snow gear, a confidence in her stance. And it was obvious she could ski better than me.

I heard him laugh. I looked behind me to see if anyone else noticed, but Julian was still keeping his eye on Hailey. I turned back around just in time to see Caleb with his arms around the girl, her face pressed up against his, everything monochrome and buffered through the goggles.

But then I second-guessed myself. Because the world was the wrong color, and the edges dulled, sunlight and ultraviolet rays filtered, and reality was skewed. I looked again, and he was skiing away. Like the last second hadn't happened.

Later, back in the locker room, when I was taking off my

gear and handed him back his goggles, he said, "Go ahead, Jessa. You can ask me."

"Ask you what?"

He looked at me, widened his eyes. "What I know you're wondering."

Had he seen me there, watching them? Before, or after? He hadn't acknowledged me standing there, one way or the other. "Okay," I said. "Who was that?"

"Ashlyn Patterson. We went to sleepaway camp together a few years ago."

"You went to sleepaway camp?"

He smiled, amused this was my biggest take-away.

"I did. And, before you ask, yes, she was my girlfriend."

I remembered his laughter, the way her face was pressed against his as they hugged, and I felt something twist inside. "Is she confused about whether that position is still available?"

He laughed out loud this time, peeling off his boots. He leaned closer. "Not anymore," he said. Then he kissed me quickly on the lips as we sat beside each other on the wooden bench.

"Hey," he said, when we stood in our regular shoes, carrying the remaining gear back to the cars. "Thanks for not freaking out."

I bristled, wondering what he really thought of me. Or if it was because he saw himself as older, somehow more mature. That he could kiss an ex-girlfriend on the cheek in greeting, calmly express his lack of availability, wish her well, see me watching and not saying anything—but know I'd be worried anyway. I told Hailey about it on the walk back to our car as they drove away, lingering on his comment.

"Thank God," she said, "the spell is finally broken." I remembered her holding an imaginary wand, asking for her friend back.

She cut off my look by circling her fingers around my wrist. "Look," she said, "I'm just saying, it's normal to see the good and the bad, you know? It's not all sunshine forever."

I nodded. Like I had finally removed the filter from my eyes. Seeing all the sides of Caleb, along with his past, and finding a way to work with it all together.

On the drive home, I kept replaying the image, filtered through red. The rush of snow and adrenaline. The curiosity making me pause and look again.

"Like, what do you even *do* at sleepaway camp?" I asked, staring out the window.

Hailey erupted in laughter. "Oh my God. You're doing it. You're totally freaking out."

"About what?" Julian asked.

Hailey did not catch the look I gave her in the rearview mirror. The one that said *My brother does not need to know any of this, oh God, please don't.* But Hailey was up for any sort of conversation with Julian, even one that included me and my boyfriend.

"Caleb ran into his ex on the slopes. Some girl from sleepaway camp."

Julian frowned, cutting his eyes to me. "That so?" he asked.

"Oh my God," I said. "Hailey, get with the eye-signal program already, huh?"

She smiled back at me. "Let's see, sleepaway camp. They hike," she said, holding up a finger. "And swim in lakes. And sleep in tents or cabins. And get generally filthy. And have subpar water pressure and soap. Everyone's kind of gross. I'm surprised they were even able to recognize each other."

I laughed, and even Julian smiled. "Do you want me to drop you home, or are you coming back to our place, Hailey?" he asked.

I rolled my eyes, and didn't need to turn around to imagine the glow of her expression. The way he'd spoken just to her, using her name, smiling at her joke. "Your place, please," she said, not even trying to mask the excitement in her voice.

Now, I think back to that letter I found in his book, wondering if it could've come from her. This Ashlyn Patterson. And if so, why Caleb kept it, if he truly didn't care anymore.

Lacrosse Stick

Underneath the goggles and the ski poles is the helmet he wore for lacrosse in the spring. The thing I remember most is not his games, but the way he looked in the gear. With his face behind the helmet's cage, it was hard to tell him apart from his teammates. They were all covered in shoulder pads, thick helmets, faces hidden behind masks. I could only recognize the different players when they faced away, catching a glimpse of the name printed on the jersey.

Buried deeper inside the bag are his shoulder pads and other pieces of protection, and then the lacrosse stick.

I pull it out, a trail of dust clinging to the base. The tape at the edge partly unwound, and still unwinding. The sticky part clinging to dirt.

It was early April, spring break, and I'd just gotten back from the Keys, five days with my parents and Julian and sun and snorkeling. Hailey was still in Puerto Rico, visiting her grandparents. Caleb had spent the whole time home, though.

The air felt crisp and welcoming back home. I could still

feel the heat of the sun in my burnt shoulders, the fabric of my shirt rubbing at the raw skin underneath.

Mia answered the front door, still in her pajamas, even though it was noon. She hugged me around the waist, asked if I wanted to make necklaces. She had beads spread out all along the living room floor, organized into piles, by color.

I smiled, thinking she and Caleb shared the organization gene. "A little later," I said. "Where's Caleb?"

She pointed to the dark stairway, then led me up the steps, the way she liked to do it now. She threw open Caleb's door without knocking, and announced, "Jessa's here!"

Caleb was sitting on the edge of his bed without a shirt, like he'd just woken. He'd been staring out the window, his eyes narrowed from the light. His confusion turned to a smile, and he said, "You're back."

I nodded. "I called."

He held up his phone on the bedside table, currently plugged into the wall. "Dead battery." Then he looked at Mia beside me. "Hey, Mia, can you make Jessa a necklace? Her favorite color is blue."

Mia took off down the steps, and he walked toward me, stepping over his lacrosse bag to close the door behind me.

"I missed you," he said, pulling me toward him.

"Ow," I said, his hands brushing over the sunburn on my back.

"Ow?"

"Turns out we were closer to the equator than I thought."

He dropped his hands, pulled the edge of my collar aside. Shook his head. Instead he kissed my wrist, the inside of my elbow, where he knew I was ticklish, and I laughed, relenting. I let him fold me up in his arms and drop me onto the bed, both of us laughing. "Still hurt?" he asked.

"Nope."

He lowered himself slowly, slowly, until his mouth brushed mine. I wrapped my arms around him, pulling him closer.

He was easing my shirt over the sunburn when the door flew open, and he jumped back, like my skin could burn him.

I yanked my shirt back down. Mia stood in the entrance.

She blinked slowly between us. "Max is here," she said, thumb jutting behind her at Max on the steps.

But Max was already cringing, looking away. "Yeah, I'll just, um. Later, guys. Come on, Mia." He took her by the hand, and she looked once over her shoulder, but Max kept moving.

Caleb laughed deep in his throat, sitting on the edge of his bed.

"Oh God," I said.

"She's eight. She doesn't even know what she saw. But I'm going to put an end to her escorting people up the steps. . . ."

"I was talking about Max," I mumbled, standing up.

"Well, Max probably understands just fine. What we need," he said, rummaging through his bag on the floor, "is a lock."

He pulled out his lacrosse stick and wedged it across the door handle, jamming it between the dresser and the wall. He pulled the door handle, which opened an inch before getting jammed on the stick—not enough to see in. He turned around, smiling. "Good enough," he said.

"Oh no," I said, hands held out in front of me. "No, no, no. In case you didn't notice, the moment is totally ruined."

I looked out the window. No Max.

Caleb followed my gaze. "Seriously, Jessa? You're embarrassed about Max? We've been together for almost a year. I'm sure he assumes far, far more."

It was the beginning of April. I scrunched up my face, doing the math. "Closer to half a year," I said, dissecting the statement from all angles. "And assuming and seeing are two very different things." Then I was thinking: Does he tell Max about me, about us? Confiding in him about the things we had done, and not done? I had always thought Caleb was like me, keeping those details to himself. But suddenly I wasn't sure, and I couldn't stand the thought—that *I* might be a secret, to be shared.

I gathered up my things, removed the lacrosse stick, and jogged down the steps, sure to make enough noise so they would know I was coming.

I passed Max sitting with Mia at the kitchen table. She had Max's earbuds in, and he was playing something for her. When he saw me, he looked up at the ceiling, then closed his eyes. "I didn't know you were in there. I swear. Mia neglected to mention that part."

"You're making it worse by refusing to look at me now."

He laughed then, dipped his head, looked at me, smiled. Smiled too wide. "Better?" he asked.

"Nope. No. Definitely not."

I spun out of the room, out the front door, and waited for Caleb to meet me there.

I heard Caleb and Max behind the closed door. "Sorry, man."

"Whatever," I heard Caleb say. "I don't get why she's making this into a whole thing."

It was true, we'd been going out for the whole school year, more than seven months now. He was my boyfriend. We were clothed (mostly). Mia was one thing, but Max? I groaned out loud, covering my face with my hands.

Caleb met me on the porch steps. "I'll come over when my mom gets home, okay? Anything going on at your place today?"

I shrugged. "I think Julian's planning to watch game tapes or something. And my parents are still in vacation mode. You can come over whenever."

He scrunched up his nose. "We can go to a movie. There's one I wanted to see anyway."

"What's wrong with my place?"

"Nothing, Jessa."

But it wasn't nothing. I realized then how often we came here, instead of going to my house.

He looked over his shoulder, at the laughter coming from inside, from Mia. "Every time I show up, your family seems surprised to see me."

I laughed. "It's denial, Caleb. I'm the youngest. And Julian keeps that part of his life totally out of my parents' eyes. Or he tries to, at least."

He grunted. "And the questions," he continued. "I feel like your dad is probably running some background check on me."

"Oh my God, don't be such a baby. He is not. Questions are, like, his way of being polite."

"Guaranteed he knows my blood type."

I laughed and smacked him in the arm. But when he showed up later that afternoon, he didn't come inside. He already had tickets for that movie.

"Just, hold on," I'd said, taking out my phone. "I told Hailey I'd be around."

"You can let her know on the way," he said, already walking toward his car. "We're going to be late."

And I remember feeling, for the first time, that there were two Calebs: the person he was with me alone, and the person he was outside of his room. Was that why I spent so much time over there, instead of at my place? Because I liked him better that way? The boy on the beach, in the bunker, when the rest of the world felt far away. I wondered if I secretly wished that was all of him. And whether he felt the same about me.

The Ticking Clock

The rest of the lacrosse bag is empty, and I leave it, together with all his gear, in a corner. I know it was expensive. It can probably be resold, along with his guitar. I assume Eve will take it away, put it wherever she's keeping the boxes.

I can almost feel Caleb slipping away—the person I thought I knew. The way I felt him slipping back then. I close my eyes, trying to hold tight to him. To remember the feel of his fingers lacing through mine, the sound of his laughter, the words he'd whisper just to me.

But I open my eyes, and I'm in an empty room, alone, with nothing but the ticking of the clock for company. I can't hear his voice, just the steady *tick, tick, tick.*

And then: there he is. He's standing on his bed, leaning toward the clock, reaching for the minute hand.

"Here?" he asked, dragging the minute hand around. The curtains were open beside him, and snow was starting to fall outside the window. Icicles clung to the roof overhang; it was early February.

"No, it's before noon. You need to move the *hour* hand,"
I said.

He leaned back, looking it over. "It looks like it's right
to me."

"Only if you're operating in Daylight Saving Time."

"Isn't it only like a month until the time changes back?
At this point I might as well leave it."

"It drives me crazy," I said. I couldn't stand that it was
always wrong—like his room was a place that operated outside the rules of time and space.

"Jessa," he said, tapping his hand against the clock, "this
is a commemorative Giants' Super Bowl clock. It's meant to
drive Sean crazy. Not you."

Sean was an Eagles fan, and so Caleb took extra pleasure
in these items, as if they could keep Sean from his room, just
by threat of seeing them.

Now, looking at the clock, it seems like it tells the perfect
time. The second hand ticks steadily along; nothing else
moves.

I finally can't take it any longer, the steady ticking, each
beat farther and farther from a world where Caleb existed. I
pull his desk chair to the wall, stand on top, and then I tear
the blue and red clock from the pin in the wall—and still, it
ticks in my hand. I turn it over to fumble for the battery pack,
to make it stop, because it seems the only fair thing to do—

But there, tucked into the wire casing, is a rectangular
ticket, like all the stubs he kept in his desk.

I slip it out, and it's a bus ticket, from the spring—never used. Never taken. It leaves from here and goes to some town I've never heard of in Pennsylvania. I look at the dates—to be used within a year of purchase. I can't figure out how this was Caleb's. If he had any intention of using this, and why.

I open the map program on my phone, pull up a search page. I plug the name of the town in, and the map zooms in to the northern edge of the state. There's nothing there that seems familiar. I zoom back out to see the path from Caleb's town to there. It crosses the river, the border of the state. Something registers from the edge of my memory—the familiarity of the region.

I think of the name on the picture, of us on the hike. Delaware Water Gap. I wonder if this was some halfway meeting point.

I try to remember the dates on the pictures. I'm trying to remember why we went there. Why *there*. I wish I had the pictures, but they're home. And now I'm wondering if we went there for some other reason, unbeknownst to me.

Maybe he went back; maybe it was a central meeting point that he was scoping out. I picture a girl, a hug, a smile. It seems obvious that's who the letter was from, and this is the purpose of the bus ticket. Maybe he was supposed to go meet her there, where she lives. Maybe it's Ashlyn Patterson, and they started up again after the ski trip. Though he has a car. He *had* a car. Surely he could've driven himself there just as easily?

Eve's footsteps echo from the floor below, and I quietly ease the blue door shut. I unzip the lacrosse bag in the corner and wedge the stick over the handle, behind the dresser, trying not to make any noise as I do, like Caleb once did.

This other life of his gnaws at me, until I have to know. Until the voice that says *What's the point? He's gone* is silenced. Because the point is that it's not only Caleb's story, but mine.

And because his story is also mine, because we're woven together—his arm on my side of a photo, my hand on his—I have to know.

I slip the bus ticket into my back pocket and log onto his computer, a simple combination of four characters—his birthday month and year—I'd seen him enter a thousand times. Even Mia could've figured this out. His documents are all there, the English essays, saved homework assignments. His music folder, organized into playlists. On impulse, I click the playlist with my name, and the familiar melody fills the room: a scrapbook of songs, whether we liked them or not, but that told the story of us. Homecoming, the lyrics I got so wrong that Caleb couldn't help but sing them every time he heard them; the song that played all summer, words belted out in the car on the way back from the beach.

And then abruptly I turn it off.

There's something too close about it, that brings me right back.

Instead, I focus on this other Caleb. The one who received letters and hid them in books. Who had bus tickets to places I've never heard of. Who took Max's money. Who left my race and was on his way to somewhere unknown when he was swept away.

I wonder if there was someone else, all along. I remember the way I'd find him sitting at the computer over this last summer, turning off the monitor screen when I walked in. I assumed it was college stuff, but the moments become recolored in my mind. I open the Internet program and see that he's cleared his browser history. But I do the same. It's a habit, from when I shared the computer with Julian and accidentally stumbled onto his last visited site—realizing the same could happen to me. I wonder if Caleb was messaging someone through the computer app, but I don't know his password for that, and his phone is gone, swept away with the river, and him.

I *do*, however, know his email password. At least, I used to.

I'd been sitting at his desk, spinning in his chair, while he did homework on his bed. It was the middle of last school year, just before our ski trip. "Hey," he'd said. "I need to print something out from my email. Do me a favor, log me in." He barely glanced up from his notebook.

I typed his username, but the password wasn't saved.

His eyes were fixed on the screen beyond when I looked back. "GreenRiver36," he said.

"Huh?"

He gestured to the screen. "My password." Then he looked back down, as if it wasn't a big deal.

Except it was. To me, I imagined it was like giving someone the key to your apartment. Permission to be there when they were not. To check in, if you so desired. It was a combination of his lacrosse number, our school color, and our school name.

▲ ▲ ▲

He knew I knew it, so part of me wonders if he changed it after the breakup. Or maybe before. Maybe when he started getting secretive, he changed it right then.

Still, I try.

I type in his email account username, and then his password, and I'm not surprised when I get the message telling me that the *Password is incorrect*.

But what makes me pause, what makes me freeze, my hands hovering over the keyboard, the words blurring, is the line below:

Password last changed 49 days ago. If this is incorrect, please click here to report.

I pull up the calendar on my phone. Look at the dates. Forty-nine days. I do the math. Check again. Look over my shoulder at the lacrosse stick wedged against the door.

His password was last changed two days after he died.

SUNDAY NIGHT

▶ ◀ ▲

"Jessa?"

His mother's voice funnels up the steps, the second before her footsteps. I exit out of the program so she won't think I was snooping, shut down the computer, and turn the monitor to black before racing to the door. I slide the lacrosse stick from its position, opening the door just as her hand turns the knob.

"Hi," I say.

She tips her head to the side gently, probably noticing I'm out of breath and flushed. "I wasn't sure if you were still up here. It's been so quiet."

I nod, gesturing to the boxes. "I did the drawers. The sports stuff."

My mind is swirling, the words on the tip of my tongue: *Someone changed his email password. Someone else has been through his things. Through his email. Through here.*

My first thought, the first image I see, is of Caleb, hovering over a computer screen somewhere, changing his password. But I shake the thought, the painful hope, before thinking of all the other possibilities: Eve, Mia, Max; a nameless girl whom he knew just as well, who sent him letters, who he met up with—

Eve frowns. "Will you be coming directly from school tomorrow?"

It's then I notice that the sky has gone dark, the shadows from the fan slanting across the walls.

"I think so," I say. I grab my purse and brush by her, my body trembling.

She grabs my bag as I pass, our bodies filling up the narrow stairwell. "Leave everything."

I flinch. "I did."

Her fingers don't let up, but they don't tug harder, either. "Can I see?" she asks.

I nod, offering my purse over to her. I have this fear that she will bar me from this room, from their lives, once more, and I'll never know what happened. I have this instinct that she doesn't trust me up here all alone, and I'm scared she will change her mind—that just as I'm peeling away the top layer, everything that is Caleb will be gone for good.

She unzips the bag, runs her fingers along my wallet, my phone, jangling the pack of gum and ChapStick, the spare coins, the extra tampon. The pictures are in my room, safely transported the day before. The bus ticket is wedged into the back pocket of my jeans. If she sees the strip of condoms I've stuffed into the bottom of my purse, she doesn't say.

"Okay?" I ask, but I'm already pulling my purse away. I want her hands out of my things—*my* things—but I don't want her to keep me from coming back. It's a tightrope, and I don't know how to manage her. It must be the same for her:

that she both wants me here, doing this for her, and doesn't want me here, my hands in her son's things, reminding her of the start of the chain of events—Caleb at my meet, the beginning of the end. All I know is there is not space for both of us in this room.

Eve says nothing, but she doesn't object as I make my way down the staircase, my feet moving Caleb-speed, my body trembling, the air thrumming. I move quickly, terrified that she'll notice the outline of the ticket in my pocket, that she'll stop me, and call me back.

I burst through the front door and race to my car, and it's not until I have the car running that I put my hands on my head and take a deep breath. I breathe slowly with my eyes closed before placing my hands on the wheel. The front porch light flicks on, and as I pull away, I see the curtains move.

There's a note on the kitchen table: *Took Julian to train station.*

My house is too big for just me. The kitchen gives way to the living room and the dining room and the foyer, all at once. The staircase is twice as wide as the one at Caleb's house, and the balcony overlooks the open layout of the downstairs. Our rooms are spread out upstairs beyond the balcony in the back half of the house, the windows facing the inclined backyard and the stone patio that's rarely used once the weather turns.

Everything echoes here.

I leave on the light near the front steps and make my way to my room, keeping my door open so I can hear when my parents return.

I want to sort through the photos from Caleb's room, which I've stored in my closet, on the shelf just out of reach. Now, I fan them over the blue bedspread on my full-sized mattress, adding the ticket from my pocket to the mix. There's a canopy overtop the bed, strung from the bedposts, from when I was younger, and it's blocking the light.

I remember Caleb running his fingers over the gauzy white material the first time he was up here, whistling between his teeth.

He fell onto his back, his hands behind his head, looking straight up. "I'm just trying to see it," he said, "the world according to Jessa."

My room might've been bigger, but his had far more privacy. He walked around mine that first day like he was in a museum gallery, his hands hovering over the decorations, the jewelry box, but never touching. Like there was something untouchable about the world I inhabited, still.

Now, the photos take his spot on the bed. The only thing out on the surface of my dresser is the broken dragonfly necklace, not put away, not replaced on a new chain, just waiting there, as if I'm not sure what to do with it. All it does now is remind me. He's everywhere now. Even here.

I sort through the photos, pulling out the shot of us at the Delaware Water Gap.

I lean closer to the photo of us at the waterfall, Caleb staring back, his eyes locking on mine through the lens and time. I turn on my computer, to try to map it exactly, remembering where we were, the details from the sign. I check the photo to see if there are any mile markers, something that might map to our final location. I look at various images from other people's hikes at the Delaware Water Gap, trying to find an exact match.

There's something similar in several of the photos, but nothing that captures this exact perspective. There will never be another shot like this—the two of us on the rock, an arc of water in the background, our faces frozen in place and time, a feeling I can remember just from my expression alone.

There's a knock on the door downstairs, and I shut my laptop and stack the photos, sliding them into my top drawer. I check my phone for messages, thinking Hailey would've texted first. But there's nothing. The bell rings as I walk down the steps, and it echoes, sets my nerves on edge.

The lights are on in the foyer downstairs, and my car's in the driveway, so I can't pretend I'm not home. I check the front window and see a car I don't recognize. The bell rings again. I peer through the peephole, and it's Terrance Bilson, my brother's ex-teammate, current alumnus, previous giver-of-questionable-look at the coach's meeting.

My shoulders relax as I pull the door open. "He left already," I say. "Sorry."

But Terrance doesn't move. He peers over my shoulder into the empty spaces, the darkened rooms. "I didn't have your number, or I would've called first." He angles his foot across the threshold, and I tighten my grip on the door. "I wanted to talk to you," he says.

I don't open the door any wider, because I don't really know Terrance all that well, other than the fact that he played baseball with Julian and Max.

He must sense this fact, because he steps back. "Will you come out for a minute?"

It's cold, and the neighbors are home, and his car is in the street, and anyone can see. "No, it's okay. Come on in."

Terrance looks around briefly, lingering near the entrance. He doesn't speak, doesn't really seem to know how to start.

"So, what are we talking about?" I ask. I remember the look he gave me Saturday night, and it puts me on the defensive.

He blinks, his gaze shifting back to me, as if remembering. "Caleb."

My jaw tenses, the word echoing in the foyer with the too-high ceilings, and I know my body language must give me away.

"I saw him, in September," Terrance continues, and then I understand. I remember.

"The college visit. Was that with you?"

He nods. "It was supposed to be. He showed up, but then he disappeared."

"What do you mean, he disappeared?"

"Just that. He checked in, but I didn't see him again until he was leaving. He came back Sunday afternoon for his luggage. He had a bag from the school store in his hand, and he looked like crap. He apologized, and left, and I never saw him again." His voice trails off, because his words have an unintended finality. I wonder if everyone has their own story for the last time they saw him. A story they each tell anytime the name comes up, becoming more embellished over time.

Caleb's phone had gone to voicemail during that trip. We had fought about it after. All I had to go on was my imagination then, and now Terrance is here, making those images even more real.

"Why are you telling me this now?"

"Because I think it's a dick move, what they're saying."

I almost say *What are they saying?* just to watch him squirm, but that would be a dick move too, so I don't.

What they're saying: *He came to see her, and she sent him away at the race. He looked angry. She sent him away, he was upset, and he crashed. He drowned.*

It's the precipitating event. There's no logic to it, but it's the simplest explanation. All I'd said was, *Please hold this for me. Please be careful.* But it was too far for anyone to hear, so the words become anything, become everything.

What they believe: Caleb had come to ask for my forgiveness (one rumor), or to try again (another rumor), or to confess he was still in love with me (uncorroborated, but a nice sentiment), and I'd said no. Something I did caused him to leave angry, and he wasn't paying close enough attention, and then he died. Cause. Effect.

"I mean, he wasn't this perfect guy," Terrance continues, filling the silence. "It's not your fault, right?"

"I never sent him away," I say. I hadn't told anyone this before—first, because I was in shock, then because I wondered if it was true, and now because it didn't matter anymore what I said: it was too late. But something about

Terrance in my foyer, a stranger giving me secrets—I was a sucker for them. "I asked him to hold my necklace. He disappeared. That was it. He didn't say anything. I don't know why he left. I don't know where he was going." It was another student and a parent who gave that account—who both said they saw him standing in the crowd after, that he looked upset. With nothing else to go on, the story filled in around it.

Terrance nods, unsure what to do with the information, whether to believe me or not—then seems to decide on something. "Okay, there's one more thing."

"What is it?"

"Someone came looking for him that weekend, at my dorm room."

I flash to the letter in his book. An image of the girl in the ski gear. The blond braid, highlighted even in the winter. *Ashlyn*, he'd said.

"Tall, skinny dude," he says, and I can't reconcile the image in my head with his words. "I don't know what he wanted with him. But he showed up while Caleb was gone. Said he wanted to leave a package for him. I said sorry, that I had no idea who he was talking about, because that seemed like the right thing to say. Guy kind of freaked me out a little. And I'm not holding some *package* in my room for anyone else, sorry."

He hadn't been answering my calls. I'd imagined Caleb drinking, at a party with girls, living it up. Not dealing with some guy with a package for him. Not coming back with a headache because of some other reason. The whole event that precipitated our breakup was not what I'd thought it had been.

"Anyway," he says, taking a step closer. "I've been meaning to get this to you." He pulls something from his pocket.

"What is that?" I say.

Terrance holds a white plastic bag, wrapped up in his fist. "He left it behind. I was going to call your brother, but then I saw you yesterday. I just didn't know what to do with it. I didn't find it until I was packing to come home for the weekend. I think it was for you."

"We broke up," I say, staring at the bag. As if I am no longer entitled to its contents. I don't reach for it, at first.

"When?" he asks.

"After. Right after."

"I didn't know that," he says. He lifts his hand toward me. "I don't know if this will make it better or worse."

I stare at his closed fist. In his hand is the bag from the school gift shop, wrapped up around something small. I take it from his grip, letting it unravel, and I peer inside.

"That's your name? Your full name?" Terrance asks, and I nod.

"Thank you," I say, trying not to choke on the words. I'm shaking by the time I shut the door behind him.

Keychain with My Name

Inside is a keychain, with the logo of the school mascot. But that's not what has me frozen.

In my hand is a gift he had bought me, and never given. We were always on the lookout for my name on magnets or keychains or ornaments. It was an obsession of mine, because I could never find it. And there in my hand, the letters glittering in the light of the foyer, is the word *Jessamyn*.

I'm trying to imagine if there might've been a different sequence of events if he'd brought this out of his pocket that Monday morning when he returned. If the conversation would've steered out of dangerous territory. I'm trying to imagine a different string of events than what really happened that day.

We were standing in a row of lockers in the student center the Monday morning after his visit, our voices carrying no matter how low we spoke.

"What were you doing, that you were too busy to call?" I wanted to know. We were already there, on the edge. It had gnawed at me all summer, this something I couldn't quite put my finger on. But it was such a big step, such a big leap to make over nothing. Undoing everything we had become, over nothing more than a feeling.

I wanted a reason. Something to cause the final split. But instead we hovered around it. I wanted to say he had done something, something to give voice to the feeling.

"You don't trust me," he said.

"Should I?"

He didn't answer. The silence was worse than anything he could've said.

"If you don't, then you don't. Nothing I say or don't say will change that," he said. He had adopted this air of condescension, affected a level of maturity I had presumably yet to reach.

It was his tone that pushed me to it. "I guess I don't then," I said, crossing my arms over my chest.

He slammed his locker shut, spun the numbers on the lock. "Well, then I guess that settles it." Like we were in turmoil, and now the pieces were settling after a storm, onto opposite sides of the line.

Except it wasn't settled yet. He found me after practice that day, forcing the point. Making it a moment impossible to come back from.

"Just say it," he said. His hands were up in the air, out to the side, as if he were bracing himself.

You don't love me.

I don't love you.

It's over.

But instead I shook my head, the words too foreign. A year together. Our existences too wrapped up in each other.

We were standing on the grassy hill after practice. He was in jeans. He'd been waiting for me. He'd been watching. I was sweaty and thirsty and the muscles in my legs burned, and I felt outside myself, like I always did after a long run— that I was overdosed on air. My hands started shaking.

Caleb looked over his shoulder once. Like even this part didn't require his undivided attention. He was split in two places, even then, already gone—already ten minutes from then, a day, a week. This just an item on one of his to-do lists that needed to be crossed off.

"Just go," I said.

Caleb narrowed his eyes, the muscles in his face hardening. "That's it? That's everything? That's *all you have to say?*"

But didn't he get it? I didn't want to give any more of myself away. I'd given everything, and now it was time to take it back. To hold on to the mystery, and leave him wanting instead.

"Yeah, Caleb. That's it."

He looked at me like he was surprised to suddenly realize he didn't know this person standing before him at all.

"Wow. Well, what can I say, I'm so glad we did this, Jessa."

I'm so glad we did this. His words rang in my ears. *This.* This conversation? This breakup? The entire last year?

I turned to go, walking down the hill to the water cooler, where everyone was still gathered, stretching after practice. Watching. "Hope you're happy," he called after me.

I didn't turn to look, but I knew when he left because everyone shifted their focus from him to me.

I felt their eyes on me, and I knew I needed to say something, that the rumors would begin whether I said it or not. "Turns out I could use a ride home," I said.

Hailey took a step closer, and Max was still staring at the empty spot where Caleb had just been.

"What a jerk," Hailey said, because that was what I would say to her if our places were switched. She placed a hand on my shoulder, squeezed, then said, "Oh, crap, guess I'm going to need a ride home, too." Then she let out the slightest giggle.

And then I was laughing too, both of us, a fit of inappropriate laughter, to mask the moment, to mask the tears.

I knew Max would wait for us, after we got changed. I knew in a way that didn't make me have to ask him, or him have to say it, even though his allegiance was to Caleb in that moment. But I knew, because of how he once pushed back through the crowd for me, how he said *You just left her*, to him after.

We dropped Hailey off first, on the way, and we were almost to my place when he said, "Want to talk about it?"

But I just stared out the window, resting my head against it. I felt the reality filter in, all the changes. I wouldn't take out my phone to text Caleb as soon as I was alone in my room. He wouldn't pick me up tomorrow. I'd have to ask my parents if I could use Julian's car for school. They'd have to ask why. I'd have to say it. All this talk, and now I just wanted silence.

"No," I said. He pulled up at my house, and I grabbed my bag from the backseat. "Max?" I said. "Thank you for the ride home."

He nodded once, his face stoic.

I went to close the door, and he called my name. I turned back. "We're friends, too. Whether you're with him or not. We were friends before." I'd known him forever, it was true, but the last year with Caleb had really cemented our friendship.

I nodded and looked quickly away, feeling the knot in my throat, the burn in my eyes.

Max's words were both true and not. We could be friends at practice. He could give me a ride home if I needed one. But we couldn't just pick up the phone, or meet up at the beach, or fight over riding shotgun.

All of this changes, too.

MONDAY MORNING

▶ ◀ ▲

The car is mine alone again, now that Julian's gone. I park in the far lot, with the rest of the juniors who have their licenses. My eyes scan the lot for Caleb's preferred spot from last year—under the tree, facing the athletic fields. Not the most convenient spot for morning class, but the best location for leaving at the end of the day. Caleb was like that, always planning for the parts that came later.

I grab whatever spot I come across first, ready for another day of the places Caleb does not exist. The combination lock has been permanently removed from his empty locker. I won't hear his voice in the hall, his laughter around the corner, or see the top of his head in a crowd, his eyes locking with mine over the people between us. All empty spaces, a gap in the world as I know it.

But something's different today, and I think it's from spending so much time in his room. Now I'm seeing him everywhere. Not just the emptiness, but the things he's left behind, instead.

Now I see the paint scratched off his locker, from the lacrosse stick, and the memory flickers through my mind: Caleb spinning around too fast when I whisper *Boo* in his ear, the stick hooked through the bag on his back scratching the metal. In first period I pass the open door of his class and see his seat, now occupied by another guy from his team—but at first it's Caleb waving his hands over his head, recounting a story. Sitting in math class before lunch, staring out the glass window of the wooden door, my eyes are drawn to the remnants of glue, a corner of adhesive—and I see Caleb biting his lip, scrubbing at it as I walk by.

As part of school spirit week last year, the lacrosse team had plastered our school flags to each classroom window. Which probably would've been fine, but they'd added a line in black marker, about their opponent. Specifically, referring to how badly, and what, they sucked.

Which was why the team was back out in the hallway after school with buckets of water and sponges and soap, scraping the glued signs off with their fingernails, or using the ice scrapers from their cars.

Sitting in math now, I imagine him there on the other side of the door, working at the window along with the rest of his teammates as I walked by.

I'd passed him in the hall, making a tsk-ing sound, laughing at the look he gave me in return. He ran a soap-streaked hand through his sun-bleached hair and gave me a self-conscious smile. I paused across the hall, my hand on my hip. "You missed a spot," I said.

One of his teammates said, "Can't you get your girlfriend to help?"

And he said, "Why would I want to subject my girlfriend

to stripping glue from glass? Run, Jessa. Run while you can."

Everything inside and outside of his room still reminds me of him. I catch my dimmed reflection in the glass of the classroom door, and even that, even the image of *me*, conjures up Caleb.

Someone calls my name, and it takes me a second to realize it's the teacher. And by the time I do, by the time I look in my notebook, ready to answer, he has moved on, unsure of what to do with me, either.

The bell rings overhead, and the rest of the students leave.

I hear the distinct tread of shoes turn in the hallway, entering the classroom. They're purple, with a strap and a black heel. She taps one toe beside my bag. "You ready?" she asks.

Hailey has her long dark hair swooped up into a ponytail. She's trying to make light of this moment, and I suddenly see how lucky I am, because I do remember the last time we spoke. It wasn't at the service; it was the next day. She'd come by my house, and after my parents let her in, I cut her off with one-word answers and asked her to leave. Her last words: *I'm trying to help here.*

Yeah, well, you're not.

Don't wreck this, too.

Too. That little word. It dug itself under my ribs, and every time I heard her speak, I'd feel them stabbing my heart.

"Hailey," I say, trying to find the right words to apologize.

"There are french fries," she cuts in, tapping her toe

148

again. "You know how the line gets on french-fry day. I'm just saying."

I swing my backpack over my shoulder and give her a grateful smile. "Let's go," I say.

On the way to the cafeteria, Hailey tries to lead me in the other direction. She tries to distract me with gossip about her latest date.

"What the hell is that?" I ask, as Hailey pulls me past the display.

But it's too late. I've already seen it.

Evers Athletic Shirt

There's a pen hanging from poster board, and sheets of paper stapled to it. It's a petition, I see. A petition to rename Coats Memorial Bridge to Evers-Coats Memorial Bridge. There are at least a hundred names. There's a photo of Caleb at the top, the same one from his school ID, and beside that, mounted to the wall in a glass frame, is his gray athletic T-shirt, folded into a square, so his name is visible under the logo for our school.

"Where did they get this?" I ask.

"His locker," Hailey answers. "Come on." She pulls me by the arm, but I don't budge.

"When?" I ask.

"His mom came, that first week, when you were ..." She trails off. She doesn't need to say it. When I was in my room, in the dark, not answering my phone or texts or the doorbell. When she showed up and I wouldn't see her, and I went running late at night, by myself, after everyone was sleeping—sure, at times, that I could hear the rumble of a river in the distance.

"Then why is it *here*?" I ask. I know Caleb always kept a

change of clothes in his locker, the Caleb he would become at three p.m. But something about this piece of him out on display, not in his house with his mother, doesn't sit right.

She shrugs. "She showed up and wanted to cut the lock, but Max knew the combo, so he was with her when it opened." She points to the wall. "That's all that was in there."

"That's all?"

"Yeah, other than pencils."

It's a T-shirt from a fundraiser for the new athletic center, from the year before. I have the same one. Only mine says *Whitworth* on the front left corner, under our school name. His says *Evers*. We all bought them and wore them on game days, and other times as well.

"She gave it to the school?"

"She gave it to Max. Apparently she changed her mind, and didn't want the things inside his locker. And Max didn't know what to do with it, so he gave it to Caleb's coach, like a tribute or something."

"And now, here it is," I say.

"Here it is."

Here it is, staring me in the face, like the last time I went to his house. The last time I saw his room, until this week.

That day on the hill after cross-country practice was not the last time we spoke. I had showed up at Caleb's house the next day, after the breakup, hating how we left things—the anger in his expression, the nonchalance of his cutting words. Everything we had been, reduced to this.

Mia had let me in, and I climbed the flight of stairs alone.

"What are you doing here, Jessa?" Caleb's arm blocked the doorway to his room. There was a mess behind him, items scattered across the floor, the room in disarray. Music was playing, something loud and grating, uncharacteristic of the Caleb I thought I knew. And it turned out I did have something to say.

But standing in the stairway, it was impossible to force out the words. It was too dark, and he was too angry. The state of his room seemed to signify that. "I left my project." It was a report that I'd been working on for the last week, articles cited, all stuffed into a folder and left at the foot of Caleb's desk the week before. I'd avoided asking for it back, like that alone would be the final break. But I needed it. I needed to turn it in.

He shut the door in my face, but I heard his footsteps moving across the carpet on the other side. He opened the door with the folder in his hand, pushing it toward me.

"Caleb," I said. A year, just gone. His face impassive. A segment of my life that was forever over, and permanently closed.

"Hey, Mia," he called, his voice booming off the walls. "Come say goodbye to Jessa."

I clenched my teeth together, and gave him a look I hoped he would remember, and regret.

So we would not be like him and that girl on the ski slopes, meeting up, kissing cheeks, laughing at time gone by.

I turned around, keeping my eyes on the steps, so sure this would be the last time I descended this stairway.

"By the way, Jessa," he said, his voice falling in an unfamiliar cadence. "I know."

I paused, my steps faltering. And then I kept moving. I kept going.

The memory has me on a mission. Because I realize there are parts to Caleb's life I didn't know at all.

After an awkwardly silent lunch, where Hailey talked about classes, and I nodded in reply, both of us pretending I was okay, I take a detour, swinging by the school library and logging onto a computer before heading back to class. I think about that town name in Pennsylvania, the tickets behind Caleb's clock, and I remember the girl in the ski gear. Caleb didn't believe in social media accounts. (*Lame*, he said, *for people who don't have better things to do.*) I cringed when he said that, because he was of course implying that *I* did not have better things to do. Still, I'm glad I have accounts set up now. It makes the search easier. I type in *Ashlyn Patterson*, and there are suddenly more Ashlyn Pattersons than I thought possible.

Scanning through the images and locations, I see one that could possibly be her. Her profile is set to private, but her school is listed. She's a senior at a big public high school in northern New Jersey. It doesn't account for the ticket to Pennsylvania, but it's possible, I think, that they were using this location as a common meeting spot for some reason. Though it's not exactly the most central location.

I send her a message. I cut right to the point: *When was the last time you saw Caleb Evers?*

MONDAY AFTERNOON

▶ ◀ ▲

Hailey's with me when I see Max by the lockers Monday after school. I'm not sure whether it's because he's been looking for me, but we end up walking stride for stride on the way to the parking lot.

"I wanted to talk to you. About yesterday. I wanted to apologize," he says.

He's walking backward, and Hailey and I keep moving. Hailey wants to know if I'm driving home—now that cross-country season is over, she's ready to leave right after school as well. I don't answer Max, and Hailey doesn't acknowledge him, in a show of solidarity, I'm guessing. She doesn't even know what cause she's supporting, but Hailey's like that, and I've always loved her for it.

"I have to go to Caleb's house," I tell Hailey, letting that be a response for Max as well.

"Will you let me help you at least?" Max asks, still keeping stride with us in reverse.

"Eve doesn't want that," I say. *I* don't want that. It's a delicate balance, me in that room. If he's there, tearing things apart with his own motivation, I might miss some-

154

thing. I might lose something. I feel like Caleb is a mirage, and every time I think I have him, that I can track the path of him—his motives, his journey—he flickers and fades, and I was wrong.

Someone calls to Hailey, and she looks at me. "That's my ride. Or, it was supposed to be my ride."

"I'll call you tonight?" I say. It's a question. I'm asking her.

"Later," she says. She squeezes my arm, gives Max a look, and spins around.

I focus on Max, really looking at him, and I say it point-blank. "Was he cheating on me?" I ask. He knew Caleb better than anyone. Better than me, I'm realizing now. This, at least, would be an answer that would give things more shape.

He looks surprised by the question. "No." Then he opens his mouth and closes it again. "I don't think so."

My stomach falls. "You don't think so?"

"He didn't tell me everything." I see his throat moving. He lowers his voice. "I didn't tell him everything."

But I remember Caleb's words that last day, as I walked down the stairs. "Are you sure? Because he knew, Max. He knew."

He looks up at the sky, as if it will absolve him. "Not from me, Jessa. Besides, there was nothing to know."

"For you, maybe."

He shakes his head. "It was the moment. It wasn't you."

It feels like a line, and I wonder who else could possibly be blamed for it. "You're the one who stopped me," I say, "if I'm recalling correctly. So I think you get a pass."

"I didn't at first. Not fast enough."

"You did." I remember the embarrassment. I remember thinking to myself, *Oh, so this is mortification. Yes, now the word makes sense.*

"I didn't want to, Jessa. I really didn't."

His words echo in my head the whole drive to Caleb's. But even thinking about them now feels like betrayal.

Mia's bus is letting out just as I arrive at Caleb's. I watch, like a creeper, as she walks with her purple backpack hanging too low, and her dark hair swooped over her shoulder. Suddenly, she turns and stares directly at me, as if she knew I was here all along.

I quickly exit the car, to seize the chance to speak with her, but Eve opens the front door at the same moment and Mia skitters in behind her. Eve holds the door open until I'm inside as well.

It smells stale in here, like nobody's cooked in ages. With the packing, I'm starting to get a whiff of the house itself, all plaster and wood polish and dust, like everyone's been on a long vacation. I'm starting to notice things, now. Like the laminate peeling in the kitchen, and the grandfather clock that doesn't chime, and the empty drawers, the sounds the house makes on its own.

I remember the police had been here that first day, when Caleb was just missing, before his fate was decided, and official. And how different his home had looked then, from a different angle, with too many people crowded into the doorway.

Thinking about it now, it seems obvious the police must've accessed his email somehow during that early investigation, and then changed the password. Maybe they even shut down the account.

I'm standing across from Eve in the entrance, staring into her green eyes. I realize I'm the same height as her, that her teeth are clenched together, that she lost her first husband, and a son. And I don't know how to ask the question. I circle around it, stalling. "Did the police look through Caleb's email? To see if they might know what he was doing?"

She shakes her head, looking at me funny. "No. He was eighteen. He accidentally drove off a bridge. There was no cause for the police to gain access, which would've taken a subpoena to the email company. Whatever emails he had sent or received did not matter. There was a flood. It was an accident." She frowns, like she had also considered this and asked.

"Not even after . . . ?" *After he was declared dead. Say it, Jessa.* But I don't. Not to her. She fought against it, at first. Saying there was no proof, that there was always hope. Until weeks later, when the current shifted, and the larger pieces of his car began washing ashore. If the current could do that to steel, well—the rest was unspoken.

"Not even then. Not even with a death certificate. His account was with one of the services that won't transfer access after death. It seems people are entitled to their privacy, even then." Eve speaks the words I don't, the word *death* coming out choked, a note higher than the rest. She says it when I will not, as if daring me to do so as well, or proving that she is stronger.

Then she leans closer, and I smell the sharp scent of her perfume, the coconut of her shampoo. "Why, do you know his password?"

I shake my head, the easiest explanation.

So it wasn't the police. And it wasn't his mother. And it wasn't me. That left Max.

"What's the matter, Jessa?"

I'm a terrible hider of secrets. Caleb must've been able to read them in my expression. Instead, I scramble for something else I can use. "I still can't find his glasses. I'm just wondering where he was going, why he needed them."

It's like when I was at school, seeing all the empty places Caleb used to be. Seeing only what's not there, what *should* still be there, if fate were fair.

But Eve gives a little sad shake of her head. "He was going to see you, Jessa. Like always." Then she leans a little closer. "You never told me, what he last said to you. Don't you think you owe me that?" As if reminding me why I am here. Why *I* am here.

He didn't say anything that day. And it's only then, when she asks, that I realize that I too am searching for those words. To go back and have him say something, so I will understand. So I will be absolved. *Going to the library.* Or *I'm hungry, might grab a bite to eat.* Or *I've been seeing someone else, and I'm going to visit her.* Even just *I feel like taking a drive.* Just something. The weight of the unsaid words presses down on me, and all I can tell his mother is the truth:

"He didn't say anything." A hard, sad thing to admit. The last words spoken from him to me were in the stairway from his room, said to my back, in anger.

She waits a beat, as if the answer will suddenly change. But when I don't flinch under her unrelenting stare, she steps aside, so I can ascend the steps.

Championship Trophy

I've got to talk to Max again. Now that I know it wasn't Caleb's mother or the police who went through his email. I think about calling him, but I know voices carry in this house. I think about texting him, but I don't even know what to say. He's been through this room. Maybe he's been through his email, too. *Did you hack into Caleb's account? What were you looking for? Did you find it?*

Can I see it?

I look out the window, but there's no movement at his house. And anyway, Eve is downstairs. I can't just leave with no explanation.

Instead, I start on what's left on the shelves, boxing away the trophies (karate, youth soccer, math Olympiad, lacrosse championship). All gold figurines that look identical, frozen in time.

Caleb Evers, Captain is written on the bottom of the prep state championship trophy. My nail hooks and locks in the groove of his name.

▲ ▲ ▲

Hailey and I had driven nearly an hour. Well, neither of us had our license back then yet, so Max drove. Except Max didn't have a car yet (*Still saving*, he mumbled, anytime we teased him about it), so he borrowed Caleb's, since Caleb was on the team bus.

"Sophie said you guys broke up," Hailey said from the backseat, leaning between the center gap.

"Yep," Max said, keeping his eyes on the road.

"Hmm."

I spun in the passenger seat, gave her a look. One that said *Stop*. It had only supposedly happened the day before. Caleb would be thrilled, I thought. Though he seemed to have grown to like Sophie just fine. Or, he tolerated her, for Max's benefit. Honestly, I didn't get the animosity. She was perfectly unimposing, unassuming, un-everything.

"What happened?" Hailey asked.

"Hailey," I said.

She gave me the *What?* look.

"Nothing," Max said. It was the beginning of May then, and they'd been together longer than me and Caleb. It seemed like a long time to be together to call it off for no reason.

"There had to be *something*," she said.

"Hailey," I said.

What? There does, her look said.

"No, nothing happened." He paused. "Nothing ever really happened."

"Oh," Hailey said.

"Oh," I said. It seemed a long time to stay together without a reason, too. But then I thought, maybe it was easier to stay with the stream of momentum, no concrete cause to call it off. And I got this slight unease in the pit of my stomach.

"And if you repeat that, Hailey, I will throw your favorite shoes into the river," Max said.

"Violent threats really aren't necessary," she said. "I'm already trusting you with my life right now. This car does not feel like the safest means of transportation, no offense to Caleb."

The demarcations in the pavement sounded like a steady beat as we drove along the highway in silence for the next half hour, passing exits and town signs and strip malls.

Caleb called while we were still on the way. "Hey," he said, "bus just arrived. How's Max doing with my baby?"

"His hands are currently at ten and two, no worries."

He laughed, dropping his voice. "I wasn't talking about my car, Jessa."

I warmed, picturing him tipping his head, speaking lower. All unease currently gone. I tucked myself into the corner of my seat, lowered my voice. "We'll be there soon. Really soon."

"Tell Max to drive faster."

"Max," I said. "Drive faster."

"I need to see you before the game," Caleb said.

"We'll be there."

I had felt so essential to his existence then. So important, as his teammates parted to let me through before the game. So needed as we snuck into the locker room to fool around in the ten minutes before their pregame warm-ups.

Until his phone buzzed in his pocket, and he groaned. He frowned at the display and said, "I'm so sorry, I have to take this."

Then he walked away, leaving me in the corner of the guys' locker room, to plan my own escape.

His voice echoed in the empty space. "Yeah. I'm here. Are you?" I assumed it was Eve, who was set to arrive later with Mia. He hooked around a corner, and I heard a door swinging open and shut.

And then I thought: *Oh, crap.* And then: *What the hell?*

I saw too many shadows passing the front door, and didn't want to be caught exiting on my own. I looked for other escape routes, then heard a stampede of cleats as a group of guys entered the locker room. I hid in the closest stall, and texted Hailey: SOS. *Stuck in boys locker room. Hiding in stall. Ideas??*

Two minutes later, I heard the door fling open, and Hailey's voice booming through the room.

"Turn around, boys!" Hailey declared. "I need to use the bathroom, but the line's too long next door."

The shock must've gotten to them, because nobody said anything, and nobody stopped her. I opened the stall door when I heard her footsteps approach, and she raised an eyebrow. "Ready?" she asked. She held up her fingers, counting down from three, grabbed onto my arm, and then we bolted.

And because it was the opposing team, they didn't know us by name. Could only guess as Hailey and I darted by in a blur.

Max was laughing from the bleachers when we returned,

apparently in on the plan. "Never a dull moment with you two," he said.

I saw Eve arriving, and Mia abandoned her mother to scramble up the bleachers toward us instead.

Max got up to make room for Mia to squeeze between us, and I leaned toward Hailey and asked, "Do you like Max?"

She grinned noncommittally, leaning over to check him out as he was engaged in conversation with a guy on the other side. "What's not to like about Max?" Just then, his eyes shifted to mine—a wide smile that reached his brown eyes.

Tall, with dark hair and a lean, athletic build, and a way about him that felt effortlessly comfortable, that put others at ease. It was true: there wasn't much to dislike about him. Not the way he looked, or smiled, or acted. He treated his friends well. He treated everyone well. I remembered the way he came back for me in the subway station, the way he gripped my hand and got me through.

"So?" I said, prompting her.

"So he just broke up with Sophie, who happens to be a friend of mine. That kind of makes him off-limits. It's in the code. Like, if I were to hook up with Caleb one day."

"Oh my God, don't you dare," I said.

She smiled, her eyes squinting. "See?" She leaned around me once more, to look. "Damn shame, though. Seriously."

Seashell

Behind the trophies, stuck against the wall, I see a white and brown seashell, spiral shaped, long and narrow. My heart plummets into my stomach. I can't believe he kept this. I never knew he had it, tucked behind a stack of gold trophies, a row of achievements throughout his life.

Valentine's Day. Caleb wanted to take me to the beach. He said restaurants were overrated, and besides, everyone else would be doing that. Everything, according to Caleb, would be crowded and expensive and lame. And anyway, we could trace our beginning to the beach. That first picture on his wall. The moment he knew.

It counted for more, he said. It had meaning.

It fell on a weekend, and he picked me up at three, and we drove out to the beach, which was vast and abandoned—a cold beige, a deep blue. For as far as we could see, it was empty, and it was ours.

The wind whipped up off the water, and he took my hand, wrapped an arm around me on second thought.

But here's the thing about the beach in winter: the sand scratches at your ankles in the wind, and it's somehow more intimidating. It roars, cold saltwater spray stinging my eyes so tears formed at the corners.

"This is the least romantic thing ever. I was so wrong," he said, laughing. He pulled me closer, and I buried my face in his chest.

"It's terrible."

"The worst." I heard the words through his chest, alongside the howling wind.

I bent down, my fingers digging into the sand. "Here, have a shell. There was once a living creature inside it, but now it's probably dead."

"You shouldn't have. Truly." He held it to his face. "I will treasure this always. Just as soon as I get the stench of dead marine life out of it."

He tipped my head up, and I wrinkled my nose. "I think there's sand in my shoes."

He smiled, his eyes shifting to the violent ocean behind us. "I thought candlelit dinners were cliché and lame, but I'm beginning to see the error of my ways."

"All I want is heat," I said, clinging to the front of his jacket dramatically.

"That can be arranged."

"Not at your house."

"Not at my house," he agreed.

"And not at my house," I said.

He seemed to think for a moment, two, and then said, "Okay."

Ten minutes later we pulled up in front of the county library. "Um," I said.

"Just trust me," he said. He took my hand in the nearly empty parking lot, and made a big show of pressing the automatic door button, gesturing for me to enter.

The hallway outside the library entrance was quiet and lined with posters made by children. There was a display of flowers, and hearts from the children's craft hour in alternating bursts of pink and red. Through the double doors of the library itself, a woman briefly looked up and smiled, then went back to her book.

"It's empty," I whispered.

"It is Valentine's Day," he said.

We walked the stacks, his arm around me, taking in the warmth and the quiet, like we were strolling the beach. He led me through the fiction aisles, to the row of computers, hidden away in cubbies. "Come on," he said, tugging my hand and leading us toward the periodical desk. It was empty, and there were a few single cubbies for working scattered around the perimeter.

"My favorite desk," he whispered, leading me toward the cubby pressed against the window. He quickly looked over his shoulder before opening the bottom cabinet. Inside was the computer tower, humming. But there was a shelf above it, with a separate drawer. Caleb opened the drawer, reaching deep into the dark, and pulled out a handful of candy, the wrappers echoing in the silence.

"This is yours?" I asked.

He smiled. "They give me a hard time about bringing

food in. But you know how I am about food. So I keep some reserves on hand, just in case." He patted the top of the desk, and I hopped onto the surface. He unwrapped a candy, offered it to me.

"They never find it?" I asked.

"Nope," he said. "I've been using this desk for a year. Nobody checks the drawers." I peered inside the open drawer. There was also a pen inside, and what looked like his math homework, half-completed. "Promise you won't tell," he whispered.

"Promise," I said as the taste of butterscotch filled my mouth.

"Come on," he whispered, pulling me off the desk. "We're not done here yet."

There were large, uncovered windows facing the trees. Beanbag chairs in the shapes of animals, in the kids' section. A framed print of an atlas map on a wall, signed by the artist.

He kissed me in the travel aisle, and I wrapped my arms around his neck, and I thought, *I love him, I love him. I really do.*

In the days after his death, I'd spent plenty of time with the map program open, looking for where he might've been heading.

The bridge was on the route we took for the beach, so I was familiar with the passing landmarks. I thought of the food places we'd stopped at on the way, or on the way back. Picking up ice at the gas station for the cooler we were hauling with us to the shore. The ice cream shop, open seasonally during summer hours only. I supposed it was possible he was in the sudden mood for a hoagie. But there were closer places, on the way back from the meet to his house.

I had traced the roads that forked off after the bridge, looking for any possibilities. I'd thought, briefly, of the library again. He was the only student I knew who used the library outside of school. Most of my classmates, if they needed a library, used the school facility. If they were going to a study group, they'd meet at someone's house.

But he really would go study at the library. I think he liked getting out of his house. I think he liked the silence. If I drove by his place and he wasn't home, and he didn't answer his phone, I'd know where to find him.

He had found himself some solace there.

For a while, I was convinced he'd been heading there. After the meet. Except he hadn't brought his backpack with him, that day. It was, I had heard, still in his room. He had taken nothing with him that might tip us off. And so everything circled back to me.

A Gold Ribbon

I have a lump in my throat, standing with the shell in my hand. I want to keep this. I'm scared his mother will find out. Still, I take the risk, sticking it into my purse. I remember the moments later on when I felt it wouldn't work between us, that there was too much to mend, but as I work my way back, I remember this part as well.

These moments when I was so sure, so one hundred percent made of a single feeling, that I know it wasn't a mistake.

That I can take the pieces together. I loved him, once. I loved him, once, despite everything to come. I loved him, and I lost him, and it makes sense, then, that I would feel pieces of myself in this room, too.

I know what I'm looking for, with this endless search, where I can't seem to get enough, no matter how much more I find.

He took parts of me when he went, and I can't seem to get them back, and now I'm digging through everything, trying to piece together myself as well.

I clear off the rest of the trophies and books, and all that's left is the marked-up white shelf, and a piece of gold fabric wedged in the gap against the wall. I pull on the fabric, and a trail of ribbon emerges.

It was Christmas.

He pulled this off the box I'd wrapped, tossed it behind him over his head. Balled up the wrapping paper, and did the same.

It was snowing, the big, fluffy kind that piled up on the windowsill, coating everything in softness. He opened the box, revealing the keychain in the shape of a flattened metal helmet, flipped over to show the signature of his favorite player—my dad knew the player's mom through a mutual business partner, and got the signature for me. I'd been looking forward to giving him this for the last few weeks, and couldn't stop the smile from spreading as he pulled the keychain from the box.

I held my breath as he dangled it on his pointer finger.

God, the look on his face.

Purple Glass Shards

I stand on my toes, looking to see if there's anything else wedged behind the gap in the shelves, but there's nothing. I bring one of the new boxes over to the side of his room and drop the contents of his shelves inside, kneeling beside it as I tape it up. I plant my hand against the carpet behind me to push myself upright, and a sliver of glass hidden in the crease against the wall digs into my palm. I brush it off and hold it up to the window. It's clear, the shape of a triangle, with a slightly purplish tint. I move my hands around the edge of the carpet, digging my fingers deeper into the fibers, and find another shard.

There are two more by the time I'm done, all scattered against the wall beside the bedside table. I leave them on the wooden surface, moving them around like a jigsaw puzzle. But nothing fits. There are too many missing pieces. I try to think about something breakable that had been here, that's now gone. Something on the surface that could've been knocked over.

There's the lamp, the wires from his chargers, an empty plastic cup from a sporting event. Maybe a glass cup was also here, I think. Maybe a picture frame. I close my eyes, envisioning the surface of the bedside table once more, but nothing comes to mind.

But what does come to mind is the way he'd always knock things off the surface. *The Danger Zone*, he called it. It became a joke: *Don't put anything there if you fear for its safety.*

Caleb threw his arms out in his sleep. He said he'd once knocked over a lamp when he was younger, so he made sure the new lamp was out of arm's reach. When I came over one day in May, I remember him turning over his hand, the scratches from the broken glass across his knuckles. He said he'd broken something in his sleep. But for the life of me, I can't remember what it was—what item is currently missing from his room.

"Caleb," I'd said that day, thinking he needed to have this looked at, get stitches, or at least put on some bandages. But then he caught sight of Max outside his window, and his face switched to a smile. Max had a towel thrown over his shoulder.

"Max!" he called. "Be right down!"

"Come on," Caleb said to me, and then he pulled me down the stairs behind him, grabbing two towels from the linen closet on the second floor. I frantically tried to keep up the pace.

"I thought we were doing this tomorrow," Caleb said, walking out the back door to meet up with Max.

Max looked up at the sky. "Might rain tomorrow. Today's better," he said. Then he nodded at me, an afterthought. "Jessa," he said.

I looked at the sky, which was a light gray, and said, "What's better about today?"

Caleb's smile stretched even wider. "You'll see."

The bridge is one town over from Caleb's place, on the way to the shore. The Old Stone River snakes through his town and the next, before making its way to the inlet, emptying into the ocean. Most days, it doesn't look dangerous. The water looks peaceful, from above.

The three of us stood pressed up against the guardrail of the single-lane bridge, Caleb's car parked around the bend, off the side of the road.

I was shaking my head. I'd started shaking my head as soon as I realized what they expected me to do, and I hadn't stopped since.

"What are you scared of?" Caleb asked.

"Sharks," I said. "Drowning. Hitting my head on the way down. Breaking a leg. Getting arrested." They were both watching me, neither sure if I was serious. "Do you want me to keep going?"

"Sharks don't live in rivers," Caleb said.

"A, I know you've seen *Jaws*. B, it's inspired by a true story. C, a story that happened *here*."

Caleb smiled wider, apparently amused by the many forms my fear took. "There's no sharks in the river *today*." And Caleb had this way about him that let me believe him.

"What about the rest of the list?" I said.

"I'll go first. I'd never let you drown."

And then, before I could protest, he stood on the metal guardrail, still facing me on the road, placed his arms out to his sides, smiled, and stepped backward.

I lunged to the edge just in time to see him break through the surface of the water, and heard him let out a shout. "Come on, Jessa! The water's nice." He shook his hair out from his eyes, treading water.

I thought of the cut on his hand. Sharks under the surface. Rocks and roots and mud. And then I felt something vibrating under my feet.

"Car!" Max called to Caleb, and then he grabbed me by the hand, sprinting down to the far end of the bridge, ducking into the tree line at the road. I was breathing heavily by the time the car went past.

Max dropped his voice to almost a whisper. "Listen. You won't get arrested, because it's a narrow bridge and the cars have to go slow. We can feel them coming before they see us. You won't break your leg, because it's deeper than it looks. The water's higher than last year, and I've never hit the bottom. And you won't hit your head, because you're going to lean forward, and I'll hold on to you until you tell me to let go. Okay?"

It was humid, and he was talking low, and he felt closer than he should be. I nodded. "Okay."

He stepped back into the road. "Then let's do this."

I made my way back to the jump spot and watched as Caleb treaded water below.

"Ready, Jessa?" he called.

I kicked off my flip-flops, held on to the guardrail as I

stepped onto the opposite side. Held my breath. Max put his hands on my waist while standing behind me on the other side of the guardrail. "Lean forward," he said. And I did.

I looked down, which was rule number one of things you shouldn't do. Caleb was chanting my name. The water looked motionless and the deepest blue, from this angle. Max's hands tightened on my waist, his fingers gripping the fabric of my shirt, holding me steady.

I closed my eyes, held out my arms, imagining I was someone else, who was unafraid.

"Let go," I said, and then I felt the absence of his grip— and I was falling.

The water was hard and crisp and it took my breath away when I hit it, and I was already swimming for the sunlight at the surface. I broke through, took in a gasp, and noticed Caleb smiling, swimming toward me. He was laughing, and then so was I, as he reached me. "See?" he said. "You loved it." He reached for my arm. "Told you I wouldn't let you drown."

Max took a running leap straight from the road, pushing off the guardrail with his back foot, tucking into a cannon-ball that sent ripples through the water when he hit the surface.

We swam for the riverbank, and when we were back on shore, Caleb said, "Told you she'd do it."

Max grunted and climbed back up to take another jump. Caleb looked at me, like I'd done something to make him proud. "Sophie never jumped," he whispered.

I wanted to tell him that I didn't jump at all. That all I

did was tell someone else to let go, and gravity took over from there. Max did it for me, holding on to me until I was ready. I leaned forward, and then I fell.

In Caleb's room now, sitting on the edge of his bed, I smell the river, as if we're still there, or as if it's here instead. I feel the water moving faster, the current picking up. And then I picture darkness, nothing but water, pushing us faster, pulling us under.

To-Do List

I tear open the drawer of his bedside table, thinking there might be pieces of whatever had broken inside. But it's practically empty. There's a pencil, a paper clip, a list written in his handwriting, crumpled up and flattened again. It looks like it's a list from the end of last school year, projects due. It says *English Final. Library. Science Final. 22. Card for J.*

I think back to June, when we were taking finals, wondering what *22* could stand for. And what he could've been giving me a card for. I can't think of anything. I don't remember any cards at all. And then it becomes clear. The *J* is for Julian. The 22nd was the date. The day of his graduation party.

Caleb hadn't shown up. I tried not to let it show on my face, when Julian was so happy, and his friends—our friends—were all there. Knowing how hard they'd all worked for this moment, and my parents too, and all the mixed emotions that came with getting him to this point but also letting him go.

I tried not to let it ruin my time, either. But it was late

afternoon and Caleb hadn't been answering my texts or calls all day.

My dad was grilling and my mom was talking to the other baseball parents. I was checking on the drinks. I was getting more ice, when needed. I was answering the call of *Jessa, can you* that I'd come to expect, and for once, I let it take the place of the circle of thoughts running through my head: Why wasn't he here? Why didn't he tell me? Why wasn't he answering my calls?

"Jessa," my dad called from the back sliding glass doors. "Can you do me a favor and check on the boys. Just make sure they're not doing anything *too* stupid, okay?"

I stopped arranging fruit. "You're going to have to define *too stupid*, Dad."

"Just . . . ," he said, and he looked up at the sky for an answer, as if filtering an explanation for his teenage daughter was too much to ask. But I knew what he meant. There was an ice bucket of cheap beer that had recently gone missing from the back deck. There were sounds of cheering from the side yard. But he wanted to give them space. Let them celebrate.

"You mean, I should make sure they're not, like, sacrificing virgins to the Greek gods or anything?" I'd said, trying for humor.

But his face turned red, almost scarlet, and I realized I'd used the V-word, which was strictly against protocol in father-daughter conversations.

"Something like that," he said, taking the fruit platter from the counter.

Just then, Hailey walked in, in a sundress and ballet flats, red lipstick, wrapped gift in hand. I greeted her with a smile and our mission.

"Can you define *too stupid*?" she asked my father.

My dad groaned at the ceiling and mumbled to himself, and Hailey didn't get why I was doubled over in laughter.

"We're on it, Dad!" I called after him, as he carried the fruit out back.

Around the side of the house, in the flattened area sheltered by trees, Julian and some of his teammates were playing a pickup game of football. Except after a moment, I realized it wasn't really a game of football—it was Julian trying to make it past a team of five alone.

"Hey, Julian," Hailey called, and he paused, looking over his shoulder. "Need a teammate?"

He shook his head and took off, before getting brought down by Max and Liam, just shy of the makeshift end zone, his arm extended into the strip of grass between trees, which currently housed the missing cooler of beer.

"That counts," he said, one hand inches from the container.

Max pulled a beer from the cooler, handing it to him. "Only because it's technically your beer," he said, and they laughed.

Max waved from the end zone, and Julian called, "Who's next?" and Hailey turned to me with a grin. "Do you think this counts as too stupid?"

Hailey slipped off her shoes, held out her arm for the ball. "Over here," she called. "Except we're a team of two."

I laughed, stepping out of my own shoes. But Julian

shook his head. "Uh-uh. No." He looked firmly at each of his friends.

But Max was smiling, and he tossed the ball in my direction. "Let's see what you got, then!"

I caught the ball and turned to Hailey. "Ready?" I asked.

"Wait a minute," she called, tying up her hair.

Hailey crouched low, and I smiled in her direction.

"Okay, go," she said. It was on.

I threw Hailey the ball first, let her weave her way as far as she could get, until Liam picked her up in a bear hug and she screamed, "My dress!" And when he put her down, she laughed and took off, calling "Suckers!" over her shoulder.

She headed straight for Julian, who I knew would not let her by no matter what, because to do so would mean letting his younger sister and her best friend get at their beer. And without looking, eyes still locked on Julian, she tossed the ball to the side, knowing I'd be there. All I had to do was make it through Max, from my side.

I ran straight for him, a game of chicken, guessing he would let me by rather than knock me down. But he didn't budge. Shook his head just slightly as I approached, and I tilted my left shoulder into him as I ran. Max was much taller than me, and there are certain unbendable laws of physics, and I knew he had me stopped. His arms came around my waist, and my momentum ground to a halt. But at the last minute, he seemed to lose his balance as I tried to push him away. His body tilted back, and we were falling.

He let out an *oof* as he landed in the grass, my weight

on top of his own, his arms still around my back, the ball cradled against his chest.

And from the background, I heard Hailey cry, "Victory!"

I was laughing, and so was Max. "You okay?" I asked.

He dropped his arms, rested his head back. "I will be, when you get up."

I dropped the ball, stood, smoothed my dress down, reached a hand down for Max.

I heard Hailey taunting Julian in the background. "You think you're the only Whitworth with moves, Julian? Allow me to introduce you to your sister."

Max hung an arm over my shoulder, breathing heavy. "Well played, Jessa."

Hailey was rummaging through the cooler, with Julian watching, his arms crossed, face frozen in a frown. Then I felt Max stiffen, quickly drop his arm, and call, "You gonna take your shot, Caleb?"

My shoulders tensed. I turned to the house, saw him leaning against the corner, watching. "Hey!" I called, jogging over to him. But his face was unreadable. "You made it."

There was something indecipherable in his expression. And meanwhile I was thinking, *Where were you? Where have you been? Why didn't you answer my text?* But he had an envelope tucked under his arm, Julian's name printed on the front. And all he said was, "Sorry I'm late."

The day was supposed to be a celebration, not about me at all. "Come on," I said, hooking my arm through his, "I just earned you a beer."

And all was forgiven.

▲ ▲ ▲

"I guess this explains why it's taking so long." Eve's words yank me from the memory. She's standing just inside the entrance to the room in bare feet, her toenails painted a dark maroon. She's caught me staring out the window, with the list on the surface of the bedside table, but she doesn't seem to notice the paper.

"I was just remembering something," I say.

Eve takes a step closer. "What were you remembering, Jessa?"

I swallow, feeling cornered, like this room is a bunker, exactly as Caleb described it, and there's no way out. A narrow flight of stairs beyond his mother. A window behind me, too high off the ground, with nothing but concrete down below.

"Christmas," I say, nodding my head toward the ribbon on the shelf, the last rays of twilight catching the shimmer. "That was from a present I gave him."

"Any other surprises?" she says, and I can't tell whether she's asking out of curiosity, or if she knows. I wonder if he brought this other girl back to his house. If his mother knew all along, and is using this to punish me—hoping I discover it for myself.

"No," I say. I do not take the bait. Not from her. Not from anyone. I step back slowly, circling my hand around the post of his headboard.

Except as I'm saying the word, my fingers brush against a thick string, a cord. Something that blended in with the grooves of the headboard.

I try not to look at it; I need her to leave me alone up here. "I need to go soon," I say. "I have a test tomorrow. I'm just finishing up."

Eve is upset with me, and I'm not sure whether it's because I've had to remind her that life keeps going for me, and I must pretend to care about trivial things like tests and curfews, or because I am bailing on her, and it's taking longer than she expected. She must want me out of here as much as I want to get through it.

Except it's getting harder and harder to leave. With each piece that I put aside, there's less and less of Caleb remaining. I don't want to move any faster, scared there will be nothing, and scared there will be too much. Things I didn't want to know. Pieces he never shared, and hid away.

"I have off last period tomorrow," I tell her. "I'll come right away. I'll get more done."

She doesn't speak, just walks back down the steps, and I see a second shadow on the landing—Mia, hidden just around the corner, listening.

As soon as Mia retreats to her room and Eve is out of sight, I follow the cord hanging from the back of his headboard, follow it to the item wedged between the wall and the back of the bed, hanging beside his window.

It's a small pair of binoculars, and I'm pretty sure these don't belong to Caleb.

I spend a few moments holding them in the palm of my hand, a memory of warmth, followed by a sharp chill.

I quickly shove them in my purse, and I leave.

MONDAY NIGHT

▶   ◀   ▲

I leave in my car, but pull around the block, determined to fit the pieces together. As if by fitting them together, all that we've lost will suddenly be found again.

I knock on Max's front door with the binoculars in my hand, but nobody answers. I ring the bell, but nothing. His car isn't here, either. I consider sending him a text, but we don't do that anymore. Not since the day of the flood.

"I'm home," I call when I walk through the front door of my house. But I head straight up the steps to my room.

I flip through Caleb's pictures, trying to find what had been on his bedside table, what glass had broken. I scan through all of them until I find the one of me and Mia on his bed. There's a lamp behind us, and there's a small glass figurine beside it.

I remember, suddenly. It's a unicorn. Mia gave it to him. If I had noticed it missing, if I'd given it any thought at all, I might've assumed it had been moved to a different shelf, or a drawer, or maybe that Mia took it back for her own collection, changing her mind.

But I didn't really notice. And now I know it was what had shattered that day. Shards of it ground into his beige rug. Another victim of his arms thrown out in dreams, or in nightmares.

Something settles inside me, this piece of information, as if I can make sense of things after all. Part of a movie scene, played in reverse: fragments from the floor un-breaking, un-falling, resettling on the surface of his bedside table. Everything slips into place, and I believe once more that I can trace the start and end, the cause and effect, the trail of events that led to Caleb in a car, heading east.

Logging onto my computer, I see I have a message. My pulse picks up, and my finger hovers over the icon. It's from Ashlyn Patterson, and it's like there's another version of Caleb in the screen tucked just beyond here. I can almost see him, waiting there.

She has written a single line in return: *I don't know who you are, and I don't know any Caleb Evers.*

I groan out loud and go back to scrolling through the images on the other profiles, but no other Ashlyn Patterson fits the description. They're either too young or too old, too unrecognizable.

I keep scanning faces until my dad calls me for dinner.

Downstairs, I eat in the dining room with my parents, but my heart isn't in it. My stomach isn't in it. But my parents let me be, ignoring the fact that I'm just moving the food around my plate. I've been in and out, here and gone, since that day in mid-September, when Caleb drove off the bridge. I've quit cross-country, but I run alone, at night, in the dark, with nothing but the sound of air rushing in and out, the imaginary rumble of a river between my gasping breaths.

I've also taken to my room, for days on end. My mom brought food up to me instead, when I didn't come down for it. They've been trying, I can see that. They've said all the right words, alternately given me attention and then given me space. I think they've read a book on dealing with your teen's grief. Everything feels like a sound bite.

"Do you need anything?" my father asks, clearing his throat. And I know he's asking about more than the food. Opening the lines of communication. I feel I must've run them dry by now.

"I have homework," I say. "But thanks for dinner."

"Jessa," my mother calls after me, but something in her voice makes everything too close. Spending so much time in his room, it all feels too raw.

I have to get out of here. I pack up my backpack, throw the binoculars in the bag, and blow down the stairs. It's almost eight—Max must be home by now.

"I'm meeting Hailey," I call, and I leave before they can call me back.

I ring the bell, and this time I hear footsteps coming down the stairs. Max throws open the door wearing worn jeans and a thin T-shirt, and I think he's been working out. But he holds his breath, seeing me there.

"Max, did you go through his email?" I ask.

He shakes his head, his mind trying to catch up. "Did I what?"

"His email. You went through his room, looking for money. And his email password was changed."

We're standing in the dimly lit kitchen, just to the side of his front door. "And you think that was me?"

"I'm running out of options as to who else had his password."

"I didn't know his password."

"You never saw it?"

He doesn't answer at first. He doesn't just lie and say no. "I don't try to look. But I know part of it."

"Which part?" I press.

"Thirty-six. His lacrosse number."

I nod. "Yes. And now it's changed."

"So he changed it."

But I'm shaking my head. "After, Max. Someone changed it *after*."

He has frozen, both believing and disbelieving. "What do you want me to say, Jessa? I said it wasn't me."

I want him to tell me the truth. I want to look in his eyes and know. I want to see the lie, the expression shutter, his gaze shift to the side. Instead I unzip my bag and pull out the binoculars, watch as his throat moves as he swallows. The way he instinctively takes a step back, as if remembering that night himself.

Binoculars

The binoculars hang from my hand. "Are these yours?" I ask, not quite meeting his eyes.

"Oh," Max says, reaching for them. He lifts them to his face, but the string is still wrapped around my hand. "Maybe. I think so. Where did you find these?"

"In his room," I say, and Max's gaze fixes on my own. "You didn't give them to him?"

He shakes his head. "No." His eyes narrow on the binoculars, and he says, "The last time I saw these, I think they were still in my car."

The moment hangs between us, all the unspoken things filling up the space around us.

Things changed after the day in New York. The way Caleb looked at me. The way Max looked at me. Each the inverse of how it was supposed to be. At the river; at Julian's graduation party; at the beach.

In August, Caleb went on vacation, a family trip. This was after Sean left, and Eve pulled Caleb in closer, relying on him a little more. They went away to a cabin in the Poconos, where there was no cell reception, and no Internet. Caleb was just gone.

In August that same week, I ran into Max at the mall—Julian had driven, and I said I'd call if I needed a ride later—and we hung out just like we would've if Caleb were there. Going to a movie, hanging out in the food court, all normal things, it seemed. Unless you paused to think about it. Unless you noticed the part that was absent.

It was me who suggested going somewhere else, who didn't want the day to end, who said *Ice cream*, and then, when it turned dark, *Did you know you can see Saturn tonight?*

The day had been a string of moments that I didn't want to pause, or stop. There was a pull of momentum, and we had to keep going. "There's too much light," he said, staring up between the streetlights by the ice cream shop.

It was Max who suggested grabbing the binoculars from his house. He left me in his idling car while he ran inside to get them. They were small, the type I've seen people use at ball games. But it was me who suggested driving out to the fields behind the school, now abandoned. Who found a spot to sit in the middle of the goalposts. The night air cooled and the grass tickled the backs of my legs as I raised my finger and pointed it out.

I took his binoculars and tried to focus on the object in the sky, but everything blurred as I moved them too fast.

"I mean, I think that's it. Maybe we should look it up," I said, laughing to myself.

Max took out his phone, pulled up some night sky app.

"Wait, you have a night sky app?" I'd asked, pushing his shoulder, teasing.

"Oh, yeah, let's all make fun of Max until nobody can figure out where Saturn is."

He realigned his phone, scanned it across the horizon, moved my arm to point in the other direction. "There," he said. "You were nowhere close, Jessa. Seriously."

Max's fingers circled my wrist, and we were both looking at the bright spot in the distance. We didn't need the binoculars at all—everything in the universe feeling suddenly so vast, and so possible, all at once.

It was me who turned my face first. It was me who talked low enough to make him look, whose eyes drifted shut first, who leaned closer.

But he put a hand on my shoulder firmly, stopping me— my face hovering an inch from his, so close I could feel his breath.

"Oh God," I said. "I'm sorry. I just . . ." *What?* I was thinking this was how it should be, with the clarity of the night sky and the boy I liked beside me. Only it wasn't Caleb beside me.

He shook his head, not looking at me, and stood abruptly.

I was on my feet, even though the rush of blood from my head made me dizzy. Max had his car keys out already. "Oh God," I said again, because that about covered it. "Please don't say anything. Please, Max. You're *my* friend too." I was begging him at this point; this wasn't how to break up with someone, by breaking their heart in the meantime.

He wouldn't look at me. "Okay," he said.

"Max," I said. "I don't know what I was thinking."

I was still holding the binoculars on the way home, wrapping the cord tighter and tighter around my hand, winding and unwinding. Until he pulled up in front of my door, and I left them on his passenger seat, neither of us saying a word as I left.

Now, Max is still staring at the binoculars, as if remembering the same moment I am.

"Had Caleb been in your car? Since then?" I ask, not wanting to elaborate on *then*.

"Yeah, sure. Plenty of times. Even borrowed it once or twice. I think there was some sort of issue with his car. He probably saw these and figured he'd borrow them, too. It's not like they're expensive or anything. Where were they?" he asks.

"Hanging from the back of his bed." Hidden, I want to say, but I'm not so sure if that's true. "Why do you think he took them?"

Max shrugs. "Anything, I guess. A ball game?"

"Was he *going* to a ball game?"

"I don't *know* Jessa," he says. The frustration on his face evident. "Did he say something to you?"

I throw my hands in the air. He told me nothing. His actions don't make sense. *He was going to see you, Jessa. Like always,* his mother said. Nothing makes sense.

I can't reconcile the two Calebs.

The one who was lying to me, in places he kept hidden. And the one who took me to the library, kept the seashell, unwrapped the ribbon on his box. The expression on his face. That wasn't a lie. It couldn't be.

I can't reconcile the two Maxes, either. The one who drove us carefully to the game, the one who came back for me in New York; the one who tore through Caleb's things, in his anger.

But if I've learned nothing else, it's that nobody was who I thought. Everyone had secrets. Trust is a luxury for fools. The more I discover, the less I trust my own memories, even.

"Max?" a woman's voice calls from upstairs. "Is someone here?"

Max looks at me, backs away. "No, Mom," he says. As if he's pushing me back once more. Reminding me that there's a line between us, that I've forgotten.

I hear her steps coming downstairs, and I step back. I've barely turned around when I hear the door latch closed behind me.

This is a story of losing more than Caleb. This was where I lost Max, too. This was the boundary never to be crossed, not then and not now. If anything, it was worse in death. I would always be Caleb's girlfriend. I could be nothing more.

TUESDAY MORNING

▶ ◀ ▲

When I wake, there's a text from Max, asking me to meet him early at school. I jump in the shower, dress quickly, and grab a Pop-Tart as I run out the door. It's the first text I've received from him in nearly two months. Part of me thinks Max must've remembered something. Something about the binoculars. Something that will slide effortlessly into place and suddenly everything will make sense: the missing piece that will trace Caleb's path from the race to the bridge; the what and the why. I'm so anxious I have to remind myself to slow down as I drive to school.

There are security cameras on storefronts on either side of the bridge. One, about a half mile down the road, caught the blur of Caleb's car in the dark streaks of the torrential rain. The other camera isn't for another mile or two beyond the bridge, and it's angled more at the parking lot than the road, but it would register a vehicle going by.

It never did.

This is the certainty.

This is what prevented the hope from growing too strong, before they pulled the pieces of his car from the river, with finality.

I think about that now, anytime I'm driving somewhere. I think about who's watching, or inadvertently acquiring evidence. I think about that now as I pull into school early—wondering if there are cameras on the buildings, inside or out as I pass, and what people will think if they watch the tape.

Max's car is the only one in the senior lot, and the engine is still running, the exhaust white in the winter air. I rub my hands together to fight the chill as I make my way across the junior lot, to Max.

I knock on the door before pulling open the passenger side, so I don't surprise him. I've always loved Max's car. He got it late last school year, and it's used, with fabric seats. There's something appealing about it all, where you can imagine a whole story—the people who sat here, what they were like. It feels broken in. "It feels *broke*," is what Max said, laughing, when I told him this. "But it runs. Most days."

Now, I feel the heat sputtering from the vents, loud and rattling behind the plastic. Max turns down the radio dial, all the way until it clicks. He still hasn't looked at me. His hand is shaking, and I'm not sure if it's from the cold.

"He knew," he begins. My shoulders stiffen, and he shakes his head and starts again. "He knew how I felt about you. That's all."

"How *you* felt about *me* . . . ," I repeat, letting the thought trail.

"He knew because you asked us to join cross-country, for fun, and I did. He knew because of the day in the city, at the ball game. He knew because I always asked if you were coming with us."

He licks his lips, and my gaze drifts to his mouth.

"So I wasn't really paying attention to what Caleb was up to right then, I'm sorry. I can't answer your questions. I was trying to hold together a friendship with him, when he knew I liked his girlfriend. I could deny it all I wanted, but he knew me too well. I was too busy trying to hide it to see what was going on with him." His hands grip the wheel, though we're parked, and his knuckles blanch white. "I don't know where he was going. I don't know who he was talking to. I don't know why he showed up at the race that day, and then left." He turns to look at me then, his eyes wide and searching my face. "He'd been distant, but I thought it was because of something else. I'm sorry."

This is Max in the front seat of his car: He has these faint dark circles under his brown eyes; his dark hair sticks up at odd angles, like he's run his hand through it over and over; you can see the lines in his long arms, the muscles flexing in emotion. His lips are parted and his eyes trace over the contours of my face. I'm trying to find a place for his words. Fit them in the moments when he pushed me away, addressed me with apathy, when he picked me up that last night and drove us around for hours.

"Max," I say.

"I know," he says. "I know." What we both know: we are forever and permanently bound to Caleb. The line is drawn, at his home, at school, even in this car. We're here in secret, so people won't see, won't talk.

But I think of Caleb saying those words: *I know.*

What must he have known, or thought? Was he merely grasping straws in the dark? "But he said it to me," I say. "Not you. Me."

He tips his head down, and I can see he doesn't want to say it, the thing he's thinking, the thing we're both thinking. That if Caleb saw it in him, he must've seen it in me, too.

And then I'm there, in the passenger side of Caleb's car, after he sees us at the meet, laughing before lining up at the start of the race. *He was angry,* they said. I see him driving away, the wipers slashing through the torrent. I'm there when he comes upon the bridge, where we all jumped, where he promised I wouldn't drown, and Max held me until I fell. I feel Caleb lose control of the wheel, confused by the change in weight, and traction, and direction. The tumbling and disorientation as gravity takes over, and then the current, metal tearing, water pouring in from every seam—

Max's hand is on my shoulder, and he's calling my name, and I can hear my own breath. "What I'm saying is, it's not your fault, Jessa. It's mine."

But I've had enough of fault, and lines, and words. How can I trust his when I'm discovering all these things I never knew about the person I thought I once loved?

Another car pulls into the lot, and I know it's time for me to go. But my gaze is locked on the small plastic smiling face on the dashboard of Max's car—one of those bobble toys that's been here forever. A disembodied happy face. And everything about that terrible night comes tumbling back.

A Smiling Face

That day in September, after the race and the rain, Max had called as I was getting out of the shower. I heard the ringing as I was stepping into my bedroom, then saw his name on the display. I held the phone in my hand for several seconds, deciding whether I should answer, before doing it. We had been careful about boundaries, since the day we found Saturn. We didn't hang out without Caleb, except for at practice, with other people around. We would text, with specific questions, like *What time is the bus leaving for the meet*, but we didn't call each other.

Finally, the moment tipped, and I answered. "Hello?" I said.

His voice was low. "Please tell me Caleb is with you."

I looked around the room, confused. Wondering why Max would want Caleb to be with me. Why the undercurrent of desperation. Nothing made sense.

"No, Caleb isn't with me," I said, feeling my face contorting with confusion.

He didn't respond.

"Max?" I said, wondering if the line had gone dead.

A beat of silence, and then, "Jessa—" It came out in a choked whisper, and I sat on the edge of my bed.

"What is it, Max? *What?*"

I could count the heartbeats echoing in my head in the moment before he answered. "They think his car went over the bridge."

I felt the air rush from my lungs. "What? They *think?*" There was nothing substantial about his sentence. I had just seen him. He was just *there*.

It was all maybes anyway. I could do maybes, too. "Then they're not sure. He's probably getting food or something. Or at a friend's house."

Anyplace else.

"The guardrail is missing," he said. "Caleb is missing."

But I was shaking my head. There was another explanation. He had my necklace. I'd asked him to hold it for me. The last time I'd seen him, from the starting line of the race.

"I'm coming to get you," Max whispered.

I had gotten dressed and run down the stairs and waited on the front porch, mumbling some frantic excuse to my parents, who were too confused to object, who seemed to sense that we were fighting against some inevitable outcome.

I had thought Max was coming so I could help in some search, so we could figure out where Caleb truly was, and we could all breathe a sigh of relief. But he wasn't. He drove to their house, with the cop cars in front, and the men framed in the doorway, and then he kept going, and I realized he didn't know where to go at all, so we just kept driving.

After a while, I focused on the smiling face of the

bobblehead toy on the dashboard in front of me, and nothing more. Watching as it bounced along. Something so normal, so simple.

We drove and drove, for hours. Until his phone rang in the cup holder, and he pulled over to pick it up, and I could overhear, with finality, in the moment he squeezed his eyes shut.

He picked me up so we wouldn't be alone, when we heard.

Max sees me staring at it now and says, "That was his, you know."

"No, I didn't."

"He won it in one of those toy vending machines on the boardwalk. Determined it was a piece of crap. Stuck it there on the way home. Said it fit the décor."

I laugh, slightly. We were always teasing Max about his car.

"But he was right," Max says, grinning. "It really does."

The whole time I'd been focused on this, trying to keep my mind from drifting to Caleb—when really it was him, all along.

TUESDAY AFTERNOON

▶ ◀ ▲

No one answers the door at Caleb's after school. The car is here, and after enough time has passed, I try the handle. It turns, and the door squeaks open as I gently push it ajar.

"Hello?" I call, my voice echoing off the walls. I peek inside, and the paintings and pictures are down. The area rugs removed, so all that remains are discolored squares of wood, darker than all the rest.

"Eve?" I've beaten Mia's bus by at least an hour, given that I've left before last period, like I promised. I take out my phone, standing just inside the entrance, and scroll to the contact she's entered in my phone. I send her a text: *I'm here.*

I hear a chirp from somewhere in the house—through the kitchen. Eve is nowhere to be found. I call her name again, softly. I don't see her phone anywhere. Peering down the hall, I see her bedroom door is closed. I send another note: *The front door was open.*

This time, the chime comes from close by. Through the closed door leading to the garage. I place my ear to the door, and I hear something moving across the floor. My phone chimes as I'm reaching for the handle: *Go on up. I'll be there shortly.*

The door to Mia's room is open on the second-floor landing, and the floor looks exactly the same as the last time I peered into her room. As if even the disarray and life I had envisioned was an illusion. Maybe everything was frozen in time here too, after all.

As I step through the entrance of her room, the surface of her desk beside her bed comes into view, covered in books and pencils and crayons. Everything's scattered. And then I see a navy blue edge, and I'm propelled across the room on a mission.

Half-buried under an open sketchpad is the case for his glasses.

I wasn't even looking for them today, but here they are, in my hand. The last piece of Caleb that I thought would lead to some other understanding, that could lead me to where he might have been going. But instead they have been here, in Mia's room, all along.

And I realize the truth then, have to look it in the face. That maybe I'm only seeing what I want to see. That maybe there is no other place Caleb was going. That his mother was right, and he was coming back to talk to me, and he was angry, and he lost control of the car, and he drowned. And it's as simple as that—what everyone already thought.

And then I hear footsteps, coming from above. From Caleb's room. Down the stairs. I'm trapped. If I go out into the hall, try to make it down the steps, I'll be seen. So I hold myself very still instead, hoping the footsteps keep going.

But they don't. They round the corner, and suddenly

Mia's standing in front of her open doorway, staring at me—holding Caleb's case of glasses.

"I just wanted to know where they were," I say. I'm appealing to a child, I'm begging, I'm pleading. *Please don't tell.*

"Give them back," she says, stepping closer. Her eyes are wide and she speaks with a strength I've never heard from her before.

"Okay." I hold them out in my hand, and she swipes the case from me, gripping it in both hands. I wonder what story she has, what piece of Caleb she sees in these glasses. I want to tell her, suddenly, about the moment I saw him in them, and loved him. I want to hold the glasses and tell her the story and let her see it, too.

"He can't read without them," she whispers.

I open my mouth, but nothing comes out. The words I want to say are caught in the back of my throat. I crouch down in front of her, nod, try to think of some comforting words, something someone else would say. "You can keep them," is all that comes out.

She shakes her head, quickly. "They're not yours." She juts her chin up high, daring me to say otherwise. Then she steps aside so I can see the door, and understand that she's sending me on my way.

I pause in the entrance, confused as to why she's home this early. "Why are you home from school?" I ask.

"I'm sick," she says, like it's obvious. Then she shrugs, as if she can tell how flat the lie falls. "We're moving anyways."

I'm just glad she's talking to me, and I try to keep up the momentum. "Do you know where you're going?" I ask.

Then she narrows her eyes and closes her mouth,

remembering who I am, why I am here. "My mom was right. You're sneaky."

I jerk back. "No, I'm not. I'm just . . ." Is that what she thinks of me? That I'm in here doing something I'm not supposed to do? "I'm just asking because I'll miss you," I say, and I realize that's true.

But Mia just steps aside from the door, until I get the message. "You were sneaking around my room," she says.

"I saw the glasses from the hall. I had been looking for them."

"They're not yours, Jessa," she repeats.

Her gaze shifts to the window as I repeat my own plea. "Please don't tell."

Old Sneakers

I'm still shaken by the conversation with Mia. About what she said, and what she thinks. What else am I supposed to be doing in this room, other than sorting through his things? That's the entire point. Eve *asked* me to do it.

I'm getting down to the basics up here. There's the bedding, the computer, the backpack, the odds and ends. But the shelves have been cleared, and his desk drawers have been emptied; his clothes have been packed away, and the walls are bare.

I can't bring myself to strip the bed. It feels so violent, and final.

Instead I go for the closet, empty of clothes, now just an assortment of shoes and shoeboxes and whatever lingers on the shelf up high. Most of his shoes are lined up in pairs, and I leave them paired this way, stacking them in a large brown box. There are cleats and snow boots, flip-flops and sneakers—all different angles of the same Caleb. And then, in the right corner, there's a pair shoved into a plastic grocery bag, tied at the top.

I rip it open, and immediately understand why. There are

sand granules. And the pair of old sneakers smells like the ocean. I picture Caleb in front of me, kicking up sand with each stride. The burn of my lungs and my legs, and the glare of the sun off the ocean.

I was supposed to be training on the beach, which I hated, the sand kicking up and the ground giving way, everything in slow motion, like running in a dream. If hiking was Caleb's thing to introduce me to, this was mine. It was a run I needed to do as part of summer training, but hated doing alone. Something about being on the beach by myself, before anyone else was up. Something about the feeling that at any moment a tidal wave could sneak up on us, wipe me out, with nobody knowing.

"Hailey, come on," I'd begged her on a weekend in mid-July, while we all sat on beach blankets, side by side.

"I'm not doing that. I hate running in sand."

"Hailey, September's going to hurt."

"Then let September hurt. I'm enjoying my summer."

Hailey was also naturally faster than me, not needing to train as hard, or as consistently, to be able to stand on the starting line and run just over three miles in under twenty minutes. She could transform from "girl in a dress with red lipstick" to "girl who can kick your ass in red lipstick" in the time it took to slip on running shoes.

"We should do it," Max had said to Caleb while I dug through my bag for more sunscreen.

Caleb made a face, but then he saw mine, so hopeful, lean-

206

ing toward him. *Pleasepleaseplease*, I mouthed. I was one step away from asking Julian, and I really didn't want to ask Julian.

"Fine," he said. "Looking forward to kicking your asses tomorrow."

I rolled my eyes. "Wear old shoes," I'd told them.

"I thought people ran barefoot on the beach," Max said.

"You don't want to do that for five miles."

Max pursed his lips. "I'm regretting this decision already."

I didn't know precisely how fast Caleb was until that day. I'd seen him on the lacrosse field, and I'd seen him doing line sprints during practice, but I had no idea whether he'd be able to pace himself for a distance run in sand.

We sat on the worn wooden steps leading down onto the beach while Max retied his shoes. "So," I said, squinting from the glare of the sun on the ocean, "we head that way until the pink hotel." The pink hotel was as good a landmark as it got on the beach. I'd mapped it out beforehand. "Then we turn around and come back."

Caleb nodded. Max leaned over the splintered railing, peering down the beach.

Caleb grinned. "Loser sings the national anthem on the corner of the street."

"Oh my God," I mumbled, "what *is it* with you two and the national anthem?" There was always some variation of that, in a bet. Singing it in the middle of class (Caleb), or at the sports banquet dinner (Max, before he got shut down by the athletic director), or on the train into the city (Caleb, but then the whole train got into it, and we all sang, so really that one didn't count).

Caleb shrugged. "Ready?" he asked.

I started jogging, and Caleb took off at a near-sprint, his sneakers kicking up the sand in front of me.

"Dammit," Max said, and he kicked into another gear, desperately trying to keep up. Max played shortstop, and I knew he could sprint. But they were both going to burn themselves out in the first hundred meters, I decided. I was going to beat them both within the first mile.

Except I didn't.

I caught up with Max halfway to the pink hotel, but Caleb kept getting farther and farther ahead. He looped back, passing us, never letting up speed. "Jessa," he called as he blew by, "don't you dare let him beat you or you'll be belting 'The Star-Spangled Banner' in the parking lot!"

"What?" I shouted back. I had assumed the bet was only between the two of them. I dug in deeper and pulled away from Max, but in the last section, he pulled even. He was breathing heavily, nearly spent, but his strides were twice as long as mine and he was going to win, I could feel it.

I closed my eyes, imagined this was a race and not practice, that the person beside me was any other person and the ground below was solid and I was stronger than them, and had practiced harder, and longer, and I had more left in the tank. I felt my steps pull even with his again, and in the last few meters before the spot Caleb sat on the steps, I sprinted with everything I had, and I beat him.

I collapsed onto the sand in front of Caleb, who was smiling. It seemed he was just barely out of breath.

Max groaned, crossed one leg in front of the other, and fell onto the sand. "I let you win," he said, his chest heaving as he lay on his back beside us.

"There is *no way* you let me win." I kicked sand onto his shins.

Max rolled onto his knees, kicked off his shoes, peeled off his shirt. "I'm just gonna . . ." He trailed off, making his way to the edge of the water. He walked in up to his knees, his thighs, then turned around so he was facing us and let a wave hit him in the back. He stumbled, fell, let the wave push him up onto shore.

"God, Max, you're like a beached whale," I called.

I turned to see Caleb staring at the side of my face. "Going in?" he asked, switching his expression to a coy grin.

I tipped my head at Max's shoes in the sand. "Someone has to guard the sneakers," I said.

He laughed. "You're so full of crap." Then he picked me up over his shoulder and started running for the shoreline.

"No, no, no, no!" I yelled. "Wait." I pounded his back. "At least let me take off my shoes. They're expensive."

He placed me on the sand, and I stepped back as I bent over to peel them off.

"Take yours off, too," I said, but he only watched me, grinning.

Then I turned and sprinted down the beach, but Caleb was ready for me, and he caught me in three quick strides. I squealed while he tossed me over his shoulder and ran straight into the surf.

He dropped me into the water, and the cold felt so good, so shocking, but I panicked for a moment, until I got my feet back under me, felt the sand giving way under my weight. We were deeper than I thought, and I automatically scrambled back toward shore.

"Ugh, I hate you!" I said, but he was laughing, holding me up.

He carried me on his back as he walked back out, as he had the month before at the river. "I told you, Jessa. I'm not gonna let you drown."

On the beach, he took off his sneakers, caked with wet sand and salt water. He tipped them over, and the ocean streamed out. "I told you, Caleb. Take off your shoes."

Max was lying on the sand, drying in the sun. There were other runners on the beach now. "Please tell me you brought water," he said. "Please. I'm unprepared. I think I'm dying." A girl stared at him lying there shirtless as she ran down the beach, and he raised his hand at her, smirking.

I reached a hand down. "Drinks are in the car, hot stuff."

At the car, Caleb opened the trunk, and they each grabbed a Gatorade from my cooler. "You guys should do this with me. Cross-country, I mean. You're fast, Caleb. And you'll both stay in shape."

"I notice you did not say that I was fast," Max said.

"I said you'd stay in shape." I smiled wide. "Come on, it's fun."

"That wasn't fun," Max said.

"You'll feel awesome later."

"Somehow I doubt that."

"You both just did five miles from nothing. That's harder than most of our practices. Come on, Max, I see you in the weight room, trying to keep in shape until baseball season. I've seen you on the treadmill."

He focused on me then, took a long sip, brushed the wet hair from his eyes. I held my breath, waiting. "Yeah, okay," he said. "Okay, I'll do it."

We both turned to Caleb, who was looking Max over. He turned to me, took a deep breath. "Sorry, Jessa. Not my thing."

Then he looked at Max again, and there was this awkward silence, where I wasn't sure what we were doing here, standing in a circle, a feeling I couldn't put my finger on. Then Caleb finally said, "Come on, Max. We're all waiting here."

Max handed him the bottle of Gatorade and climbed up on the hood of Caleb's car. He walked onto the roof, stretched his arms out to the sides, and belted the lyrics, "O say can you see—"

The sneakers are beach-worn, waterlogged, completely spent. I hate that I have to throw these out, but they're ruined. I warned him, I think. I told him. But Caleb was like that. He didn't like to be told what to do, even by me.

Shoeboxes by Letter

The top shelf of his closet is partially lined with a tower of shoeboxes. They're black and orange, and have miniature images of cleats, or sneakers, or boots. They're all in his size.

During the middle of last school year, I remember Mia telling him in the kitchen, "I need a box, for a diorama."

Caleb saying, "Go get one from the tower."

And Mia shaking her head, her eyes wide.

Caleb grinned. "There aren't any monsters up there."

"But I hear them," Mia said.

Caleb groaned but bounded up the stairs and returned a few moments later with an empty shoebox.

"You have a tower of boxes?" I asked.

"I do," he said. "I started out keeping my shoes in them, but then I also just started keeping them for projects and storage, and now, what can I say, I'm the person who has a tower of boxes in his closet."

"This is how it starts with cats, right?"

The first few boxes I pull down are empty, as I recalled them being. But then there's the sound of shaking, something loose and rattling inside the one at the base. I pull it down, open the top, and see it's full of Legos. I smile, imagining a smaller version of Caleb sitting on the floor of this room, building a town, or a spaceship. A few pieces are still stuck together, in half-towers, half-robots, shapes I can't quite decipher.

The box, I realize, has an *L* on it. And others are labeled as well, as I pull them down and open them. Old figurines, collectibles, baseball cards. The boxes are labeled in marker, with a single letter—a code. *L* for *Legos*, *B* for *Baseball*, *P* for . . . *People*, I guess? They're action figures, G.I. Joe, stuff like that.

I hear Eve come back in the house, and Mia speaking to her below. I can only hope she's not telling her about finding me in her room. I hold my breath, waiting for footsteps on the stairs, but eventually the voices settle, the house settles back to silence.

Near the bottom of the boxes, there's a *D*, and it's sealed extra-closed with a rubber band, and I worry for a moment that this is it, some girl, an ex or a new one—something he didn't want me to see. But the first thing I see inside is a photo of a very young boy beside a man. They're holding fishing poles. They're standing knee-deep in a river. Some instinct makes me flip it over, and I see, written in faint pencil: *Delaware Water Gap?*

It's his father. It's so easy to see, from the distance, from the shape of them. Now that Caleb's older, you can see the resemblance between him and his father from over ten years ago. They've met at the center, from opposite directions. Separated by fifteen years or so now. He's got the same build, the same hair. Which I figured, since Eve's hair is so dark, and she's lithe, with green eyes and pale skin, like Mia. But nothing else is in detail. Instead I imagine the man in the photo turns to face the camera head-on, and it's the replica of an older Caleb, one I will never see, but who once existed in another lifetime.

Then I think, *Maybe that's what we were doing there, on our hike. Retracing the pattern of his father's life, with places they had once gone together.* I move the photo to see what's below, and there are a few more pictures. They're all of Caleb and his dad. There are none with Eve. They have years written lightly on the back, with question marks. Words like *home; backyard; summer; winter*. There's one of the two of them cleaning an old black car. There's a corner of a house behind them, and something about the angle, and the trees behind, make me wonder whether it's the house we stopped at on the way to Max's game. In the photo, the younger Caleb has the hose, his father has the sponge. They're both in bathing suits. Caleb points it at his father, and his father has a hand up—but he's laughing.

I close the lid, my fingers shaking.

I was doing the same thing Caleb did. Creating a single box remaining, to tell the story of someone I loved, that would one day be stored in my closet.

I don't know what to do with this. If these photos once belonged to Eve, Caleb took them from her for a reason. He was trying to figure something out, something his mother wouldn't tell him. If he asked, *Where was this taken?* surely she would answer. But his father was an off-limits topic. I wondered if they had divorced first. I never knew. Didn't pry too much, into a thing I couldn't understand and didn't want to push Caleb back toward. All I knew: His father died in a car accident when he was five; his mom met and married Sean a few years later; Mia was born when he was nine; and they all moved here just before he started middle school. That's all I knew of the Caleb before we met.

I let him show me what he wanted to show, and I saw the things I wanted to see.

I've started my own box—the box in my mind, that's marked C for *Caleb*. It began with my pictures. I've taken the seashell. And now these pictures sing in my hand, as if they belong together. I close the shoebox back up and tuck it under the bed, and figure I'll wait for a moment—when Eve is out, or occupied again. I listen for sounds of water running through the walls, but all I hear is the silence, and the ticking of the grandfather clock, up two flights of stairs.

Flashlight

I stand up and reach my hands to the top shelf, feeling for anything left behind. There's an assortment of ties, and what look like shin guards, maybe from soccer, though I don't recall him playing soccer.

My hands brush something larger that rolls when I bump against it, and I strain my fingers, then close them around a rubber edge.

I pull down a flashlight, in black and red, with a switch at the base. I run my fingers over it, push it on, and shine it into the corners. I feel him behind me then, hear his whisper in my ear as this flashlight was in my hand, surrounded by the cold night air, and the dark.

Turn it off, he says.

It was sometime in the middle of March and we were not supposed to be out. Caleb had gotten into some fight with Sean, and Sean had grounded him. But Caleb maintained that Sean didn't have the right to ground him, daring him to say otherwise.

"You're not my father," he'd said. We had come home from school, dropped the keys on the entrance table, and had made it halfway to the steps when Sean rounded the corner from the kitchen. Caleb had not expected for Sean to be here. Apparently he hadn't expected us either.

"I thought you were supposed to be studying at the library," he said, raising an eyebrow.

"I thought you were supposed to be at work," Caleb answered.

"Of course you did," Sean said. "Is this what you do instead? You tell us you're busy so Mia has to go to the sitter's, and then you bring your girlfriend here? You lie to us, and Mia, so you can screw around with her?"

I jerked back. "Hey," I said. The tone of his voice made me stiffen my backbone, plant my feet.

But Caleb stepped forward. "We came for my books, Sean."

"Sure you did."

He brushed by him, pushing his shoulder into his. Sean grabbed Caleb's car keys from the table.

"Why aren't you at work, Sean?" Caleb asked, not backing down.

"Leave," Sean said to me, over Caleb's shoulder. But I had nowhere to go. Caleb was my ride. I thought, briefly, of heading to Max's place. Thought about knocking and saying, *Caleb's stepfather kicked me out*. Thought about calling Julian, or my parents.

There was something off in the dynamic—I wasn't sure whether he had caught Caleb, or Caleb had caught Sean, but neither was backing down.

And then, before anyone could make a decision, the

lights flickered once and went dead. The washing machine wound down—I hadn't realized it was on until that moment, when I heard it stopping. Sean frowned, flipping the wall switch a few times.

"Seriously?" Caleb's eyes bored into Sean's, and I remembered that night from November, when the lights turned off, because they hadn't paid the bill.

"It's just a surge," Sean said, his words on the offense, instead of the defense as I had expected.

Caleb rolled his eyes. "This house is falling apart." Then he grabbed the flashlight from the kitchen drawer and opened the door to the garage. I followed him into the darkness. Then he called back into the house, "What do you do with the money, Sean? Really?"

The door slammed shut behind me, the lock turning. I felt the gust of air from the swinging door, pushing me inside.

"Watch your step," he said. There were two wooden steps down until I hit the concrete floor.

They didn't put cars in here—it was mostly for storage. It smelled of paint stripper and gasoline and wood shavings. He flipped the flashlight on and made his way to the circuit board, where he flipped the switches back and forth in one smooth motion, like he'd done it a hundred times, and the house rebooted.

Then, staring at the door back into the house, he hit the garage door opener instead. "Let's get out of here," he said.

We both went to Max's house, and stayed there until after dinner. His mom ordered pizza for us. Max didn't ask what we were doing there, and Caleb didn't offer up the information. My parents had called twice—once to wonder if I'd be having dinner with them (no), the second to ask if I was still at the library. I hated lying to my parents. I was terrible at lying to my parents.

"I'll tell Julian to pick me up here," I mumbled. I'd owe him one, I'd have to put up with the questions in his silence, but I knew he'd at least keep it between us.

"No," Caleb said. "I'll drive you." But I thought of Sean with his keys, in that house. Still, he didn't seem to want to talk about it in front of Max, so I agreed.

He handed me the flashlight and we walked through Max's backyard, shining it in our path.

"Turn it off," Caleb whispered as we approached his gate. We walked in the dark through his backyard, the frost-covered grass from the remains of an early spring snow crunching under our steps.

At the back door, we could hear his parents arguing, muffled through the walls.

"Probably about me," Caleb whispered. "Don't move," he said. He took the light and shone it into a window on the second floor. Then he turned it off and did it again. Eventually, Mia's face came into frame. Caleb mimed opening the window.

"Mia," he said. "I need you to get the spare keys. They're in Mom's purse."

We waited in the darkness until Mia reappeared. She held out her small hand and dropped the keys into Caleb's below.

He shone the light in his face, so you could see his smile,

now eerie from the angle. He mouthed *Thank you*, grabbed my arm, and we left.

I wonder now if he snuck back upstairs after dropping me off. If he kept the flashlight because he didn't want to make any noise.

I asked him the next day, what happened, and he said, *Nothing, Jessa. Nothing happened.*

Hidden Door

I use the flashlight to illuminate the corners of the closet, to see if there's anything else I've missed. Other than the wooden bookcase in the corner of the closet, stacked with old textbooks, spines cracked through the labels, I believe I've finished the closet.

I empty them out, heap them in the middle of the room, ready for a box of school supplies to donate. Caleb would like that. He was big on that.

He didn't get why we had to buy textbooks each year; why they couldn't be property of the school, used year after year. Instead we had to purchase them fresh, or make it down to the basement book sale where people purchased used versions from each other, for a discount.

But these are all from last year: Physics, Trig, Spanish 3. Where were the rest, from this year? They should be here, or in his school locker, but his locker was empty.

I don't remember seeing them in his car, in his backpack, or on his desk, and something eats at me.

I don't remember seeing them at all.

▲ ▲ ▲

I'd gone down to the basement the first day of classes, look-ing for Caleb after school. But I'd only seen Max. I'd asked for Caleb, and he shrugged. He had a stack of books he was carrying and said, "I guess we can share, if he needs to. Or he can buy the new ones."

But I worried Caleb had just forgotten and would be upset later. I'd sent him a text: *Want me to get books for you? Send me a list if so.*

He'd never responded, and I added it to the list of calls and texts that felt like they were disappearing into the abyss. After practice, when he was giving me a ride home, I asked him about it. "What?" he said. "Oh, I took care of it."

All these non-answers he'd given me. How little he'd really ever told me at all.

I stand on my toes to see if there's anything left on the top shelf of the closet, but I can't quite see. I figure if I tip the empty bookcase, I can use it as a step stool. Which I do.

Only once I have it in position, I see what was behind it, when it was upright. There's a door. A hidden door, lower to the floor, for storage. Dragging the bookcase completely out of the closet, I walk back into the closet and see the door comes up to my rib cage.

There's a doorknob, but I have to crouch down to see inside.

Hailey's house is like this on their top floor. Most of their third floor is a guest suite, but there are all these little doors, leading to unfinished rooms, attic spaces under the eaves, for storage. Her father added locks to the outside of them years ago, when Hailey's brother used one in a game of hide-and-seek in the summer, and by the time they found him, he was dehydrated and nearly unconscious from the dry, oppressive attic heat.

I open the hidden door inside Caleb's closet now, and instead I get a shock of cold.

The space opens up to part of the attic.

The wind sounds louder inside, unprotected by the added insulation. There's pink foamlike material clinging to the walls at the entrance, but no light, and as I run my hand along the unfinished entrance wall, I find no switch, either.

I think about where he left that flashlight—right within arm's reach of this door. I go out to his room, grab it from the box, then return to the closet, crouching down in front of the opening, shining the light inside. I've got my other hand on the door, ready to swing it closed—I'm not sure why, what exactly I expect to find. Some animal living up there, maybe.

On the floor, there are only attic beams with plywood below. I think I probably shouldn't step directly on the plywood, unsure if it'll support me. Either way, this space was not expected to be used. It's unfinished, and there's no solid floor over the beams for storage.

The wind blows against the siding, and something rattles up above. I jerk the flashlight in that direction on instinct, and suddenly I'm staring at an insulated duct with a hanger swaying from a bolt hook. It slows as the wind settles, but I'm already maneuvering farther through the doorway, balancing on the beams of wood. Once I'm through, I stand and reach for the hanger, holding it still. It looks like all the rest of the hangers in Caleb's closet. Metal, but thicker than the wire ones that come back from the dry cleaner at my place.

I don't understand what it's doing here. Spinning slowly around, I shine the light in the rest of the space. The walls are covered in the pink insulation, and pinpoints of daylight filter through where the slanted angles of the roof meet the flooring. It's dusty, and musty, and smells of wood and fiber. The beams are coated in a layer of dust, or debris.

But then my light hits a smoother surface, unmarred by a layer of dust. The wooden floor beam under the hanger. The surface is bare, and shinier than the rest, as if it's been wiped clean from there to the entrance of Caleb's closet. It's a streak of dust-free wood. Maybe as if something has been dragged across the floor.

And then I hear voices. They're coming from directly underneath my feet, unfiltered by the plaster and carpeting of a bedroom. It's Mia, speaking to her mother. Her voice rising and falling in a familiar rhythm. I freeze, realizing that if I can hear them, they can hear me.

"We can't just leave—" Mia says.

But Eve cuts her off. "I told you, honey. He left. He's not coming back. We can't afford to stay here."

I realize they're talking about Sean. First, her father left, taking a good chunk of their income along with him. Then her brother died. Eve told Sean he had to leave in the summer, and he did—taking his car, and not much else. Caleb and Sean had been fighting more, pushing up against each other, and I thought the tension would dissipate after Sean finally left. But it didn't. It still lingered, unplaceable. I wondered then whether Eve secretly blamed Caleb. If Eve held it against him that she was forced to take a side, driving a wedge further between their fracturing family. Knowing her the way I do now, I wonder if she even bothered to keep her blame a secret.

"It's not *fair*," Mia wails, in the way that only a child can get away with.

"Of course it's not," Eve says. "But this is life. And now you have to decide. This is your bag. Fill it with what you want to keep. The rest we'll have to sell."

I crouch lower as the words become more muffled—they must be moving across the room now. I'm trying to hear better, when something catches my eye. There's something shiny that has fallen between the beams, stuck in the insulation.

My fingers carefully push the material aside to keep from getting splinters from the fiberglass insulation, and the hairs on my arms rise in a chill. But I pull out the item. It's a house key. And it's attached to the keychain I know so well—the one I bought him, that he opened on Christmas, signed and personalized. My hand shakes. I don't understand. I don't understand why this key is here, in this room, under a hanger.

I don't understand how it got here. Why it wasn't with Caleb when he disappeared.

I'm crouched down in this attic room, running through the day in my mind again—*He tosses his clothes on the floor.*

He changes. He leaves—so I don't hear the footsteps coming up the stairs until it's too late.

And all I can do is stay put. I pull the attic door shut, and huddle into the corner of the space.

His bedroom door creaks open. Someone moves around the bedroom. They don't speak. My purse is still there, at the foot of the bed. I silently curse myself. Then the steps move with purpose, into the closet, straight toward me, and the door swings open and it's Mia, poking her head inside, her eyes watering, her mouth hanging open.

I turn the flashlight on, and her face falls. She sits back on her heels. Her face looks ashen. "It's you," she says.

And I wonder, for the flicker of a moment, who she expected to see instead.

She's holding his glasses, I see. Like she intended to give them back to him.

I crawl back toward her so we're both out of the unfinished space. "Who did you think I was, Mia?"

She shakes her head, catches her breath on a hiccup, like she's trying not to cry. "I heard his footsteps," she says.

"It was just me," I say. We're sitting in the floor of his cleared-out closet now, and she's letting me hold her. It's the closest she's let me get in months, and I take it. I'm scared to make a sudden move, to move at all.

"No," she says. "Before."

I feel a chill rise on my arms, the back of my neck. The ghost of someone else here beside me. "I've been working in the closet," I say, for her and for myself. She must've heard my footsteps there.

She looks at me then, like I don't understand. "When he was here, sometimes I would hear footsteps at night. I thought it was a monster. But Caleb said it was just him. His closet is just over my room. I didn't know about *that*." She points to the open doorway, the cold coming in with the dark.

I stroke her hair, just letting her speak. Letting her remember.

"But I also heard him there, after the police came," she whispers.

My hand stills. The air stills. I wonder if someone was going through his things. Maybe that's why the desk is in such disarray. Where nothing is as it should be here.

"It could've been the police. Or your mom."

But the key. The hanger. I'm holding my breath. That painful hope that doesn't settle right with what I know is true.

"He was here, Jessa. A few days later. I heard him at night, after my mom went to bed."

"Did you see him?" I ask. I realize this is a ghost story, and I'm letting her tell it. I'm feeding it myself, giving her pieces, letting her weave them into a tale, wanting to believe.

She ignores the question, as if she knows that by answering truthfully, the story will shatter, and Caleb will vanish again. "I thought he was looking for his glasses. He'll come back for them. He has to."

"Did you tell your mom?"

She nods, then drops her voice. "She said not to tell you, though. She said not to talk to you."

I smooth back her hair, and she curls herself onto my lap, and I feel, for a moment, like Caleb. I wonder if she feels it, too. Like I am filling a gap that keeps growing, and we're both here desperately pushing back against it.

"Mia," I say, speaking gently into her ear. "When, exactly, did you hear someone up here?"

TUESDAY NIGHT

▶   ◀   ▲

She thinks it was two days after the night the police came, but she's not sure. That's what Mia kept saying. But she believed it enough to come straight up here, to the closet, expecting to find someone else.

There was a hanger. A bare piece of wood. His house key.

Mia's words become a life raft. They become something tangible, with weight. Even if they are a lie, they are something to cling to.

She heard footsteps in the attic two nights after Caleb was swept out to sea. When the police were still searching the river. When the shock waves were still rippling through school, and the rumors were laced with my name. When the looks were not apathetic, but cutting.

But. His key is there. *His key.*

Maybe she didn't hear anything. Maybe she wanted to. Or maybe she did, and it was someone else. But Caleb had been in there at some point, because his house key had fallen.

I imagine him taking something from the hanger. Dragging something across the floor. Dropping his key, and not realizing it.

There are too many unknowns: the money he supposedly took from Max, that we cannot find; the unused bus ticket; the story Terrance Bilson told me about his college visit, and the man who showed up looking for him. As if Caleb had this whole other life, hidden underneath.

And I'm back where I started, the very first day I began, as if I've been running in place all along: *Where were you going, Caleb? Why?*

By the time I leave—grabbing my purse from the foot of the bed, escorting Mia to her room, descending the rest of the steps on my own—my feelings shift until I'm angry. Angry at Caleb, and angry at myself.

This is all so Caleb, honestly. Every bit of it. Everything that keeps me tethered to that room, even now.

It was the secrets that hooked me from the very start, the things that he doled out to me, in pieces. Letting me believe I was always getting closer, seeing more of him. But now I'm realizing how much of it was only granted to me because his hand had been forced. Three months before he said a word about his father, and only then because I didn't understand his family's money situation; a chance encounter with an ex-girlfriend before I even knew she existed.

I'd believed myself worthy not only of his affection, but of his trust. Except I'd misread the signs. Everything had been situational, a reaction, an answer to a question I had to first ask.

There was always something just under the surface, that

230

I was trying to reach. He kept things just hidden enough to keep me hooked on the intrigue. Doling out the secrets—*I don't like my best friend's girlfriend*—to mask the ones he kept.

The way his eyes turned slightly downward at the edges, pulling me closer, so I could decipher him. The physical differences from his mother, a window to the father he must've once known, but whose picture I'd never seen.

The history of the marks on his body: lower stomach, appendectomy; outside of the knee, skiing accident; between the thumb and forefinger, a kitchen knife.

But he'd never let me all the way in. Kept that box of photos for him and him alone, now hidden underneath his bed.

Meanwhile, I gave him everything. What it was like living with Julian (like a shadow), exactly what I had done, and not done, with my last boyfriend (it wasn't much), a trail of names, an open book. What I wanted to be (a pediatrician), where I wanted to be (somewhere warm all year round), what I wanted to do (Doctors Without Borders, see the world).

He answered by telling me what he wanted to be (happy), where he wanted to be (here, with me), what he wanted to do (not answering, instead giving me a smile that cracked my heart wide open).

I thought because he told me where he was born, brought me to see that old house, told me about his father and the trust fund, that he was letting me further in. That he was giving me everything.

But all I'm left with are these pieces of our lives,

sharp-edged fragments that don't fit the picture of the Caleb I thought I knew.

I'm shaking by the time I make it home, everything on autopilot. Running through the last day again in my mind: Caleb showing up at my race; seeing him while I stood at the starting line, and handing him my necklace. *Please hold this for me. Please be careful.*

What had he come back for? Where was he heading?

I see glimpses: The rain. Caleb launching himself down the steps. The bridge. The phone call. The police. Driving around with Max. The moment we heard.

Pieces of his car. Pieces of his life.

My phone dings in the cup holder, and I jump, too accustomed to the silence, to being alone. The message is from Hailey. It's a time and location: *The pizza place on South Ave. Six p.m. Be there!*

It feels a little like neutral ground, like a baby step before we hang out at one of our homes again. Like we're starting over. The clock in the car ticks forward. I can make it if I leave now. And I have nowhere else to be, no one else to talk to, just my own memories—and even those begin to feel like lies.

I can talk to Hailey, work it all through. She will calmly tell me that I'm not being myself, that I need to get out of that room, that it's getting to my head.

▲ ▲ ▲

But when I get there, I realize that's not what this is at all. The pizza place is busy, full of people I know.

It's a cross-country team get-together. Hailey waves me over. The coach places a hand on my shoulder and squeezes. There's no animosity. I wonder if I've manufactured it. Or if it's just time, dulling the sting for them.

Life goes on, and these things are the same: Hailey will make the decisions, and others will follow; Oliver will take out a pack of playing cards at some point; Vivian will sit beside Brandon, in a well-timed maneuver; Brandon will pretend not to notice, but he does, everybody does; and nobody can put away as much pizza as a cross-country team.

I am the only element not the same, who seems to have forgotten her role, and her lines.

Max is there. Sitting in a booth across from Brandon and Vivian. He freezes for a moment when he sees me, then raises his hand and gives me a small smile. I'm a mirror image, doing the same, confused as to why I'm here at all.

Hailey makes room for me in the booth across the aisle, and I slide in beside her. She doesn't even break conversation as she sets a paper plate in front of me. "Well, whatever, Brandon's way hotter."

"I'm sitting right here, Hailey," Brandon said.

"I *know*," she says. And she smiles while she takes a bite, leaning around me to look him in the eye. Only Hailey can make eating pizza look good. "I'm explaining why we have the better team. Obviously. I mean, so what if you can't beat him in a race. Ever."

He throws a balled-up napkin at her, but he's laughing.

"Next year, fellas," she says.

"Too bad I won't be here to help you out," Max says, and the table laughs. Max never got much faster than that day on the beach. He's not slow by any means, but he's a solid middle-of-the-pack cross-country runner, same as me. He picks up points for the team, but he doesn't win. He's essentially the male counterpart of my role.

I was a solidly above-average runner, but I wouldn't be recruited for it. I had to work twice as hard as Hailey, just to be half as good. I didn't even want my parents to come to my races most times, because it made me feel like they could only see the things I lacked—in comparison to their other child, one of the best pitchers in the state; a skill that had come so naturally for him.

If my coach has missed me, it's only in that I'm a body that picks up the number five spot. But my replacement isn't much slower. My presence isn't critical to anyone but myself. If I were to quit (as I sort of did), not much would change.

The soda feels too carbonated, and the pizza too hot, and I'm all jittery energy until Hailey places a hand gently on my arm. "You okay?" she asks, when no one else is paying attention.

Everything in the now feels so far away, as if filtered through a thick layer of plastic. Hailey dulls. Her voice fades. The scenes from earlier today sharpen into focus instead, and I keep replaying moments: Mia in Caleb's room, Mia's words, her memories. She's nine. Still, that doesn't mean she's wrong.

"Caleb's mom has me cleaning out his room," I say, as a way to explain my current demeanor.

But she frowns, and cuts her eyes to the rest of the table. "Stop doing that," she says, nearly whispering. "It's not healthy, Jessa."

I think back to what Hailey said, about his mother cleaning out his locker at school. "When did his mom clean his locker?"

"What? I told you. That first week."

"No, when? Which day?"

She shakes her head quickly, like this is both pointless and also an impossible memory to recover. "I don't know . . . it was the same day as the school-wide meeting. Someone came to get Max after that. So, the Friday, I guess? Does it really matter?"

The meet was Tuesday, the day Caleb drove over the bridge. Two days later was Thursday, when Mia said she heard Caleb upstairs, and told their mom. Eve was at the school the very next day. Could it be coincidence? Did his mother wonder what Caleb was up to, as well?

Hailey sees me thinking, and places a hand gently on my wrist.

"Listen, a bunch of the girls are coming over to my place after this. Why don't you come? It will be good for you. Get you out of that place."

I feel sick. Like I either ate too much or not enough, and I'm not sure if there's room inside me for anything other than my own thoughts. "Next time?" I ask. I give her a smile so she knows I'm grateful. Because I am. But I also need to get answers, and I can't do that with five other girls in Hailey's basement, streaming HBO Go.

"Do you need a ride tomorrow?" I ask, because Hailey

doesn't turn seventeen until later in the year, though she already has a car waiting for her, for when she does.

She wrinkles her nose. "Craig Keegan is picking me up."

"Craig?" I ask, as she tips her head back and laughs.

"I know, I know. Attempt number two went much better than the first date." That first date, Craig had gotten lost in a side conversation with Stan from the city, asking what other tickets he could hook us up with, effectively ignoring Hailey. She was not one to be ignored.

Hailey slides out of her seat, and the stream of girls trails after her, calling their goodbyes back to me. Vivian pauses beside my seat, says, "We've missed you, Jessa," before heading out.

Hailey silently mouths *Bye* while waving her fingers, and I feel like I'm making my way back to my old life, just slightly out of sync. But I can almost touch it as I watch it go—my shadow beside Hailey as she piles into a car at the curb with our friends.

When everyone's leaving, I catch Max in the hall leading to the bathrooms, or Max catches me. Either way, we're standing in the hall, inches apart, the rest of the sound dulled and far away.

"I need to talk to you," I say.

Max leans against the opposite wall. The light's too bright, and it makes us look sick, blue-tinted.

"I talked to Mia, and . . ." I let the thought trail. Then I close my eyes, forcing the words out. "She heard something.

Two nights after." I don't need to specify after *what*. We've set our calendars to the same weighted moments.

Max is holding his breath. "Heard something where?"

"There's this hidden attic space, the door was behind a bookcase in his closet. I was up there, and I found something. His house key was there."

He narrows his eyes, just slightly.

"He took your money," I add, begging him to line up the pieces in the same way. To hear the same ghost story, imagine the same moments, see the same outcome.

And so I say the thing I've not given voice to, but the thing that's been whispering in my head. That terrible hope. "Max, what if he's not dead?" I whisper through my fingers.

But he shakes his head, eyes closed. "Don't do this, Jessa."

"Don't do what?"

"Make it harder. Make it worse."

"How is him being not dead making it any worse?"

He looks over my shoulder, at the lights on the wall. His face changes as his eyes water from the glare. "I want to believe you, that's why."

I was Caleb's girlfriend, but that's not the hardest. Max was his best friend. How many years of his life were mixed up with Caleb's? And now I was feeding him this hope, from nowhere, when he had already grieved for all we had lost.

WEDNESDAY MORNING

▶   ◀   ▲

Max isn't at school. I've checked the parking lot, and I've waited by his locker, and he's not here. The warning bell rings, and it's time to make a decision.

I've called him. Twice. Once last night, after we left in separate cars from the pizza place—he didn't pick up, and I didn't blame him. I figured he didn't want to hear it again, the ghost story I let Mia feed me, that I wanted so desperately to hold on to.

But I tried again this morning, and nothing. So I send him a text: *I'm worried.*

Because it's not a cool thing to do, to not answer. Not for us. Not for people who know where it might lead.

He responds right away: *I'm fine. Not feeling well.*

I know I've done this to him. So I make a decision. The second bell rings, and I'm officially late, and *Screw it*, I think. For the second time in my high school career, I skip a day of school.

I drive by his house, but nobody appears to be home. His car is gone, but I ring the bell anyway. I wait one minute, two, and when the silence stretches on, I send him a text: *I'm standing outside your front door. Where are you?*

He writes back immediately: *Just thinking. Go back to school.*

Which means he's not driving around. I can think of two places off the top of my head where he'd go to think, if he was thinking about Caleb. There was just one place if he was thinking of the things I whispered to him last night.

I drive slowly, expecting things to look different on the approach. But it's all the same, perfectly normal: the strip of stores lining the road, a restaurant, then thicker trees, and a sign: BRIDGE FREEZES BEFORE ROAD.

Max's car is tucked onto the shoulder of the road just before the bend. I ease my own car next to it, rocks and unpaved dirt crunching under my tires. I'm surprised by the change in incline, the way the car leans too far, and I'm suddenly caught in a tangle of fear—that there's a tipping point, and I have to be careful not to breach it. But the car remains steady. I remain steady.

It's chilly outside, but the sunlight hits the road, and the glare burns my eyes as I step across the divide from pavement to bridge.

I find Max in the center point of the bridge, sitting on the spot where the guardrail has been replaced. It's a little brighter, a little smoother, and it draws the eye, standing out. Max is staring deep into the water, and he doesn't notice me approaching.

"Max," I say. He swivels his head, but nothing more.

I cannot stop the way my heart melts at the look. The way I can't help moving closer.

"You shouldn't be out here, Jessa."

I don't know if he means because it's a school day, or because of the bridge, or because of him.

"Neither should you," I say.

"The cameras saw his car pass the bridge, and never come back. They found *pieces* of his car in the river." He chokes on the word *pieces*, forcing it out.

"I know," I say.

"And it happened before, years ago, with the Coats guy. With the ocean currents, they didn't find him for another four months."

"I know that, too," I say. It's why the police are still checking, still waiting, but they aren't holding their breath in the meantime. If the river wasn't moving as fast; if the weather formation and the Gulf Stream weren't crossing that exact same time of year . . .

But my mind still clings to this terrible hope, picturing him kicking out the window, swimming for the shore, pulling himself up onto the mud, coughing up water, catching his breath. Did he walk back up the slope, to the road? Did he make it?

But there's one piece that doesn't fit. That makes the whole puzzle fall apart: he didn't come back.

Max must be thinking the same thing. He's staring off down the meandering river, the current a deceptive calm, a still blue. "I don't know anything about him. I don't know why he took that money. I didn't understand what was happening."

"Because he didn't tell us," I say.

I stand beside him, on the safety of the road, and he pivots his head. "What kind of best friend was I, then? That he wouldn't tell me? That I wouldn't notice?"

I know what he's thinking, because I'm thinking it, too. We had been preoccupied. We thought we were getting away with something. We thought we were the ones with the secret. And we tiptoed around him, grateful when the conversation slid to anything mundane.

We did not want to hear, *I need to talk to you about something*.

We did not say, *What's the matter, Caleb?* Because we were scared what that might force into the light instead.

"Remember the day you jumped?" Max asks, looking straight down, where his feet dangle against the concrete below the guardrail. I want to reach out and grab his shirt, keep him from falling.

"I didn't jump," I tell him. "I wouldn't have jumped on my own."

He shakes his head. "We thought we were invincible. That nothing could really touch us." He looks at me. "I lied to you. You could've drowned. Or hit your head. Or broken your leg."

And it's then I know what I must do. It feels inevitable. I cannot stop the momentum. I take off my sneakers, placing my socks inside. I strip off my sweater, but leave the rest. I'm standing in the November chill in a tank top typically worn underneath a sweater, and the black pants of my school outfit. I start to shake; I have to move.

I stand on the edge, just out of Max's reach. "Jessa," he warns, and then I leap. The cold air beats against my face, and it feels like it might carry me for a moment—and then I fall, and fall fast, the relentless pull of gravity drawing me toward the harsh and bitter shock of water.

I hear Max hit the river a moment after me, the sound echoing under the water, and when I break the surface, he's calling my name in the shadows of the trees.

"I'm right here," I say, after I manage a breath. The cold was shocking, and it stole my breath, seized my lungs. I tread water in the middle of the river, slowly making my way closer to shore. But Max swims arm over arm, his face focused in concentration.

He's angry when he reaches me, when his arms snake around me, so he's sure he has me.

Max is struggling to swim, weighed down by his jeans and his thick sweatshirt. "You were supposed to take off your sweatshirt first. You're going to be freezing," I say. And suddenly I'm the one helping hold him up instead.

He's coughing. I can't tell whether he's laughing when we make it to shore. I pull myself out, and Max stands beside me. My body is covered in goosebumps. I'm shaking anyway.

He steps away, looks me over quickly. "He would hate me right now."

"He would be too cold to hate you," I say, wrapping my arms around myself, fighting for some extra heat.

"Fine, then your brother would hate me." His teeth chatter as he speaks, the whole effect vaguely unsettling, like the words don't quite count right now. "Remember the party your parents had for the baseball team at the end of the year when I was a freshman? Before you were at school with us?"

But I don't, not really. Not until he starts telling me the story, and I see the memory playing out, through his eyes. "You were in the kitchen and you poured me a soda and I don't even remember what we were talking about," he says, "but I guess I was laughing, because when you left the room your brother stood like three inches from me and just said, *No*." He smiles now, thinking about it. "Just that. No. I'll be honest, it was pretty effective. I was terrified of your brother."

I reach for his hand, cold and clammy at his side. And when he doesn't object, I rest my forehead on his shoulder, breathing him in. But all I get is river.

His body is close, shivering, he's wound tight. I feel his heartbeat against my ribs, but he's looking beyond me. His other hand rests against the back of my head, and I feel his fingers move gently through my hair.

I press my lips to the side of his jawbone, and he softens. He lowers his head. "Jessa, I'm not him," he says.

I run my hand up the side of his face, feel the contours that make Max *Max*.

He's not, it's true. *He's* the one who got me to jump. The one who drove me home after the breakup. The one who picked me up when Caleb went missing. The one who came back for me when I was lost in the crowd.

"I know," I say.

I hold my breath. I wait. The trees are hiding us, and the cold is inside us, and I was a girl who just jumped on her own. For a moment, we are not ourselves. Separate from all the events leading up to this, and the ones that will soon come after. The words we say here don't count. The things we do, only half-real.

Only maybe they're not. Because as he finally lowers his lips to my own, I think I have never felt something so real.

Max's house feels warm and welcoming, even as I'm shivering in someone else's clothes. I've followed him back here, after we separated. After he pulled back and said, his forehead still resting against mine, *You're going to get hypothermia, seriously,* and we walked back to our cars together, like nothing at all had happened.

The front door leads to the kitchen and the living room together, the only parts of the house I've seen before. There are family photos on the beige walls; Max is an only child, so it's all him, except for a photo from his parents' wedding.

My living room is like this too, covered with images of me and Julian, and in that one moment I realize what's missing from Caleb's. There are no pictures of him when he's younger on the walls of his house. There are pictures of Mia, and Caleb with Mia, both not until he's older.

"Eve doesn't have pictures of Caleb growing up," I say. "Downstairs."

But Max frowns, turning back to the fridge to scrounge for food, and I realize my mistake. I know what he's thinking: everything I say, everything I see, is in comparison to Caleb.

Max: taller, leaner. His kisses more tentative, unsure.

My first thought down on the riverbank, when he finally lowered his lips to mine, was frustration that he was pulling away and stepping back, until something tipped and he pulled me closer, our clothes cold and clinging to our skin, my body trembling against his. Everything natural and easy from there, where Caleb was all anticipation and surprise; it was as if I'd known Max forever, and this was the way it was meant to be.

I wonder if it was just the moment, two people missing the same thing, seeking comfort in each other. If now that we're back in his kitchen and reality, he will say something like *Listen, Jessa—*

Things that felt possible an hour earlier seem suddenly overexposed in the reality of our lives. He looks like he wants to say something, like he's on the cusp, but instead he looks me over again. "You're still shaking," he says.

Our clothes are in the dryer, and Max has changed into something warmer. Meanwhile, I'm wrapped in Max's sweatshirt, and a pair of his mom's pajama pants. Still, the chill lingers.

"I'm freezing. It seemed like a better idea an hour ago."

He cracks a grin, and a laugh slips through. Then he bites it back, as if remembering why we are here. "About earlier," he starts, and I lean forward. Earlier, as in when I kissed him, and he kissed me back? Earlier, as in when I threw myself into the river and he followed? Earlier, as in when I told him that Caleb might not be dead and he started to believe me?

But before he can continue, there's a sharp noise from the back of his house, like a waiter dropping a tray of dishes.

I jump, on edge, while Max walks to the living room

windows, peering through the blinds. "My neighbor," he says. "Dumping the trash. It's garbage day tomorrow. We keep the containers in the alleys behind our houses until garbage day, when we drag them around to the front."

I stand beside Max. The neighbor doesn't see us. She heaves another bag into the bin beside it. The bottles crash against one another as she drops her recycling inside.

My gaze shifts to the house over the fence, and I know Max is doing the same.

Just like that, we know what we have to do. I see him staring out the back window, to the high wooden fence.

"They're gone," he says.

"How can you tell?"

He points to the window of the garage, the shades pulled closed. "The garage light is always on when they're home now." There's only darkness behind the shades now.

"Always?"

He shrugs. "Seems that way to me."

"That sounds like a really inexact science."

He turns to face me. "I want you to show me, Jessa. Show me the room. The hidden attic space behind his closet. The things that made you think he's alive."

And of course I must, we must. You can't put a thing like that out into the world and expect it to dissipate in the air. It has substance now. I've sucked him in, and now I have to prove my theory: that there were parts to Caleb that neither of us saw. Something neither of us knew. Secrets lingering just underneath the surface, hidden in plain sight.

I have a key now, I realize. The one that somehow ended

up in the attic space. I can get in his house on my own. Un-detected.

But I don't fully trust Max's surveillance techniques, which is why we end up waiting for the dryer to finish, and then check the house on foot first, walking around the block, looking for Eve's car.

"I told you," he says. But I am not one who can accept what I am told without question any longer.

Max watches the street as I slide the key into the lock, and I imagine Caleb standing in my place. The lock turns, and the feeling reverberates through the metal, into my bones.

"Hello?" I call as I push the door open, but Max grabs my arm suddenly, and I fall silent.

"Just listen," he whispers. So I do: the grandfather clock, counting the seconds; the hum of the refrigerator; our steps that seem to echo louder on the hardwood floor in the entrance. The house feels so different without the area rugs under the furniture, and the artwork off the walls. All that remains are the hard surfaces of the floors and walls, with a smattering of furniture.

"I can't believe they're really doing this," Max whispers.

They're moving. They're leaving. And they're taking the truth with them. I feel an urgent pull upstairs, as if it all might slip through my fingers at any moment. As if everything I told Max hinges on a certain moment in time. Max locks the front door behind him, and the noise resounds.

I take the stairs first, two at a time, like Caleb would do. My hands plant against the walls on the way to the third floor, and I hear Max breathing on the steps behind me. The door is closed—dark blue, in the darkened hall.

I push the door open with a creak, and Caleb's room is too bright now, without the window cover, in the noonday sun. The glare hits the bare surfaces of his desk and the bedside table. Specks of dust hover in the streams of light, and I know it's me who has set them loose, who has shaken them out, disturbing the balance of this room.

The boxes are gone.

I don't look at the bed beside the window, the backpack in the corner. It's practically all that's left.

I open the closet door, nervous that the bookcase in front of the door will be moved, or that my memory will have betrayed me, but it's there: a small door, hidden behind the shelves.

Max stands behind me, unmoving, unspeaking. I open the door, and have to duck through the opening. I stand once I'm through, and Max follows. He pulls out his phone from the back pocket of his jeans to use as a flashlight.

I step once, and the beam creaks under my feet. "Mia's room is right below here. I could hear her and Eve talking when I was inside. Mia says she heard footsteps up here two days after Caleb's car went over the bridge."

Somewhere, I've stopped saying *died*. I say *his car went over the bridge*, which, I'm realizing, is the only thing we're truly sure of. The police declared him dead because he went missing under peril. Because there was once a man who disappeared in much the same way, decades earlier, who didn't wash up to shore for months later, and there was no point dragging it out that long, and no guarantee Caleb's body would ever be found, either.

"Max?" I ask. "You know Caleb inherited that money from his dad, right?"

He nods, looking around the space.

"What happens to it now?"

He raises his eyes to mine, the wheels processing alongside my own. He doesn't answer. I thought it must go to his mother, or to Mia, but I heard Eve say they had to leave—that they couldn't afford this place anymore. I almost say as much, but then his eyes narrow, distracted. Max is taller than me, and he sees something I do not. His hand reaches for a higher beam, and he pulls down a folded red rectangle.

Swiss Army Knife

I can feel the red, folded rectangle in my hand, even though Max is currently holding it. I know there are grooves on one side, from when Caleb tried to dislodge a stubborn collection of rocks from his tire tread, but the rocks ended up getting the best of the knife instead.

It was August, and Caleb was back. Caleb told me he'd gotten home from his trip the night before, but he hadn't answered his phone the next day. He said he'd be free, though, so I figured his phone needed to be charged after returning from vacation.

I had Julian drive me over on his way out with friends. I let out a sigh of relief when I saw Caleb in his driveway, hose dragged around from the side of the house, working on his car. If he was out here, he probably hadn't heard his phone, anyway.

Julian idled at the edge of the road, but Caleb didn't look up. "You sure he's expecting you?" he asked.

I wondered. Everything about Caleb recently felt disconnected. But with Julian watching, I wanted to pretend every-thing was still fine. So I rolled my eyes and exited the car.

He was crouched down beside his back tires, working at something with a knife.

I called, "Hey there," when I stepped out of the car, but he hadn't turned around. It was then I noticed he had headphones in. I tapped his shoulder, and he jumped, spinning around, the red Swiss Army knife falling from his hand.

He quickly pulled the earbuds out and stood, resting his hand on the back of his car. "Jesus, Jessa," he said, "you al-most gave me a heart attack."

He picked up his knife, then noticed Julian still waiting and raised his hand in greeting.

His shoulders were pulled tight. The engine was grating. Everything was tension personified.

Caleb had a lot on his plate, with Sean gone, and I'd felt guilty about my time with Max while he was away. Part of me wanted to just tell him what happened—or what almost happened. But I didn't want to drag Max into it. Whatever was happening between Caleb and me, it had nothing to do with Max.

Seeing his face, I knew it wasn't the time.

"Car trouble?" I asked, trying to defuse the moment.

"Tire trouble," Caleb answered, running the side of his sneaker against the ruined tread. Then he shrugged, turning away. "Whatever, it can wait." He placed a hand on my back, gently leading me into his house. Julian didn't pull away until we were safely inside.

Caleb still had the Swiss Army knife in his hand, his fist closed around it.

"Wow, like the Boy Scouts," I said. I was too bright, too cheerful, trying to make up for the terrible mistake I'd almost made, which he knew nothing about.

"You know what they say," he said, tossing me the closed knife as he took the steps up two at a time. "Always be prepared."

I laughed, and he called, "Be right back," and it was then that I noticed the footprints he left behind on the wood—wet, and grimy, like the dirt in his wheels. I texted back and forth with Hailey while waiting.

"Boo." Mia jumped out from behind the kitchen wall, and I really did jump then, my heart racing.

"Mia, you scared me to death."

Mia smiled, but she wrinkled her nose at me. "That's not possible," she said. "You can't scare someone to death. You have to hurt them."

I jerked back, her words in sharp contrast to her easy smile. "Mia," said Caleb, coming down the steps in a new change of clothes, "stop being creepy." He picked her up and threw her over his shoulder, flipping her upside down and back onto her feet in one smooth motion as she squealed with laughter.

Then he turned to me. "You really want to be scared to death? Listen to a child tell you about the people who come out of the walls at night."

"Oh my God, stop," I said, and even though he was laughing, the goosebumps rose on my arms.

He took the Swiss Army knife back, and slid it into the front pocket of his khaki shorts. "Mia," he said, "wanna go to the park with Jessa?"

"I thought you had to paint," she said, her face scrunched up in confusion.

"That can wait."

"You're painting?" I asked.

He shrugged. "Found some paint cans in the garage. Figured it was time for a change."

"I can help," I said, feeling there was something I could finally do.

He paused, and it looked like he was trying to think up some excuse. But then he shrugged. "If you want," he said, wandering through the kitchen. I followed him into the garage, where he pulled a few paint cans from under the tool bench. There was one of eggshell white, unopened, and one of a deep blue. "Rustic Sea," he said, reading the label.

"Probably too dark for the walls," I said.

"Probably. But who said anything about the walls?"

We painted the door to the bunker that day—front and back and sides.

Now Max is holding the same knife in his hand, and I'm trying to remember what else Caleb said that day. If he ever explained the rocks in the tires, the water on his shoes. Max said he had car trouble, and I assumed he had to get the tires replaced. He hadn't driven me anywhere the rest of

August. But he came by for my birthday dinner over Labor Day weekend, and he drove me to school the first week, and he never mentioned anything about it again.

Max turns the knife over in his hand and the side of his mouth quirks up.

"The first time I met Caleb, we were eleven, and he had this thing with him." Max's voice drops lower. "I knew there was a kid my age who had moved in behind us, because my mom kept talking about it. I saw him in the yard in the afternoons, so I kind of timed it so I was out at the same time once. He was using this knife to make a sign. He was carving words in a piece of wood."

"The Bunker," I say, and his eyes cut quickly to mine.

"How'd you know?"

"I found it."

"No kidding."

"It's in a box with his personal things now."

He holds the knife in front of his eyes. "Well, that was it. That's how we met. The beginning of it all."

I'm captivated by Max's story of the knife, so different from my own.

These fragments of a lost life are not just that—they're pieces that belong to me, to Max, to everyone who knew him. We are connected through the moments.

The knife in Max's hand, where it had been in Caleb's before, and mine before that. Everything connected.

"So he was here at some point," I say, nodding to the knife. The space feels claustrophobic, and haunted.

Max frowns, opens his mouth, then shuts it because

we hear the car engine rumbling in front of the house, but there's no window from the attic space to see who it is.

"Go," he says, his eyes wide, as I scramble past him through the entrance.

Max is out right behind me, sliding the bookcase back into position, both of us heading out the blue door toward the steps.

"Wait," I say. I turn back and dive onto my knees, reaching for the box under the bed that I had forgotten, with the pictures of his father—the things Caleb was searching through. Max stands at the entrance waiting, but he's mumbling *Come on come on come on* in an endless string, even as we're on our way down the steps.

I frantically take the steps to the second floor, then turn to Max above and whisper, "Shut the door."

I slow to a tiptoe on the first-floor steps, listening.

It's Eve. I know it's Eve because there's a rhythm to her steps, something I can picture in my head, in time to the noise outside. Max grabs my hand and yanks me around the corner of the kitchen just as Eve slides the key into the lock. I am so grateful that Max locked the door behind us, so there's no evidence. We go straight for the garage door—unlocking it and pulling it open just as the front door opens.

I ease the garage door slowly shut, keeping my hand on the knob, and I listen. We're standing in the pitch dark, the roller shades pulled down over the garage windows. I hear Eve drop her keys on the entryway table, and I decide it's now or never.

I slide Caleb's old key into the door, and slowly, slowly

slide the lock back into place. I press my ear to the door and hear her steps enter the kitchen. I stop breathing. Max stops breathing.

She pulls open a drawer, and another, and another. She opens the fridge. I think maybe she's making lunch, and I know we're trapped. There's no way out until she leaves.

I stand silently in the middle of the garage as my eyes slowly adjust to the dark, the only light coming from the edges of the shades and the strip under the garage door. Max sits on a rolled-up carpet, places his face in his hands, and waits. The rolled-up carpet comes into focus, the slivers of light from the corner of the window shade illuminating the maroon around the edges.

There's a whole row of them, and I see they're all bound with plastic wrap. I look around the cluttered area, and the rest of the scene comes into focus. Boxes. Caleb's boxes. As if waiting for a moving truck, or a dumpster.

All these things I've sorted through and labeled—and for what? It sits in the dark of the garage now, shoved into corners, out of sight.

Behind the boxes are a few suitcases, but they don't look familiar. Maybe they're Mia's, or Eve's. I gently tug on the zipper of the nearest one, and see men's clothes inside. But they don't look like Caleb's. I wonder if they once belonged to Sean, if he neglected to take everything, if Eve was tasked with sorting through the fragments of the life he left behind as well.

Behind Max, there are items sitting on a toolbox that must've once belonged to either Caleb or Sean—forgotten, abandoned, along with the people they left behind. Some are familiar: the letter opener, an assorted collection of electronics. Things taken from the boxes I've packed. They've been sorted through, reordered, mostly Caleb's personal items.

Some items, though, I don't recognize, and I assume they must belong to Sean. That this is the assortment of things of value, to be resold. There's a phone, with the back removed, wires exposed. A man's wedding band. Maybe left behind when they split, a ring on the bedside table, a last goodbye. Or thrown at her feet in a rage, when she kicked him out.

And there, underneath, is one more item. I can't see it well in the dark, but my hands move over the surface, feeling the circular item, the chain attached, until it makes a small sound.

I stand straight, jerk back.

Max has stood, as if sensing something lingering in the air, in this room. I feel him approach as my hand releases the item.

He picks it up and holds it to the light, and I see a broken pocket watch that looks vaguely familiar. It belongs to a man, but it's not Caleb's. I've seen this before, heard the sound of this chain moving whenever he entered a room. The broken chain slides through Max's fingers, and it sounds faintly like music, and I know exactly who this belongs to.

Sean's Pocket Watch

This silver pocket watch with the broken chain belongs to Sean. There are certain things I know about Sean's pocket watch. I know I've never seen him without it. I know it makes the faintest sound, like a tag on a cat's collar, announcing his entrance before his booming voice.

Listen to your mother, Caleb—

Take some responsibility in the family—

I'd roll my eyes while Caleb's shoulders would tighten, and I could feel him bristling. Imagined the words he had said to Sean: *What do you do with the money, Sean? You're not my father.* There was something weighty and solid between their interactions, and I couldn't quite crack it. The truth was, I hadn't really tried. I let him say nothing about it: *Just leave it, Jessa.* I never pushed.

Sean had a tendency to open and close the pocket watch in his hand, when debating what to say. He did it a lot, whenever Caleb would talk. As if weighing his choices: *Say something; let it go; cut deep; swipe shallow.*

And I know it probably broke in a fight with Caleb.

I know because it all matches up now—the broken chain, and Caleb's face, and what came after.

He was supposed to meet me and some friends from the cross-country team out for dinner, a Friday night in late July. He didn't show up; he didn't answer his phone. But we were less than a mile from his house, so while the rest of them went out for ice cream after, I walked over to Caleb's.

I showed up at his house. All the cars were still there. And then I saw him, coming down the front steps with a garbage bag in his hand, his expression unfocused.

He stopped at the bottom of the steps, turned his face to the side, but it was too late. I saw the mark near his jaw-line. A raw cut in a straight line, the skin red and swollen around it.

"What happened?" I asked. It would've been easy to ignore it; it could've been anything: playing a pickup game of football in the road, Mia accidentally knocking her head into his. But it was in the way he hid it that pulled my focus.

"What are you doing here, Jessa?"

"You were supposed to meet me for dinner," I said.

His face went pale as I reached for the mark, and he jerked back. "Got in a fight," he said, his voice so much smaller than I was used to. He looked over his shoulder, into the house, the door slightly ajar. There was a shadow-shaped person in the darkness where anyone could've been looking out.

I lowered my voice, my eyes gone wide. "With Sean?" I asked. I peered at the entrance of the house again, but the shadow was gone.

He blew out a slow breath, took my arm, and pulled me to the side of the house. "I said some things."

"And he hit you?" He didn't say anything, just set his jaw firmer. "Does your mom know?"

He looked at the front door again. I heard the faint sound of Mia crying.

"She kicked him out," he said.

Finally, I thought. His car was still there, though.

"You can't be here, Jessa. Not today."

"He's leaving?"

"Yeah, he's leaving."

"Come with me," I begged him. And I thought he considered it, for a moment, before he closed his eyes and backed away.

"I can't. I need to be here."

"We can call the police," I said.

"No," he said. "Please, Jessa. Don't call the police. Don't make it a thing. It's over. It's done."

"But what if he comes back? What if he does something else—"

"We don't all have perfect lives with perfect families," he barked, and I jerked back. Like he saw me as a character from a storybook. My house, a set. My family, an act.

And then he took a slow, steady breath. "Please. Just leave it, Jessa," he said. And I did, walking back alone. Seeing Hailey through the glass windows, everyone smiling, everyone laughing—but I couldn't go inside. All of us, storybook characters to him. Like he couldn't be bothered to see beneath the surface.

I called Julian, asking for him to come pick me up. And I sent Hailey a text, saying I was staying at Caleb's. Keeping his secret; becoming part of it.

I called him later, to make sure he was okay. He responded late at night with a text, telling me Sean was gone, but they were going to take Mia away for a trip to the Poconos, to make it easier—and he'd let me know when he was back home.

"This is Sean's," I whisper to Max in the dark garage. I take the watch from him and hold it closer to my face. There's something brown and rusted stuck between the link to the chain. Blood, I think. I wonder if it's Caleb's blood. Dried and caked in, the only thing left of him. It's sitting in the garage, next to items I have packed up, as if maybe his mother intends to sell this, too.

I see things again, in the dark, behind closed window shades and a locked door:

Sean's clothes are still here, in suitcases. His pocket watch, his wedding band. Boxes of Caleb's things, left behind.

The rugs are gone, bound up in the garage, ready to be taken to the dump; the watch has blood. They're stripping the house down, piece by piece—and suddenly the scene replays, from a different angle.

She kicked him out. He's leaving.

It's over. It's done.

But what if that wasn't what happened at all?

Don't call the police. Don't make it a thing.

My breath catches, and I can't focus. All these things I've been sorting through. Digging deeper, looking for the Caleb I thought I knew better than anyone. Only to discover something worse, something I don't want to imagine at all.

Caleb, I think, *what have you done?*

Inside, Eve answers a ringing phone. "Thanks for returning my call. Yes, I have some large items I'd like to sell," she says, and I can hear her scribbling down some notes.

I need to get out of this garage. I pull back the window shades as quietly as I can, but the windows are just for decoration—they don't open. I suppose I could break them, throw something through, and make a run for it, but not without drawing attention to myself.

I remember where the circuit breaker is, feel Caleb beside me as I go to it. I do the same maneuver, using the side of my hand to take the entire house offline. I flick it all back on, then open the garage door, and hope she will think it's an unexpected, unexplained part of the power surge.

Max takes my hand, pulling me around the corner of the garage, in hopes we won't be seen. He has the box of photos tucked under his other arm, from upstairs. I hear the door from the house to the garage swing open, but we don't look back.

It's not until we're around the corner, tucked out of sight, catching our breath with our hands on our knees, that I realize, in the clenched fist of my other hand, I still have Sean's pocket watch.

WEDNESDAY AFTERNOON

▶ ◀ ▲

We are sitting in Max's car, but the engine is off. The only sound is of us both trying to catch our breath. The pocket watch is on my knees, and the blood looks more like rust in the light of day. Max keeps looking over my shoulder, out the window, as if expecting Eve to come along at any moment, but nothing happens.

"Did she see us?" I ask.

"I don't know. I was running." His throat moves as he swallows, and his eyes drift to the pocket watch in my lap. "What's going on, Jessa?"

My fingers tighten on the watch. "I don't know. But I think . . . I think something happened to Sean. I don't think he left."

"And you think . . . Caleb?"

"I don't *know*, Max," I say. The lies are bigger than I thought. If he is truly alive, then this is a deception, and he's done it to all of us. "I showed up at his house the day his mom kicked Sean out, and they'd been fighting. Sean had hit him. Caleb had a mark on his face, and this watch has blood on it. I assumed that's why his mom kicked him out. But now Sean's clothes are in the garage, in suitcases. His wedding band and his phone are still there, in the garage. And this." I hold up the pocket watch. "She's pulling things back out of Caleb's boxes. What am I even doing up there?"

"It doesn't make sense, Jessa," he says, but his voice is low, unsure. "You think Caleb did something and took off because of it? Where would he go?"

"I don't know." I laugh to myself, a hollow, pained sound. "And here I thought he was just meeting up with some girl."

"What girl?"

"Ashlyn Patterson. From sleepaway camp."

Max frowns. "He didn't go to sleepaway camp."

I pull up her profile on my phone, show him the picture. "I thought this was her, but she said she didn't know him."

He shakes his head, then grabs my wrist and pulls it closer. "I know her."

"How?"

He narrows his eyes. "I don't know. But I know I've seen her before."

"They were talking at the slopes, last year when we went skiing."

He wrinkles his nose. Like he's trying to place her there. Slip her back into focus. "No, no, I remember now. That game we drove to. Remember? The one when you got stranded in the boys' locker room and Hailey had to bail you out?"

The hair on the back of my neck stands on end. The phone call he got, when he left me. I thought it was from his mom, but what if it wasn't? I try to remember where we had gone. It was up north. Out of the way. Was it her school? Somewhere nearby?

"When did you see her?" I ask, though the words feel like sandpaper coming out.

"With Caleb. After the game. By the locker room. We were leaving, you guys had already said goodbye, and I went back for a drink at the vending machines. I saw the two of them, but he was saying goodbye to her, nothing sketchy or anything. I asked him who it was, and he just said someone he knew growing up. Maybe through his dad?" He shrugged. "I don't really remember. It didn't seem important."

I think about the letter I found, his name on the envelope, with no address—as if it had been left for him somewhere, and not sent. I think of all the secret places Caleb had brought me: the library, the burned-out house, that hike. And then I think of the places he never brought me, but disappeared to: when visiting Terrance in college, the man who showed up for him.

Nothing makes any sense, and I can't pull the answers out of the air. I open the message, the one from Ashlyn Patterson, and I write: *I know that's a lie.* But the message comes back as undeliverable. She's blocked me from making contact again. My grip tightens on the phone. It's her. It has to be her.

"How far is this town from here?" I ask Max.

He looks between the phone and me, and he makes a decision. He doesn't ask any questions. He looks at the clock on the dashboard and says, "We can make it if we leave right now."

"Then let's leave right now," I say.

The longer we drive, the more weight seems to fall around us, until we're trapped in silence and our own thoughts. "Max," I say quietly, and he jumps, pulled from whatever dream he'd been running through.

"Yeah?"

"Should we call the police?"

He clenches his jaw. "And say what?"

"That something happened in that house."

"What happened in the house, Jessa?"

I think about it, really think about it. If something happened in that room, I believe Caleb may be in trouble. I think Eve knew about it, and that's why she's been spending so much time in the locked garage, looking for evidence. But I can't figure out why she has me in that house, if she knows. There's a piece that doesn't fit. It doesn't make sense.

"I don't know," I answer Max. "I'm not sure. Maybe I'm wrong." But it doesn't feel wrong. The past begins to make more sense, the memories filtered through a different perspective.

"Look," he says, reaching over the console for my hand. But once he has it, he's not sure what to do with it, and he drops it again. Caleb is suddenly looming larger, between us in this car. "We'll talk to Ashlyn and figure out what she knows, and then we'll decide what to do. Okay?"

I nod, but as we pull into the high school parking lot, I realize the futility of our plan to find Ashlyn. Her school is massive. At least five times the size of our private school.

But Max seems undeterred. He walks up to the front doors, just as school's letting out, and he starts asking.

"I'm looking for Ashlyn Patterson," he says. He gets a few shakes of the head, a few tips of the shoulder, a few glances around, mumbled *sorry*s. But one girl stops and thinks. She makes a show of raising her eyes up under bangs, twisting her mouth, she adds an *um* for good measure—and I know it's because of Max. That he is our ticket in, because of the way he looks, and asks kindly, and doesn't push.

"She's probably working at the paper."

"The paper?" Max asks.

"The school paper?"

"Could you show me?" Max says, and the girl looks around for her friends for a moment, then shrugs.

She goes back inside, and Max walks beside her, and I trail behind. "It's that door, see?" It's open, and the hall is silent. "Sorry, I really have to go."

"Thank you," Max says. She nods. I don't think she's even noticed I'm standing here.

Ashlyn's just inside the classroom, and she's alone. There's a large monitor in front of her, and her glasses shine in the reflection—but it's definitely her. It's the long blond hair, and the confident posture. A pen rests between her teeth. She doesn't seem to notice us hovering near the entrance.

I knock once on the open door, and she jumps, the pen dropping from her mouth. "Can I help you?" she asks. It's obvious she doesn't know who I am, but she's working it out. Her eyes flash in vague recognition, and she's processing it as she stands. I can tell the moment she figures it out. Her body stiffens, her face pales.

"Ashlyn Patterson?" I ask, though I already know it's her. I'm blocking her exit, and it makes me feel powerful. "We're here about Caleb."

She shakes her head, looking between me and Max. "I don't know any Caleb."

"I remember you," Max says. "From a lacrosse game last spring. And she remembers you from a ski trip."

She looks between the two of us again, presses her lips together, undecided.

"Look," I say, "we're just looking for answers. I just want to know how you know him. That's all."

"You're the girlfriend," she says, matter-of-factly.

"Jessa," I say, nodding.

"I'm sorry for your loss," she adds, and then she looks away.

"How did you know him, Ashlyn?"

"Look, I just really don't want to be involved, okay?"

Involved in what? is what I'm thinking. But I can't just shake it out of her.

"I only want to know how you know him," I say. "I found your things in his room." That letter, at least, is a ticket in.

"My things?" she says. "I've never even been there." Then she relents, falling back into her chair, shifting it back and forth so the squeak fills the room. "I met him by accident," she says, "when he came by my house a few years ago. But I've never been to his place."

"He came by your house, though?"

"Yeah. To see my dad. He's an estate attorney, has an office out of his home, and Caleb and his mom meet with him once a year or so, to go over finances or something. I don't know. Anyway, we were young, and we hung out a couple times. But we lived so far away, and I mean, neither of us could drive or anything." She shrugs. "We just kind of . . . faded. I was devastated at the time. But it is what it is, right? We were just kids. It was mostly just emails and phone calls, anyway."

"You never sent him any letters? On paper?"

She frowns. "Letters? No."

"You didn't ask him to come see you?"

"No. Not at all. It was the other way around."

My stomach twists. I hate her answer. That Caleb was the one pursuing. "Then why did you pretend you didn't know him?" I ask. "You could've just said that."

"I *told* you. I don't want to be involved. I did something for him. It wasn't a big deal. I didn't think anything of it. But now that he's gone, I don't know. If anyone finds out, my dad could lose his job."

"What did you do?"

But she's already shaking her head, in denial. "I'm not even sure what I showed him, even. It's just the setup of his trust. I figured he'd seen it before, so what was the harm?" Her hand goes to her mouth. "But now I don't know. I don't know what I did. He died a few weeks later, and I'm worried it was related, even though that doesn't make sense. I'm worried it was somehow because of me." She covers her face with both hands.

"*What's* because of you?" I ask, but I know I'm coming on too strong, because I am. I'm angry, I'm strong, and I want answers.

"It's probably not," she adds, taking a deep breath. "It's probably just because he's dead, and he was my first boyfriend, and now my dad has to deal with the paperwork once probate's up, and I'm feeling this weight of guilt. So, you see? I just want nothing to do with it. I don't want to get pulled in. I've got colleges I'm applying for, and I don't want my name in the news." She points to the computers. "I'm studying journalism. I mean, the last thing I need is to become part of the news first."

But I don't see. I don't see at all.

"What was he looking for?" I whisper.

She shrugs. "I don't know. My dad says trusts are funny. They can say whatever the person wants, deciding when the beneficiary is able to get the money themselves. I figured he had already seen it, and was just checking details." She shrugs. "It looked normal enough to me, though. Pretty basic. Guardian until twenty-five. All the typical stuff."

"Twenty-five?"

She wrinkles her nose. "Honestly, that's not so bad. My dad says for some people, it goes a lot longer."

Caleb was looking at his eighteenth birthday as a way out, but it wasn't. Still, I didn't think that would be enough to make him take off, to set something like this in motion.

She takes my arm, and I smell mint from her breath. "Please don't tell," she says. I picture Caleb leaning closer, the scent of her enveloping him, the laughter on his face. Her hand is trembling. "My dad will kill me," she adds. "Listen, Caleb asked to meet me when he was going to be up at our school last May, said he had some questions that he didn't want my dad to know about. He asked if I could make him a copy of something, or take a picture. I almost did it, but I chickened out. When I saw him, I told him I couldn't do it. Then he called again at the beginning of the school year. Like, the first weekend, asking if he could stop by. I thought maybe you guys had broken up and he was coming to see *me*, but when he showed up, he was asking to see the setup of his trust. Caleb had seen the paperwork from his grandparents before, I'm sure. It didn't seem like a big deal. My dad doesn't need to know about this." I can feel she's close to tears, and I don't want to see them. They're tears for herself, not for Caleb, and I have no room for anyone else's guilt.

But something isn't sitting right, in her explanation. "You mean his father, not his grandparents," I say, my voice in a whisper, out of respect for the dead. "The money is from his father."

She stops crying, shakes her head. "No, his grandparents. He's got some trust from them."

"Right, only you're wrong—it's from his father."

"No," she says, her voice rising, her spine straightening, and I think she's the type of person who likes being right most of all. "That's kind of the catch. It skips his father. It goes right to him."

"What do you mean, it skips his father?"

"Just that. I don't know why. All I know is that it skips his father."

"His father is dead," I say. I picture the suit in Caleb's closet. The letter opener that's been passed down. The pictures hidden in a box on a shelf. The thing he was missing in his life, that he slowly let me see.

She scrunches her nose. "His father is not dead. That's why my dad's in charge of it in the first place."

Max is silent as we walk back to the parking lot. He puts a hand on my shoulder near the car, where I've frozen.

The dates line up. This is where Caleb disappeared to, that weekend he was supposed to be at the college visit, staying with Terrance. At least part of the time. He took his car and drove up here and asked Ashlyn to see the paperwork. What did he see? What had been set in motion that day?

And then there's the other issue—the one that feels worse, like I've stumbled upon answers only to discover I don't like what I've found. The knowledge that Caleb lied to me from the start. That the moment he told me about his father, rested his forehead against my stomach—a moment that made me feel infinitely close to him—was all a lie. And I'd fallen for a version of him who wasn't real, who never existed.

That he must've had a moment where the truth was right there, so close to the surface, and he looked up in my eyes, and found me lacking.

My phone rings when we're halfway home, and the name flashes *Eve*. I pick it up, and the voice on the other end feels closer, more personal. "Jessa?" she asks.

"Yes?" I say.

"Is there a problem?" she says.

I worry that maybe she knows where I am. That she knows there's nothing but problems. In the silence, she continues, "I thought you'd be here after school."

I look at the clock, realize that she probably expected me over an hour ago. I look at Max, who shakes his head. She must not have seen my car at his place.

"Yes, sorry," I say. "I'm running late. I'll be there in thirty minutes." I need what's in that room. I need to dig all the way to the bottom, because it's all that's left from him.

After another ten minutes of silence, I ask Max, "Is it true, about his dad?"

His hands tighten. "He told me he was dead, too. Ashlyn could be wrong."

"Right," I say. But everything twists inside. The more I learn, the less I feel I know. The less certain I am about anything. This person I thought knew me better than anyone, and I hadn't known anything real about him.

I feel distant, distracted. I look at Max, and wonder who he really is, too.

We park in front of Max's house, so I can get my car. There's a pang of worry, that Eve has seen my car here. I don't want her to know I've been with Max all along. But I shake the thought. What are the chances?

"I'm going to show up," Max says. "I don't want you there alone with her."

"Max—"

"I'm not asking for your permission, Jessa."

"What are you going to do?"

"I don't know yet. Just trust me, okay?"

After a long pause, where he stares at me waiting for a response, I slowly nod. "Okay," I say. Something lurks inside Max's words, as much as I want to rely on him. And I realize what it is: it's Caleb. It's the shadow of him, and all he kept hidden, and everything I thought I understood.

I drive around the block, stare up at the narrow house, trying to see the ghost of Caleb. His mother is waiting, and opens the door even before I knock.

"Where were you, Jessa?" she asks.

"School," I say.

"Really," she says, and there's something in her eyes I can't decipher. I wonder if she's seen my car at Max's place. Of course she must have. But I am bound to the lie, and so I stick to it.

There's something I'm missing. Something I don't trust, about anyone. I don't want to give anything away. It feels like a tightrope, and the answers are dwindling.

"You're almost done up there," she says.

"Yes," I say.

"Today should be the end of it, don't you think?"

I nod tightly. This is it. My last chance, before all that is Caleb disappears for good.

Backpack with a Broken Zipper

The first thing I see when I go upstairs is his backpack, leaning against the wall. His green comforter. And then: Mia. She's sitting in the middle of his bed, staring up at me like I've interrupted her.

I quietly shut the door behind me, to muffle the sound of us. "Mia," I whisper.

"You're here again," she says.

"Your mom asked me to do this. She asked me to help." I sit beside her, but she looks away.

"He's really not coming back," she says. "My mom was right."

But I say nothing, because now I'm not so sure. But then I think, *Maybe she's talking about Sean. Maybe she knows something.*

I drop my voice even lower. "Mia, what happened to your dad?"

"He's gone," she says, and she has this faraway look, staring out the uncovered window.

"I know. What happened?"

"He and Caleb got in a fight."

"Were you here?"

She stops talking then, turns to face me. "Yes. It's all because of you, you know. They were fighting more and more. Caleb was always making excuses, he always had to be with you. *I have to go to Jessa's race,*" she mimics. *"I have to help set up at Jessa's for her brother's party."*

"Wait, what? He said that?"

"Yeah. Your brother was graduating, right? And he spent the whole day with you instead of watching me so my parents could go away."

"He wasn't—" I cut myself off. I don't need to argue with a nine-year-old. But he hadn't been there all day. He'd barely been there at all. I think back to that to-do list I'd found in his bedside table, the date written down: *22.* I had assumed he was reminding himself about Julian's party, but maybe it was something else.

Going to see Jessa's race, he'd told his mom before taking off that last day, as an excuse. Maybe that's why he hadn't told her we'd broken up. Maybe he was using my name as an excuse. Meanwhile, where had he really been heading each time?

"Mia," I say, leaning closer, but then I hear Eve call out for Mia as well, and she scrambles to the door, down the steps, and I'm left shaking in the middle of his room. There's barely anything left. There's his comforter. His sheets. His backpack, leaning against the empty wall. There wasn't much inside, which I remember from when Max went looking for his money: just some notebooks, a few stray papers, and a pen, missing a cap.

His textbooks were never here. They weren't in the closet on his shelf, on his desk, or in his locker. And I wonder if he ever purchased them at all this year.

The backpack is a dark green, with multiple pockets. Max had already tipped the bag over, emptying the main contents, when he went through this room, in his fury.

Now, all that remains in the bottom is the pen he would tuck behind his ear, or rest between his teeth, if he was concentrating. There's an old test—a 91, circled in red—crumpled and forgotten at the base of his notebooks. In the side pocket is his student ID, the same image hanging above the petition outside the cafeteria. We all took the photos for them at the beginning of the year, and they always looked ghastly, overexposed by the printer settings and white background. But Caleb looks alive in his.

The second pocket has been unusable since last year—the zipper stuck permanently in the closed position.

It was me who got it stuck. Caleb was loading up the notebooks on top of his desk, getting ready to go study at the library. He swung it onto his back and called, "Ready?" over his shoulder

Halfway down the steps, I asked, "Do you have any gum?"

"Second pocket," he said.

We were still moving, descending the steps, and after I took a piece of gum, I tried to pull the zipper shut—but it caught, and I pulled harder. But when I tried to tug it back to realign things, it wouldn't move. "Oh, crap. I broke your backpack," I said.

He stopped moving and dropped it to the ground at the

base of the staircase, fidgeting with the zipper. "My gum is held hostage," he said.

"Forgive me?" I said.

"Always," he said.

Now, I think again, *Forgive me, Caleb.* Because I'm trying to unearth something he wanted to keep hidden. And I can feel how close I finally am.

The zipper, now, is pried open. It seems someone has taken scissors to the material around it, splitting it open, but also tearing the fabric in places. I wonder if it was just Max who tore into it, looking for the money stolen from him, and I didn't notice.

Either way, someone has been through here, so sure there was something hidden.

That pack of gum is still inside, and I laugh for the moment, imagining this was all they uncovered. The pieces are brittle, snapping in my hand. I toss them in the garbage, but the scent of mint fills the empty room, until it is inescapable. It's starting to rain, so I don't open the window, but I take Caleb's trash down the steps, outside.

I move quickly, through the drizzle. The garbage goes out tonight.

Peering inside, I see the placemats, the cookbooks. All dumped without care. It's junk. It's nothing. I tip Caleb's garbage can over, watch the contents rain down over the rest of the trash.

I dislodge a cookbook in the process, and underneath,

I see something iridescent. At first I think it's one of Mia's toys—the colors change when the light hits it. But as I move the other items aside, it comes into focus. It's a spiral-bound notebook that I last saw less than a week ago, in the passenger seat of Eve's car.

Spiral-Bound Notebook

I had gone by her house three times, without being let in, after the accident. I walked up their front steps and stood at the door, and heard muffled noises behind. I knocked, and the noises went quiet. They didn't come out. They didn't move. I figured they knew it was me and decided they didn't want to talk to me, and I tried to respect that.

I sent a card instead, a lame thing expressing condolences, which felt absolutely appalling in hindsight, but I couldn't get inside otherwise. I mailed it across two towns, a few days before the service.

I felt invisible, the ghost of a person left behind, ignored as I drove by her house, or sat in the pew of the church, beside Hailey.

And then, suddenly, she saw me. The tables turned.

My house had been empty, my parents on the way to pick up Julian. And the silence was unbearable. In the silence, I could only hear wisps of Caleb: *Just leave it, Jessa. Just say it. Mia, come say goodbye to Jessa—*

I had been standing on the front porch, just to breathe, when I saw her car, like a ghost itself, parked at the corner of my street. It was dusk, everything cast in shadows, and for a moment I thought I had conjured it from my mind. The window was cracked, the car dark. But I saw a figure moving inside. I stepped closer, just to be sure it was real. I walked down my front steps, my arms crossed over my chest, and at first she didn't notice. She was staring up at the big house behind me, and I was suddenly embarrassed by it. By the white pillars and the brick facade, the hedges all cut to the same height, the way it all felt suddenly so unnecessary. She narrowed her eyes at it—the lights on outside and inside, the curtained windows—and frowned when she saw me.

"Hi," I said as she lowered the window some more. Her eyes were dry and cold, and I wondered if she was out here for some sort of revenge fantasy. As if she could see the river rising up under the base of my car in the driveway, sweeping me away.

I took a tentative step back, unsure of everything.

"Jessa," she said, like she was confused to find me here—as if she weren't the one parked in front of my house, waiting for me. "I was going to knock."

I nodded. Waiting. She was the adult, but it seemed like she was checking out of the conversation, leaving it to me. My breath escaped in a short burst of fog. The words *I'm sorry* hovering between us. But I didn't know what I was apologizing for.

"We're moving," she finally said.

The shock of it knocked me back a step. "Oh. Where?"

But she brushed the question aside. "I need to pack up his room."

It's then that I saw the question, heard it lingering between the spoken lines. She licked her lips. "This isn't something a mother should ever have to do." And then, "The room is full of you, Jessa." It was both an invitation and a request, and I seized it.

"Okay," I said.

"We'll be ready for you this weekend." Then she started the car, with one look back at my house.

She looked so small, with me standing over her on the curb, and the childlike notebook in the passenger seat, which must've been Mia's.

My parents were due back with Julian at any moment. Memories of Caleb circled in the silence again. I was never so grateful for the headlights coming down the road, and Julian crammed in the backseat, like an oversized kid.

I was already walking toward the driveway when he exited the car.

"If I knew you'd be waiting on the curb, I would've caught an earlier train," he joked. He tucked my head under his chin and said, "Good to see you, kid."

I patted him twice on the back, thrown by the sudden display of affection. My parents averted their gaze, and I knew: they had spoken to him, warned him that I was a fragile thing that must now be handled with care.

Like a glass figurine in the box.

▲ ▲ ▲

Now I see the notebook in the trash can, under the place-mats and utensils and cookbooks, nothing else of Mia's on top or underneath.

I open the cover, expecting to see Mia's writing. But instead it looks like a ledger. Row after row of times, dates, locations. I flip the page, and it keeps going. A diary. A file. Propping it on the edge of the garbage can lid, I try to read the words in the fading light. I cup my hand around the pages, to protect it from the steady drizzle.

There is a list. An annotated schedule. I'm confused at first. It says things like: *school, home, school*, with predictable times, in an unwavering pattern of regularity.

The dates don't make sense, because Caleb wasn't there. These are more recent.

Then there are a few diversions. *Walk, 10 p.m.* Another: *Run. Out for 1 hr.* And another: *Girl shows up. Leaves after 10 min.* And then an address follows.

I look again. I know that address. It belongs to my best friend. To Hailey. I don't understand why Eve would be following Hailey. What Hailey has to do with anything at all.

I look at the dates again. This is the day after the service, and I realize where Hailey had been for those ten minutes on that day. Where Eve must've followed her from.

It was my house. She was at my house, trying to talk me out of the darkness, and I sent her away.

I see the dates again. The walks I took at night, when everyone else was sleeping. Running in the dark, where I could hear a steady rumbling, like a river.

But no, not a river. A car engine in the distance, following me.

My hands shake, and the paper trembles faintly in my grip. These are my movements. This is my path. She's been following me.

"Jessa?" Eve calls from the back door. "Is that you?"

I look up to Caleb's window, then down at my feet again. I start to slowly ease the garbage can aside, but his mother stands at the back door, watching me, frowning.

"Can I help you with something?" she asks.

I drop the notebook into the container, wipe the rain residue from my face. "I was emptying his garbage," I say, holding the can up to her. A proclamation of innocence. I didn't see. I want to force the words into her mind. *I didn't see.*

"It's getting late," she says. "Bring that back up, and we'll call it a day."

But I suddenly don't want to be alone in the house with her. Not up on the third floor, with no exit, trapped behind crooked stairs.

"I need to go home," I say, taking a step back. *I didn't see. I didn't see. I didn't see.*

I realize I'm holding my breath, and I make myself exhale slowly. My bag is upstairs, with my car keys. I can't just take off. But I don't like the way she's looking at me, like she suspects something.

She doesn't answer, just tips her head to the side, looking between me and the garbage can.

Now I'm wondering why she asked me here in the first place. That day I saw her car—had she been about to knock, as she claimed? Or was she watching me, as she had been in the weeks after Caleb disappeared? And if she was watching me, what was she hoping to find?

I'm saved by Max coming through the swinging gate. He must see something on my face, because he switches to an indifferent smile toward Eve. "Saw you guys out here," he says. "Can I help with any lifting?"

Her lips purse together. "No, honey. I've got movers coming tomorrow to take some things down to the dump or to consignment. Then we'll list it."

"Where are you going?" I ask.

She cuts her eyes to me. "I'm not going anywhere yet."

I slip back inside, race up to the room to grab my bag. I peer out his window, where Max is standing, talking to Eve. And as if she can sense me, she tips her head slowly back, looking straight up at me.

I back away. I leave out the front door without saying goodbye to either of them.

WEDNESDAY NIGHT

▶ ◀ ▲

I call Max once I get home, let him know I think Eve has been following me. That I found a notebook in the trash can, detailing my every move.

He doesn't speak at first, and I wonder if maybe he thinks I'm cracking up—if maybe I really am. When eventually he says, "She has to know, right? I mean, if something happened to Sean, she has to know. She had that pocket watch."

And now I have it instead. Oh God. I slide it out of the top drawer, the metal chain faintly chiming in the silence.

Why would she keep this if it's a piece of evidence? Proof of something she's been hiding, too?

And now it's hidden inside my bedroom.

I'll bring it to the police, I decide. I'll drive to the station. Act like I don't know what it is. I'll hand it to them, sealed in plastic, and say I found it when I was packing up Caleb's room. I'll wash my hands of it.

But then I think of Caleb. What do I owe him? What do I really know of him? I owe him at least the truth. I need to know it, before I turn this in. If he ran, I need to know why. Whether it was because of Sean, or something else.

If his mother was watching me, I need to understand what she was after.

I spend the night looking through photos, trying to make sense of the different angles to the same events. I've plugged Caleb's name into the search bar of the Internet program, but the only thing that comes up is the details of his memorial service, and a mention in the local paper, the named victim of the bridge flood.

I don't know his father's name. He never told me. Based on the letter opener with the initials, I know his grandfather's first name begins with a *D*. Is that really all I know? The closest I can come to Caleb Evers?

I search for his last name, plus *Eve*. Last name plus *accident*. Last name plus *obituary*. But the last name is too common, the search absolutely fruitless. I could ask his mother, but I don't trust anything about her. She makes me nervous, always watching, always following. She makes me want to lock the doors, and ask my parents to stay home with me.

But I can't do any of that.

I feel, for the moment, that Caleb is in danger again. In a car, tipping over the bridge, the current raging. I picture myself standing on the road, screaming his name. *Run!* he screams. *Run while you can!*

I picture him again in his doorway, barring me from his life. *Go.*

Leave.

Don't look back.

His words so cutting, so final.

The necklace in his jeans pocket, left on his floor, left behind.

Please hold this for me. Please be careful.

And I know what I must do.

PART TWO

The Puzzle

THURSDAY MORNING

▶ ◀ ▲

By the time the alarm goes off in the morning, I haven't slept at all. I hear my dad leave for work in the morning, before dawn. By then, it's too late to try anymore.

"I don't feel good," I tell my mother in the morning, in the kitchen, as she's draining the last of the orange juice from her cup. I don't even have to fake it. My stomach churns, and I catch sight of my reflection—pale in the window.

She places a hand to my forehead. "Do you want me to make a doctor's appointment?"

I shake my head. "Feels like the stomach bug," I say. Feels like betrayal. Like lies. Like disorientation.

She looks from me to the clock, as if she's debating staying home with me as well. I hold my breath until she swings her purse over her shoulder and grabs her keys. "Call me if you need anything, okay?"

I nod, and she pauses at the doorway, as if she senses something. But in the end, she doesn't press, and she waves once, shutting the door behind her.

Immediately, I lock the door. There's a piece Caleb left for me. A memory he shared. The house he grew up in. If

I had the address, I could check back through the public records, to see who owned it when he was younger. I can barely remember the town name. I have to pull up the map program, trying to remember where Max's game was—but the names all blend together. I remember there was a toll. We veered off course. I think I could find it if I retraced our route, imagining Caleb beside me as we drove.

I take a shower to wake up, then pull together the directions and head to my car.

I'm halfway down the driveway when I see Max, walking up the path. He freezes, midstride. "You weren't at school," he says.

He showed up, like I did for him. My eyes shift down the road, making sure I don't see Eve watching.

He eyes my bag, the keys in my hand. "Where are you going?" he asks.

"To find the house where Caleb grew up. He took me to it, once. On the way to one of your games. There was some sort of accident there, a fire or something. But I figure if I can get the address, I can get the names, and then some answers."

He stands farther away, an adequate distance to keep. His words travel the expanse between us. "Want some company?" he asks.

"I could use some help with the directions," I say. "I don't know exactly where I'm going."

"Which game was it?" he asks.

"Playoffs. The other team wore black. You won by one run. You beat the throw to home."

He raises an eyebrow, and I remember our last conversation about baseball, on the subway, where I told him I didn't pay attention anymore. Except I obviously was.

"I remember," he says with a grin. "I know the way."

We drive down the same highway, and I start rummaging through my purse. I have the coins out just as Max sees the sign for the toll and says, "Crap, toll."

I can't help the smile, the echo of the moment. I hold my hand out to him with exact change. "I remember this part," I say. But that's the last thing I remember well. I remember we veered off at a diamond-shaped sign, and Max and I take a few wrong turns before looping back to the exit and trying again, on a different route. "There," I say as we pass the cornfield, the thickening forest. "Take a right."

Then I'm directing by gut, by my memory of the landscape, how it led to someplace less occupied, abandoned, forgotten. There's the dirt road, I'm sure of it. I direct Max to turn, and then I see it: a little sharper than the last time.

The eave hanging off the porch. The singed steps, splintered edges. The grass that looked scorched from the sun, or more. Boarded-up windows and an overgrown driveway, with no mailbox to designate the address.

I walk as if in a dream into the house. The numbers are gone, once nailed into the post beside the door. But the shadow remains, whiter than all the rest, aged with time. *734*. I have the start of an address. Max opens the map program and reads off the street name. "Briar Rock Road," he says, and it feels so fitting, as if the road name came after the house, and all that happened here.

Then I push at the door and stand in the same spot I stood with Caleb, months earlier. But now I'm someone new, and I am propelled toward the steps to the second floor.

"Jessa," Max calls from the entrance.

"Caleb went up here," I say. "I didn't. But I have to see."

The steps creak and sag under my weight, and I'm not sure whether they'll hold me. I keep my hands planted against the walls, covered in what remains of a floral wallpaper, which is starting to give way, with the elements. But eventually I make it to the top. The dark hall with missing doors and half a wall burned straight through.

There are two rooms at the top of the stairs, one on each end. And a bathroom to share in the middle, straight ahead. There's water damage everywhere, on top of the fire damage. The hall is dark.

In the first room, there are remnants of furniture, burned, soaked, ruined. The frame of a bed. A beat-up dresser. In the room across the hall, I can tell the walls had once been blue in sections, peeking through the charred remains. There's the skeletal frame of a rocking horse, the skeletal frame of a child's bed.

I imagine Caleb standing in this very same spot, looking inside. I wonder what he saw. What he understood, that I am struggling to see. I feel, suddenly, a person behind me. "Oh," Max says. "Wow. This place has been eviscerated."

"Mm," I say. What was Caleb looking at? What was he looking *for*? I scan the room again, trying to see it through his eyes. He told me he didn't know what happened here. He told me his father was dead. Lies and more lies.

And yet, he brought me here. It's a tipping of scales that makes no sense. Letting me in, keeping me back.

"Did you hear that?" Max asks.

I didn't. And then. A footstep, on the steps of the porch. Another.

I almost say it, the word already in my throat, pushing through: *Caleb.*

Only it's not Caleb. I know the same way I know the tread of his step, the stride of his run, that this is not him. *This is not him.*

I hold my breath, and Max does the same. The footsteps disappear, and still we hold our breath. Faintly, I hear the background noise of an engine, idling at first, then driving away. And then I'm running down the steps, after the sound of the engine, as if I can catch a ghost.

I'm halfway down the drive when Max catches up with me. "Did you see?" he asks, breathing heavily.

I shake my head, staring off down the road. "Someone was here," I whisper. "I told you, I think Eve's been watching me."

"I didn't see anyone following us."

"Doesn't mean it's not true."

"She didn't see us leave, Jessa. I don't think it was her."

But the thought lingers. I don't understand what she's after, with me. Why she was keeping notes, watching where

I go, who I was talking to. Checking up on Hailey. And why she doesn't need them anymore.

I remember the first day I showed up, when she asked to see my phone, to see who I'd been texting.

As if she wanted to catch me at something. Only I don't know what it is. I don't know what I've done.

We walk back to our car, the morning seeming eerily quiet. I'm used to living close enough to the shore that occasionally we can hear the gulls in the distance, crying. Here, there's nothing. With the cold, there's no insect noise, no bird noise. Just the wind moving the leaves, the branches swaying, the world faintly sighing. We wait, with the engine running, to see if anyone comes back. Eventually, Max puts the car in drive, and we leave.

But in an unspoken agreement, we stick to the back roads. I check the mirrors, constantly. There's nothing. There's no one.

"It could've been any car, really," Max says. "Someone who took a wrong turn down a dead-end road or something. It could've been an animal, around the house."

"Right," I say. But we both believe there's something more. It's the unsettling, growing and gnawing.

It's the feeling that we might not like what we find, and that maybe we're not the only ones looking.

THURSDAY AFTERNOON

▶ ◀ ▲

We go back to my place, because the distance from Caleb's house feels safer. We have the address now. The road name. The house number. I go to the county site and look through the property records, which is a thing that Hailey taught me one day when she was sitting around wondering just how rich Craig Keegan was. Apparently her dad had taught her this trick. "Please tell me you didn't do this to me," I'd said to her.

She shrugged. "It's public information." I dropped my head to the desk.

"What? I don't do anything with the information. I'm just *curious*, is all," she'd said. She seemed more surprised that I wouldn't think to do the same.

I find the site now and plug in the property address for the house where Caleb grew up, and I pull up the listing. It was purchased by a Carlton Evers.

"Carlton!" I shout. "His name is Carlton!"

"I'm right here, Jessa," Max says, jumping from the sound of my voice. But I catch him grin, excited by the new piece of information as well.

From there, it's an easy enough search. Carlton is not a common name. I know, as soon as I type it in, I should get his obituary.

Instead, I pull up an article about a sentencing hearing. My stomach sinks. Ashlyn was right. "Oh God." I skim the details.

Caleb lied about his father; his father was sentenced to fifteen years in prison for a conviction of arson and endangering the welfare of the people inside—Caleb and Eve. Apparently the whole thing was an accident, an insurance scam gone wrong; Eve and Caleb were supposed to be out of the house. But they weren't.

It isn't hard to understand why Caleb would lie about that, discovering that a parent almost recklessly killed you for a money scam. But still, it stings. He never chose to tell me. Even later.

I pull out the bus ticket from the drawer where I've stored Caleb's things, because I have a feeling in my gut. This town. I pull it up on the map. I search for prisons, and find one. And I know, with sudden clarity, that his father had sent him that bus ticket, in hopes that he would use it.

He never did.

I don't blame him. His father put his life in danger, for an insurance scam. It's reprehensible. It's unforgivable.

At the bottom of the article, there's a mugshot, and my heart drops. He looks so different from the photos Caleb kept in his room, blurred and smiling in the distance. Here, the camera is zoomed in on his face, so close you can see the lines of rebellion or contempt.

I push the chair back. My breath catches. I've seen his face before. I've seen this man. "I know him," I say. "Max, I've seen this man before."

And so has Caleb.

The Photo

I look closer, to be sure, but the face remains the same, lining up in my memory. I have seen this man before, with the eyes a little softer, some added weight with time, and the hair slicked back, as he brushed it out of his face, water dripping from the ends.

That day at the waterfall. The man in the river, who was swimming nearby. He waded through the water, offered to take our picture.

I flip through those photos now, until I find the right one. Caleb's face is frozen in the image, as if he's staring right through it, to something beyond, and he is. He was.

He's looking right back at the camera with a haunted expression, looking right through the lens.

I think of the letter again, the one I found in his room. Begging him to show up. Three lines, to break my heart.

And eventually, when his father got out of prison, he did. But he didn't want to go alone. He brought me, as a buffer, the first time he saw him. They didn't interact at all that day. But it must've been the start.

Now I'm thinking of all the times he blew me off, when he wasn't where I thought he would be. All the excuses he gave. *Going to Jessa's. Have to help set up for her brother's party.* If that date on his to-do list was for the second time they were meeting, and that was why he told me he couldn't come at first.

Just as I think he's left me behind, I'm realizing that all along, he's been leading me closer, leaving a trail of clues. But now I'm worried what he's brought me into.

Max stares at the side of my face. I stare at the computer screen. All these pieces, tying us together.

"I need to talk to Terrance Bilson," I say. "A man came to see him, when Caleb was visiting him at college. I need to know if it was him."

Max isn't moving. He's sitting at my computer, staring at the screen, at this part of Caleb we both never knew.

"Max," I say, and he jerks back.

"I don't know his number," Max says.

"Okay. It's okay. I know who will."

I print out the mugshot image and throw everything in my purse, and already I'm making a plan. I hold tight to the items in my purse, these things he left behind. Fragments of lost memories. Now clues left behind, for me to follow. To find him.

I decide to ask Julian for Terrance's number. I text him the question, assuming he's in class. My phone rings a minute later. He's rightly suspicious. "Why do you need Terrance's number, Jessa?"

"Do you have it or not?" I ask.

He sighs, a drawn-out pause, in which I imagine the internal argument he has with himself. Then he starts rattling off a number—so maybe the pause was just him looking up his contact info.

"Thank you," I say.

"Jessa? Is everything okay?"

Julian is one state away. One train ride. One car ride. It is both close and infinitely far away. "Yes," I say.

"I can come home this weekend," he says. He doesn't even know what he's offering, but part of me knew he would do it, that I could count on him.

"Julian," I say. "You can't help with this." Julian is all rational, contained energy. He wants to believe the best of people. He believes that people want to tell him the truth. That he can fix things. But this is an emotional, gut response. You have to be willing to be wrong, and I don't know if Julian has ever risked his own image in his life. If he's willing to be the one out on the limb, who falls, who makes a scene. To lean forward and let someone else decide whether to drop you or not. To jump when you can't see under the surface, when you don't know what might be hidden underneath.

THURSDAY NIGHT

▶ ◀ ▲

Terrance agrees to see me. Not that I gave him much choice. I asked him what time would be good for me to stop by, and I must've caught him off guard with the question, because he says he'll be around all evening.

Max drives again, and I direct him. We don't speak. There's something too fragile hanging in the balance.

By the time we arrive on campus, it's dark. My mom calls, asking where I am. My car is home, and I am not. Also, I'm supposed to be sick.

"I was feeling better. Hailey picked me up. We're at the library," I tell her, and she pauses, like she can feel the lie.

"Jessa, please come home."

I wonder if Julian called her to say he was worried. Always thinking it's the right thing to do, that he knows what's best for me.

"I will," I say. "Soon. Mom. I'm just in the middle of something." I hang up, and I turn the phone to silent.

Terrance's dorm room is on the third floor of an old building with no elevators. The walls are made of something that looks like cinder blocks, painted over. When he opens the door, he looks too big for the room, which has two twin-sized beds crammed beside two desks, and another above-average-sized guy behind him. The other guy is eating Chinese food from a carton at his desk, and the scent is overwhelming.

I try to picture Caleb here, slide him into context, but I can't find a place for him.

Max and Terrance do this weird guy-handshake-greeting thing, which seems to be universal, and yet. Terrance gives Max a look that seems to say, *What are you doing here?*

And Max's look says, *I don't know what I'm doing here.*

And Terrance gives him this warning look like, *Did you think this through?*

Max, beside me, has not thought this through. Neither of us has. But we're on the same page, willing to live in the moment, seeing where it takes us.

Terrance leads us to the student lounge, where people are grouped in couches or chairs, and there's a half-eaten pizza on one of the tables.

I fish for the stack of photos in my bag. I have two shots to show him, different versions of the same man. The photo from when Caleb was a kid, standing beside his father, washing the car. The thinner man with thicker hair, smiling. And then the mugshot, printed off my computer. Hairline receding, slicked back. A little heavier. His face morose, his eyes flat. The corners turned down, just like Caleb's. A close-up where you can see the lines etching around his mouth and eyes. Neither are recent, but I'm hoping Terrance sees something inside them. "Is this the man who stopped by when Caleb was here?"

But Terrance shakes his head automatically. "Sorry you came all this way, Jessa, but the guy who showed up here was much younger. Like my age."

"Oh," I say. I had been picturing someone Sean's age, a man who had some sort of authority over Caleb.

Terrance's fingertips push the pictures around, sifting through the arc of Caleb—little boy, teenager, his life out of sequence.

"Okay, we should go," Max says, but Terrance is still staring at the photos. His fingers haven't moved from the shot of the group of us at the ball game. Sitting in the bleachers, arms around each other, Hailey laughing, Craig Keegan talking to the guy Stan beside him, the field in the background.

Terrance brings the picture closer to his face, and I'm holding my breath. He puts it back down and taps the edge. "Him," he says.

I stare at Terrance, confused.

And then he says it again. "Yeah, this is the dude."

"Stan?" Stan, the guy who got us the tickets for the ball game when we all skipped school. Max had gotten those tickets from him. He'd met us at Penn Station. Craig Keegan had spent half the game asking Stan about the other types of things he could get him.

"How do you know him?" I ask Max. "How does Caleb know him?"

He shakes his head. "From baseball. Little League. When we were kids. He's a year ahead of your brother. Goes to college in the city. I went to him for last-minute tickets, had to meet up with him to get them. We're not really friends."

"But you have his number. Was he friends with Caleb?"

"No. They met that day. Craig Keegan was pressing him about getting a fake ID. They all got his number." I'd missed that part of the conversation, but it made sense now why he blew off Hailey for that conversation. As if they all had plans each weekend to go to bars and pass as twenty-one. The idea was ridiculous.

"Fake IDs," I repeat, and Max's eyes widen. The hairs on the back of my neck stand on end. Everything in the lead-up to Caleb going over the bridge suddenly shifts, becomes a little less certain.

"Call him," I say, but Max already has his phone out.

In the silence, Terrance leans forward. "What's going on?" he asks.

"We don't know," I say. "You said this guy left something for him?"

"Yeah, a package. Like a thick envelope. But I wouldn't take it. Guess they made plans to meet up somewhere else."

"Max," I say as he's leaving a message, "when did he take that money from you again?"

Because suddenly all the fragments are realigning, shifting into place, and they reveal a plan: Caleb taking money, calling Stan, using it for a fake ID, which was delivered to Terrance's dorm room while he was driving up to see Ashlyn Patterson, asking to see the paperwork for his trust.

And earlier: a man sending Caleb a bus ticket, to visit him in jail, unused. A man leaving him a letter after his release, asking to see him. A hike, where we sat on opposite sides of the river. The briefest contact. The preliminary event.

The phone rings, cutting through the silence.

"Stan, this is Max," he says. "I need to talk to you about Caleb. About something you gave him."

I can hear Stan on the other side, something about, yeah, being down at the college for some football game, delivering something for Caleb. But not willing to say anything about any fake ID, one way or the other. "Not on the phone," he mumbles.

"Caleb's dead," Max says, and the silence that follows is excruciating. "We're trying to figure out what happened to him."

Then Stan starts talking, and Max turns up the volume on his phone as I lean my ear closer, to hear. "The police better not end up coming to me with this, Max. If that ID has anything to do with it, I could be charged with something."

I want to punch Stan through the phone. "Tell him we'll find the ID," I say.

"We'll get it," Max says.

"Well, listen, it won't be one from New Jersey or anything. You always want to get an out-of-state one, so it's not looked at as closely."

"What state?" I say, my voice scratching. "What's the name on the ID? What's the state?"

Max goes to repeat the question, but Stan must've heard. "The name is whatever we can get, I don't remember. The state I do remember, because he requested it. Most people don't care. I mean, it's just to purchase liquor." I'm holding my breath. The room is silent as we wait. "He asked for Pennsylvania."

We sit in the parking lot, with the car running, staring straight ahead, into the night sky. We don't move. We don't drive.

I think he's alive.

I think he lied.

I think he was planning this.

I don't know why.

Max smacks his hand once against the steering wheel, lets a string of expletives fly. "Who does that?" he says. And then louder. "Who does that to people?" Except by *people* he means him. I don't know what the last few months have been like for Max, but I imagine a cloud of grief and guilt, like my own. I reach out and take his hand, slide my cold fingers between his own. We sit there, with his head hanging low, until the phone buzzes in my pocket with another text from my mother.

"I need to get home," I say.

Max stares out the window, presumably trying to fit his own memories together in a way that makes sense.

My mind keeps circling, doing the same. Sean hit him. I don't know what happened after that. I don't know for sure that Sean is dead, and not gone.

But his mother kept the pocket watch. His mother has kept all of Caleb's things. And she's been watching me. Telling Mia not to talk to me. But keeping me close all the same.

▲ ▲ ▲

My mother isn't having it, the excuses.

She catches me coming in. "That's not Hailey," she says.

"No, it's Max," I say.

She tilts her head.

"As in, played-baseball-with-Julian Max."

"As in, Caleb's best friend?"

"Yes, they're one and the same, Mom. Which you know."

She rubs her temple, closes her eyes. "It's not the person, Jessa. It's the lies. We've given you time, and space, and I can only imagine what it's like. . . ." She trails off. Then regroups, says what she's been meaning to say. "But I won't stand for the lying. I won't stand for the sneaking around."

"Mom, please," I say, because I can't even focus. My whole body is thrumming.

"I've let you do whatever you've needed—a week home from school; quitting the team; ignoring us all—" She shakes her head before continuing. "But I can't say nothing when you stay home from school and then disappear. I'm worried. And I'm angry. I know I'm not supposed to say that, with everything you're going through. But there it is. You were gone, and Caleb's mother came by today and—"

I stand straight. Shocked silent. "Caleb's mom was here? Eve was here?"

"Yes, Jessa. She was looking for you."

"The room is finished," I say. "What did she want?"

"Well, I wasn't about to twenty-question the poor woman. I told her you were at the library with Hailey, but that's obviously not where you were, now, was it?" She eyes me, like she isn't sure what to do with me. I can't remember

Julian ever being grounded. But I can't remember Julian ever being caught in a lie, either. Maybe he was just better at it than I am. "She asked if she could wait for you, but I had to pick up dinner."

Eve, asking to come into this house. What does she want with me? She has my number. She could've just called. . . .

"Mom," I say, dropping my voice, "something happened. Something's wrong, about what they say happened to Caleb."

She shuts her eyes, takes a deep breath. "Don't do this, sweetheart."

"Something's wrong in that house. Something's wrong with that woman." I'm shaking my head, the confession making it all become real, out in the air. But she puts a hand on my shoulder.

"Jessa, please." She tries to pull me toward her, in an embrace, as if to calm the illogical from me.

I feel like I'm so close, that I just need a little more time. And a little more space, from this, and from Eve. I don't feel safe in my own house, not after Eve has been here. I can't be here, not with that pocket watch, with his mother dropping by. I can't go to the police, not without dragging Caleb back to whatever he was running from.

But a plan forms, even as the anger rises.

"I want to go visit Julian," I say.

Her breath releases. Yes, this is something she can manage, that she can count on.

"Of course," she says. "It would be good to get away. I'll call him now, to make sure he's free this weekend."

"I do know how to call my brother," I say.

"Right, I just, I want to talk to him anyway." She's backing away already, and I set my jaw. My teeth press together until the pain radiates to my jawbone. Of course she wants to talk to him first. Discuss the point that I am unwell, make sure he looks after me. Responsible, predictable Julian. His sister stuck in a stage of grief: denial.

FRIDAY MORNING

▶ ◀ ▲

I'm leaving straight from school. I just have to get through the day. I'm safe here, surrounded by people. Though everything sets me on edge. A door slamming down the hall. A person walking too closely behind me. The sound of the bell, signaling the end of class. I'm grateful for lunchtime, the halfway point, knowing that I only have to get through three more classes and then I'm off. Hailey sits beside me, grabs a fry from my plate since it's obvious I'm not eating mine.

Hailey taps my tray, to get my attention. "So? Are you finished? Packing that room?"

"Yes, I'm done," I say. I remember that Hailey's address was written on Eve's papers, and I want to cut the conversation short, keep her safe and at a distance.

And then Brandon from the cross-country team leans over and says, "Are they having a garage sale or something?"

I'm not sure whether they're having a garage sale, or selling things online or through a secondhand store. But his interest, the way he's practically salivating, is off-putting.

"I assume she's selling some stuff. I don't know how, though."

"Do you think you could put something on hold for me?" he asks. People are jerks, I decide. Or their memories are short-lived.

"No," I say, the venom rising in my voice. Apparently his good looks have kept him relatively protected from any requirement of manners. He bats his eyelashes once, pouts.

He pouts.

Ugh. I don't understand his appeal at all.

Then he puts his hands up toward me, palms out, as if I am an animal about to pounce, and maybe I am. I certainly feel like I am. "Okay, okay," he says. "I'd pay good money for the camping gear, is all I'm saying."

I go through the contents of his room in my mind once more. "His boots?" I ask. I knew they were expensive, but I doubted Brandon couldn't have just bought himself a pair if he wanted.

"No, the sleeping bag. It's pretty sick, all-weather. They cost a fortune, though, and my parents think it's unnecessary."

I think again, shake my head. I run through the list of things found in his closet. Under his bed. "There's no bag," I say.

"Check the closet," he says with a shrug. "It's the type you'd want to keep hanging up. All-down filling, you know? Like I said, pretty sick."

Something hanging. Something large.

The sound of the hanger swinging in the attic makes me sit straighter.

"How do you know he has this?" I ask.

He takes a bite of his food, talks around it. God, how does anyone find him attractive, honestly? "Ran into him at the outdoors store," he says. "My dad and I were getting some fishing poles. He was in the camping section checkout line. Had that sleeping bag, one of those waterproof duffel bags, too. Shame if he never got to use them."

The spot on the attic floor, empty of dust.

I grab his wrist, and he looks startled. "When?" I say.

Brandon shakes free of my grip, makes his eyes go wide and looks around the table to see if anyone else is watching. There's no need. *Everyone* else is watching. Jessa Whitworth is losing her mind. But I don't care. I prefer this Jessa to the one who disappeared along with Caleb.

He rubs his wrist, making a big show of it. "I don't know. End of the summer sometime? Geez, Jessa. Sorry. It was just an idea."

I push back from the table in a rush, off to find Max. But he's nowhere to be found. He has class this period. Lab, I think. But I'm not sure of his schedule, and as I race through the halls, peering in the class windows, I don't see him anywhere.

I send him a text: *I know what was in the attic.*

I get no response.

Instead, I race for my car, alone. Bailing on my afternoon classes. I picture Caleb again that day at my race. Standing there, watching us. The rain coming down, faster, heavier. *Now*, he thinks.

How long had Caleb waited, before seizing the perfect opportunity? What was he waiting for?

The flood, yes. But if he wanted to run, he could've just run.

All these memories, slowly taking shape.

And I remember that there's one more place I might find answers left behind.

I drive straight to the library. He was the only kid I knew who spent time working there. Between the library at school and the Internet at home, I didn't see the need. I liked bringing my research back home to work on. My house was quiet. My room was my own.

But he loved working here. He knew it so well. He took me here, even, on Valentine's Day. Told Sean he'd rather study here than at home. Hid snacks in the drawer that no one else checked, left homework there and trusted it would still remain when he went back for it.

The room smells of books, of carpet, and the air hums from the heating vents. There are people scattered in a few of the cushioned chairs throughout the space, some roaming the aisles; I hear typing coming from behind a cubicle.

I walk with purpose, like I belong here, cutting through the aisles, to the desk where Caleb always sat.

The chair squeaks gently as I sit, rocking back. The wheels catch on the plastic underneath. I place my feet in a slight indentation, and imagine Caleb in this spot instead.

The computer boots up to the main page, with the library

catalog. I pull up the Internet instead, looking through the search history. Here, there's a little more information. Not like his computer at home, which has been wiped clean. Except there's too much. Other people have used this computer, and even going back to the summer dates, it's impossible to tell what's from Caleb and what's from someone else.

I hear a printer start up at the circulation desk across the room, and a woman crosses the space to retrieve her papers, handing the man behind the desk a few coins in return. I make my way over to the desk, hoping he can help. "Hi," I say.

The man looks up, smiles with his lips still pressed together, and waits.

"I was working on a project," I begin. I give him a sad story. Except it's not a story. It's true. The details are the only thing changed. "With a boy from my school. And he died." My voice wavers, on its own. These things I've never said aloud, instead shutting myself off from the rest of the world. Disappearing into myself.

The smile withers, the man leans back. "I heard about it," he says. "I'm so sorry."

I swallow the lump in my throat, feeling like a traitor to Caleb. To everyone. And I press on. "I know he used to work here. I was wondering if you had any information for me about what he might've been working on?"

He leans forward again. Shakes his head. "I'm sorry. Yes, I do recall him working on something. He asked for my help once, about accessing public court records, and I pointed him toward a website. But that's all. We don't keep records of the material printed off. I'm sorry."

"Can you tell me the website?" I ask.

"Sure." He pulls off a yellow sheet of paper from his pad, writes down a web address, and I hold it tight in my hand as I walk back to the computer.

Typing in the address, I see it's a link for a government site, where it looks like you can make an account and access court transcripts.

Caleb, what were you looking for?

I wish the username information were automatically filled in from when Caleb was here, but it's blank.

I feel Caleb again, like I'm getting closer, and then he's slipping away.

This was where he worked when he didn't want anyone to know what he was doing, then. This was where he felt safe.

Opening the cabinet door, I hear him in my memory, unwrapping the candy—I can almost taste the butterscotch flavor, from when we were here on Valentine's Day. I slide open the smaller drawer inside, expecting to find an assortment of Caleb's uneaten candy, but there's nothing here but a paper clip, and a pencil that rolls forward with the momentum of the drawer.

I reach my hand farther, leaning down to peer inside, and instead of candy I see a stack of papers, folded in half, pushed up against the back of the drawer. They blend in with the white base. There's another pencil wedged against the papers, and some sort of energy bar that I've seen before in

Caleb's room, in the bunker. My heart's in my throat when I pull out the papers, hoping they aren't blank. Hoping he took some notes.

But they're more. Oh, they're more.

I see, on the top, the court heading. I see the details. This is the judgment from his father's trial. A summary of events, and the sentencing.

My hands shake as I skim the printout. It's not all of it. It's a random few pages, not in order. The second page, I see, contains a reference to his mother. The shock of seeing her name, of realizing his mother had testified, and for the prosecution. Her account is brief, stilted, and I can hear her quoted words as if she were whispering them into my ear. And as I do, the scene comes alive:

We had been fighting. He said I needed to get a job, that we couldn't cover the mortgage. We had a big fight, and I told him I was taking our son to my mother's. But I changed my mind, came back, and he wasn't home. I woke up to the smell of smoke. It was everywhere. I grabbed my son across the hall. The smoke was already so thick I couldn't see, but he was screaming, and I found him. He had burned his hand, between his thumb and index finger, on the door handle. I covered us with a blanket. And then we ran.

That raised scar between his thumb and pointer finger, that I've rubbed my fingers across, listened as he spun me some tale about a knife, a child wanting an apple. An imaginary story, a sweet scene—being kind to his memories. When really, his father put his life at risk. He had long believed it. His mother testified against him. He was sentenced to arson, insurance fraud, endangering the welfare of a child.

The page cuts off at the next witness. An arson investigator. It picks up in the middle of another account, from another witness.

A witness who saw a man running from the house, late at night. A man who fits the description of his father. He points him out in court.

I go back to the first page, search for the name of the witness, and it stops me cold.

Sean Larson.

I picture Caleb in this seat, reading these pages—what does he see? He had been to that house, to look for something. The scene of the crime. Something, maybe, his father had tried to tell him. Something he was now discovering for himself. A reminder, every time he glanced down at the patch of raised, discolored skin on his hand.

Him, ticking them off, lifting his shirt, "Appendectomy," tilting his neck, "dog scratch," raising his pant leg, "dislocated knee from skiing, needed surgery."

And me, doing the same, running my finger over my forehead, "Chicken pox, caught them from Julian," the white line on my chin, fading over time, "sledding accident, a dare, a tree." I was ten, and everyone had left, and it had just been me. I'd been scared to do it, and so I didn't. But I went back, on my own, because it ate at me, that moment, why I couldn't just let go. I

didn't tell Caleb this. The shorter version was better. The one I
saw him imagining to himself.

Then, pointing out the one on his hand, I said, "What about
this one?" And I watched as his face shuttered for a moment.

"I forgot about that," he said. "It was so long ago." A pause,
and then, "A knife. I wanted an apple." And I had smiled.

So many more, from the both of us, and we shadowed them
away. Hid them under the obvious and trusted that no one
would look any deeper.

Finally, I see him. I know what he was looking for, and
what he found.

Caleb had discovered that both his mother and Sean testified against his father. Back when Sean was a stranger. Was
supposed to be a stranger.

And now, so have I.

FRIDAY AFTERNOON

▶   ◀   ▲

I pass Caleb's house, and it looks like no one is home. I keep driving, and I park at Max's house, thinking maybe he's home—but he's not. He still hasn't responded. I send him another message: *Back at their house.*

And then I run. Through the backyards, to the back door, until I'm standing beside the empty spot where the garbage and recycling are usually kept—right now they're at the front of the house, awaiting pickup.

I stand back, staring at the concrete pad. There's nothing unusual about it, except that it's been painted. An eggshell white. Was it always like this? I can't remember. I've never paid it any attention.

I hear Mia's words again, the day I showed up unannounced: *I thought you were going to paint.* We'd painted his bedroom door. But now I'm wondering if *this* is what she was talking about.

There's nothing definitive here for me, only what I want to see. I barely cast a glance over my shoulder before letting myself inside with Caleb's key that I've found in the attic.

I take the steps two at a time, until I see what's left of

Caleb's room: a bed. The single bed. Empty shelves. An emptied backpack. A flashlight, on the bare desktop.

The undoing of Caleb Evers.

The carpet looks threadbare, has indentations from the pieces of furniture that have been moved, the pieces that felt so permanent. Just shadows left behind.

Vacuum tracks cover the floor. There's a faint whiff of paint, and then I see the two cans just inside the door. The color is an eggshell white. The window is open. There's a plastic tarp, underneath the paint can, fluttering in the wind, everything prepared. But she hasn't yet begun.

But there are still the marks from where the bed used to be, that I remember from last weekend, after Max had been through the room. And now I'm thinking it was moved for a reason, even earlier. A plan. An order to the chaos.

Everything had a spot, even if it wasn't obvious to anyone but himself.

This bed has been moved by Caleb.

I walk to the side of the bed, and I get onto my knees, planting my hands against the metal frame. And I push. It barely moves, with the box spring and mattress on top. I move to the other side, grip my hands to the underside, and pull with all my might, and it slides a few inches. I do it once, twice more, until the bed feet settle into their previous location.

The floor underneath looks the same, on both sides. I walk around, to the side next to the window, and my stomach falls, everything lurches. The wall that I've just exposed behind the bed, the foot of old gray paint just exposed. There's a deep gouge in the wall, like the indentations on the other side of the room, where he'd thrown the letter opener long ago. But here, it's cut down through the gray to the plaster. The swipe was strong, the line in the wall angry, starting and jumping, with force and intent behind it.

And it's inches from the window.

The fight. The fight with Sean. He wasn't lying.

If Sean hit him, what had Caleb done back? Had he grabbed the closest thing he could find? The letter opener on his desk? Had he swung it around, in a practiced maneuver?

I can picture it happening—Sean grabbing his wrist, the force wrenching the blade through the wall. Missing. Struggling. The chain of the pocket watch breaking. And then.

And then. I look to the open window. The screen is missing. Sean is missing.

I can't breathe.

Caleb, no.

The door swings open downstairs, and I want to tell her. I want to show her. *Look what happened. Look.*

Except.

She knows. My blood runs cold. She must. Sean is gone; his clothes were here. The pocket watch in the garage. She knows—she's always known.

The room hollows out: *Why am I here in this room? Why did she ask me to come?*

As I hear her heading up the steps, presumably to continue painting this room, I slink into the closet, pull the bookcase aside, and disappear into the hidden attic space, pulling the bookcase back into place behind me.

I listen to her footsteps. She walks into the room. She must see the wall I've exposed. She must know someone has been here. She opens the closet door. Peers inside. Steps back. I hear fabric moving, assume she must be checking under the bed.

It's like she can feel the presence of another.

"Caleb?" she calls.

And the name, the very word, makes him come alive. Makes everything something other than what I assumed. Her steps circle the room slowly. And then, closer now, she calls, "Jessa?"

I reach my hands up, to the spot I cannot see, where the Swiss Army knife once was. There's nothing but empty space. I know Max and I were passing it back and forth, but then Caleb's mother arrived, and . . . I can't remember what we did with it. I take out my phone to use as a flashlight, and there, between two wooden beams, the glint of light reflecting off metal.

I reach down and my grip tightens on the Swiss Army knife. It's all I have. That, and my phone. I turn the volume down, and input the numbers 9-1-1 into the keypad. My finger hovers over the button, ready to hit Send.

Because I suddenly understand exactly why I'm here. Why she was keeping me so close. Following me.

She has sent me here to find her son. She believes he's

alive. It's why she's been following me, thinking I knew something more. And when it was clear I didn't, she brought me here instead, hoping I'd find something and figure out where he was, where he went.

And I believe I have.

Backpack with Broken Zipper, Part 2

A phone rings, and I jump—it's not mine.

I hear her answer, her voice just beyond the wall. "Yes, you're here? Great. Be right down." And then the footsteps back away. They fade down the stairs. Then there's the sound of a door swinging open somewhere below. I hold my breath until I hear the door close again. I cancel the call screen on my phone. Then I leave my hiding spot in the attic, the Swiss Army knife still in my clenched fist, my phone in the other. I peer out the window, carefully. There's a van out back, at the edge of the long driveway. I assume she's rented it. She's carrying her things to the back. It's now or never, I decide. She's busy. She won't be paying attention.

Caleb's backpack is in the middle of the room, and I picture him swinging it onto his shoulder, looking over at me briefly: "Coming, Jessa?" Raising an eyebrow as he takes off, launching himself down these steps—me always running a step or two behind.

I grab the few things left in this room, shove them all into his green backpack, along with my things. I barely focus on anything else as I half tumble down the steps, out the front door, racing, racing, around the block, to Max's house.

I send my brother a text, letting him know I have after-school plans and won't be arriving until later. I don't want him worrying, and calling our parents.

I have Caleb's backpack, the flashlight, my phone that's slid into the side pocket. These shoes aren't the best, but they will have to do.

Because she knows what I know. She's been following the same path. And I've led her most of the way there.

I'll have to go the rest of the way alone. To beat her there.

It's the things that are missing that tip me off: the camping gear, the money. Eve doesn't know about those things. She doesn't know the pieces I've put together, from my memories. I know where he went. He took me there, once before.

The day is like yesterday, a hazy gray, a fine drizzle, the sky always on the verge of just breaking open. My wipers cut through the mist as I drive, and the rain seems to come down heavier the faster I go. I imagine, for a moment, that I'm Caleb. Coming upon the bridge. Deciding. Seizing the moment.

Max still isn't picking up his phone. If he's in a science lab, he probably won't be able to check it until the end of the double period. His voice finally answers: *Leave a message*, and I'm shouting into his voicemail, which I have on speakerphone in the cup holder. "Max. I know where he is. Don't tell his mother. It's the Delaware Water Gap. I'm heading there now."

The drive takes almost two hours, but alone, it feels longer. It feels like I'll never make it, that he'll always be somewhere just out of reach. I'm constantly checking the rearview mirrors, but that's crazy, and impossible. She didn't see me go. She missed her chance. I'm free of her now. Free to find him on my own.

Max calls back when I'm almost there. It's started to rain, and it's hard to hear him over the wipers. "Jessa?" His voice is frantic. I've pulled into the lot I remembered from the day months ago, and I sit there in the empty parking spot, the rain faintly hitting the windshield.

"I'm here. I made it."

"You're where?"

"A parking lot where we once took this trail. I remembered, he met his dad here. Only I didn't know it was his dad. And Brandon said Caleb had a bunch of camping gear, but I never saw it. It's nowhere. It must've been in the attic, and now it's gone."

"Wait for me, Jessa. Okay? Tell me where you are."

"I don't know exactly. It's this trail we once took. So, take the parkway to 80, and then follow signs. It's in the town of—"

"Just send me your location."

"What?"

"On your phone. Go to my contact, and hit *share location*, and I'll be there."

"Okay," I say. I hang up. I open his contact page. I see the arrow, and I hit it. *There*. He has me, I think.

And then I freeze. My finger shakes. I slowly scroll through the names, until I see the entry marked *Eve*. She took my phone, that day, when Hailey texted. She checked my text, and she entered her own information. I thought she was just being nosy, seeing who I was talking to, making sure that I wasn't lying, but a slight moan escapes my lips.

How she always shows up just after I get there, or seems to know when I'm about to arrive. How she seems to know when I'm not where I say I am. How someone showed up at that old house, just as Max and I did. Did she think Caleb would be there? Hiding out inside?

I press her name, and that same arrow comes into view, enabled. I click it, frantically, to turn it off. But it's too late. She set this up. She doesn't need to follow with a pen and paper anymore, because she could follow me remotely. She knows exactly where I am. Where I've stopped.

I've led her straight to him.

I'm bouncing on my toes, pacing back and forth in front of the trailhead. It's still daylight, but the rain is starting to come down heavier. Max is coming. But so is Eve. And if she makes it here, if she finds Caleb first . . . I don't know what happens next.

Still, right now, I have a head start. I can't wait for Max. I don't have time. I don't know if she's on her way or not. And so I run.

There's something about having Caleb's bag on my back that gives me comfort. His flashlight in the main pocket. The papers I've found, my wallet, my things.

But then I remember the hike. How everything hurt. And it does. Oh, it hurts. The trail is wetter, and I lose my footing, cutting my knee once. It seems to take twice as long, alone, in the rain, with the sun slowly setting.

When I finally come up on the view I last saw with Caleb, the wind blows and lightning strikes somewhere in the distance, and I feel too close to the sky. Too exposed.

And then I think I've made the wrong decision. That I am out here alone, and it's cold and raining, and there could be anything hidden in the trees, in the dark.

But still, I keep moving. As if I can feel something just at my back. Stepping in our steps, from long ago. Feeling our strides in sync, hearing his breathing, just under my own.

I know when I'm getting close, and I will my legs to move faster. The sound of water in the darkness feels like a tidal wave, like a flood. It's dark before I make it, and I have to stop to pull out the flashlight, shining it on the path in front of me.

I'm shaking, from adrenaline and the rain and the fact that I'm on this trail, alone, in the dark. I could turn back, I think. But I also think of Eve heading this way, and I'm not sure which I'm more afraid of. I have to move forward.

There's water in my shoes now, and it only gets worse as I plant my feet in puddles forming on the trail, over and over. And then, finally, I'm there. I hear the waterfall, shine the light in an arc in front of me, and the light reflects off the rain hitting the surface of the water.

This is it. This is the spot. There's the rock where Caleb and I sat. There's the waterfall, where the people once swam. But now, there's no one here. There's no campsite, no tent, no Caleb. It's eerily empty. A chill rises up my spine as I'm standing in the middle of the woods, so far from civilization, all alone.

I remember that he told Stan he needed an ID for Pennsylvania, and I know I'm not quite there. We're separated by a state border, deep water, a place we once called Nowhere.

Flashlight, Part 2

The beam of the flashlight shakes in my hand. I can hear his whisper almost as clearly as I could that day back in March, when we were sneaking across his backyard, and he placed this in my hand. *Quiet, Jessa.*

I scan the light behind me, around me. Across the way, trying to see through the trees. It looks so different here than the last time. It feels more dangerous, sounds more ominous.

The rain has been coming down steady and hard, and I can hear the river. The waterfall rages underneath the sound of the thunder, the rain. I know the river must swell, that it will be deeper than the day Caleb and I were here together.

I shine the flashlight across the expanse. I look for footsteps, for evidence of a campsite across the way.

I call his name, but it's swallowed up. I don't see a campsite—I can't see anything that far in the dark.

I know there's something on the other side. Caleb had plans to be in Pennsylvania, if his ID was anything to go on. That day of our hike, I remember the river being shallow, passable, that one could be nowhere for a moment, and then across the border.

But now it's dark, and loud, and this is it. And for a moment, I wonder if I'm only seeing what I want to see, once more. If the truth is that Caleb did something to Sean, and was running away, and went over the bridge the day the river rose. That he was swept away, as everyone believed, along with the pieces of his car, to the ocean.

I am scared that there is actually nothing at all on the other side. Nothing but terrible hope, cut down. That this is as close as I'll ever get, still infinitely far away.

I swing the flashlight around again, taking everything in.

I watch the path, expecting to see Eve coming down at any moment. Or maybe she's already here. Maybe she's waiting. There's nothing here but the rain, the darkness. A person could disappear here. No evidence. An accident. A slip, a drowning. A body never found.

There's one way in, and there's one way out, and there's a raging river in front of me, impassable now.

I can't stay still, so I begin to pace. But I can do nothing more, other than call his name, over and over, into the darkness.

Eventually, I sit on the rock at the corner of the river, where Caleb and I once sat—just out of sight. Nobody responds to my calls. They're swallowed up in the rain and the dark. So I sit, and I breathe, and think, *You have done everything you can.*

But that's not true. The voice whispers everything it knows is true: *You have done everything that is expected of you. But have you done everything?*

The water rushes, angry in the dark, in answer. The answer is I haven't. I have not done all I can.

The pieces I've followed fit together into the puzzle of a boy, leading me here. But more than that, it's the puzzle of a girl. Leading to this moment, this version of herself.

From that girl in the first picture, afraid of the ocean that was six feet in front of her—to this, right now.

I jam the base of my flashlight into the mud, the light shining up, like a beacon, so I can find my way back.

I close my eyes and picture Caleb. Cutting the wheel, the water rising, but his head above the surface, swimming for shore.

And I think that maybe I am not just doing this for him.

I call Max. I try to. The phone keeps breaking in and out, so far from the main road and the trail entrance. Dropping the call before he picks up.

I send him a text instead. *I'm crossing the river. I can't wait. Eve is coming. Call someone. Call for help.*

It shows that the message is sending, but it hasn't gone through. I have to hope that it will.

I'm in New Jersey. I need to be in Pennsylvania. I leave my backpack, including my phone, to keep it all dry. I tuck it all out of sight, under a tree, trying to keep it protected. All I'll have left is myself.

I remember the expression on Caleb's face on Christmas, then Valentine's Day in the library, the moment I saw him in his glasses, sitting at his desk.

I loved him once, the parts I thought I knew. I think he loved me too, the girl he thought he knew. Even if he didn't believe I was a person capable of holding his secrets, and the truth. But I am more than he thought I was.

I wade into the river, and it's freezing. I step back out, take off my outer jacket, lay it over the bag with my phone. The truth is, whether he's there or not, I have to know. Because it's not only his story, but mine.

The water rises up to my knees quickly, then my thighs, and when it hits my waist, I feel the current moving faster than I expected. *Careful, be careful.* I plant my feet gently on each rock, making sure I have my footing before continuing on.

And then, in the middle, when I'm nowhere, the ground suddenly drops away, and I'm weightless, at the mercy of a current, until I remember myself, and swim frantically, arm over arm, for the other side, my feet reaching down, and feeling nothing, until finally—a rock. My toe reaching the bottom, my next step solid, and then I'm on the way out, on the other side, with nothing but darkness and the cold. I remind myself—keep moving. Keep going.

FRIDAY NIGHT

▶ ◀ ▲

I'm standing on the other side of the river. It's completely
dark here, except for the stars. Behind me, I see the faint
light from the flashlight, the rain slanting across the view. I
can't see the path in front of me. I reach out my hands as I
walk, feeling the leaves and twigs marking the path, holding
on to tree branches, until I start to get the feel of the thing.
A path, slowly emerging in the shadows.

"Caleb?" I call. It's tentative, unsure, because I'm standing here soaking wet, and I feel outside myself for a moment.
That if I were to step back and look at the scene, I'm sure
I'd be witnessing the unraveling of a girl in the dark, in the
woods, who has swum through a river in the cold, because
she thinks her ex-boyfriend isn't really dead.

I take another step, away from the sound of the river.
There's a sliver of light through the trees, and as I move,
it disappears. And then there's the noise: like water hitting
something else. I move through the trees, closer and closer,
until I'm upon it. It's a green tent, the front flap moving in
the wind. I throw it open, my hands shaking, and peer inside,
into the darkness.

I wait for someone to speak, for a hand to reach out and

grab me, but there's nothing. I crawl inside, feeling for anything left behind. And then I hear heavy footsteps outside. A light shines on the outside of the fabric. My shadow, illuminated on the far side.

"Caleb?" I call, but no one responds.

I crawl back out of the tent, because someone's here, and I'm running for him, for the shadow, but the light is in my eyes, and I can't see who's there.

Then the shadow's edges take shape: He's older, heavier, harder. It's the man we saw on our hike. It's his father. I hold up my arm to block the light, and my steps slow. A deep voice says, "No one by that name here."

"Please," I say, walking all the way up to him. "I need to talk to Caleb." I'm shaking, because I've done it. I traced him back to this man, from the pieces left behind. I grab onto the front of his jacket—here, solid, the image of a photograph, brought to life.

He steps back, pries my hands off his jacket, looks me over again—this crazed girl dripping wet, who has dragged herself from the river, like a memory.

He shakes his head, sadly.

"I know he's alive," I say.

"Sweetheart, you need to get out of here." He looks over his shoulder, and I know he's there somewhere. I know it.

"Caleb!" I call. "I made a mistake. Your mom followed me."

The man freezes, and that's when I know I've won. His grip tightens on my arm and he drags me farther back into the woods. But I don't understand. The trees close around us, and there's no one here but us.

"You don't know what you've done," he hisses. He has

pulled me out of sight, and I think I should be afraid, but I'm not—I'm too close. I'm driven forward, to see it through.

"I do," I say back. "I know exactly what I've done. That's why I'm here. I'm telling him. To run." I hiccup, and he lets go of my arm.

I step back, and he looks down at what's in my hand. What I have grabbed from my pocket and held out in front of me, the only thing I have left. Caleb's Swiss Army knife.

He frowns. "I'm not going to hurt you. You need to go back," he says. "Now."

"I can't go back." He looks down at me then, as if just finally understanding what I've done to reach them. He turns his back on me, and starts moving, but he doesn't object when I follow him. We're on a trail, leading to a clearing. In the clearing, the sound changes, to rain on a roof.

There's a small circle of metal trailers, not attached to cars. They're rentals, I see. The door to one creaks open, the light behind silhouetting a figure. It moves down the steps, to the darkened shadows of the trees. A hood over it, to protect from the rain.

Standing in the shadows is a shape. The shape becomes human. Becomes real.

He lifts his face, to both of us. "Dad," he says.

And then I'm standing across from a ghost. Except I'm not sure whether the ghost is him or me, because he looks at me like he's never seen me before. Like he has no idea who this person is before him.

"What are you doing here?" he asks.

But all I can think is, *I've done it*. He is here, exactly as I believed, as I hoped.

"I found you." That's the only thing there is. The only thing to say. I found him. When no one else believed it, or no one else could do it, I was the one who fit together the clues he left behind, who traced the beginning and end, to here.

But I don't step any closer.

We are standing across from each other, and I am suddenly afraid. I thought I knew him, but the pieces I've discovered do not line up to the person I thought I knew.

"How?" he asks. He also does not move to come closer. In fact, I'm scared he might turn and run at any moment. That I'm not understanding something, that this Caleb was never meant to be found. That he's already gone, somehow.

"Your mom had me cleaning out your room. I figured it out. I know what happened in that room."

He cuts his eyes to his father.

"We have to go," his father says.

But Caleb doesn't move. "We can't yet. You know that."

"I'm getting the tent, Caleb, and then we're going." And then his father disappears back into the night, and Caleb turns back to the trailer. I pocket the knife, trailing after him—always a few steps behind.

"Caleb," I say, "whatever happened to Sean, it doesn't have to be like this."

Inside now, he turns to me, and I see the shadow of the boy I knew in his expression. "You know me," he says. "You know I didn't do that."

I also thought he was dead. He let me believe that. He made me believe that.

"I thought I knew you. I don't. You ran. You let us all think . . ."

He shakes his head, everything pouring back. "Sean was hurting me. He was choking me. I'd confronted him about these papers I found—"

"In the library," I say. "I have them."

"You have them," he repeats. "I accused him of framing my father. Of putting him in jail for something he didn't do. My dad swore he didn't do it, that he was nowhere near that house that day. He thought it had to be my mother, but nobody believed him, because there was a witness. Only when I looked up the witness, you know what I found?"

"Yes," I said. "I know."

"They must've been having an affair. It must've been their plan together. She convinced Sean to lie. They both set my father up to take the fall."

"Oh," I say. I know some of this, because I've followed his footsteps. But I didn't know he suspected his mother had been the one to put his life in danger. I'm starting to understand why he left, why he couldn't stay.

"He was angry. He was so angry, Jessa. I thought he would kill me. My mom came upstairs, and she pushed him off. And I used that letter opener to take a swipe at him, and he stumbled back. I didn't even hit him. He stumbled back. Near the window." He takes a deep breath. I know what comes next. The window screen is gone. The concrete has been painted.

"But he was okay. I swear he was okay. Until he lunged for the letter opener in my hand, and she pushed him."

His mother, then, coming to his aid. As a mother would.

"She was helping me, Jessa. It was because of me. He was

so furious. I'd never seen him so mad. I don't know what he would've done if he thought I was going to tell the police or something."

The day comes back into focus. "I was there," I say.

"All the evidence pointed to me, so she decided. We weren't going to tell. We couldn't do anything for him. She said, we'll say he left. And it was just like that. We said he left."

"You said she kicked him out."

"You had showed up. You saw my face. What could I say? So I made something up, but my mom thinks you know. She thinks I told you."

"Oh." The reason for her keeping such close watch. All along, she thought I knew more than I let on. She didn't know she was leading me right to it, just as I did for her.

"I have to go now, but I want you to know that. I want to know you believe that, Jessa."

And I do, I realize. I wonder: can I take both sides? The parts I do know, and the parts I missed? This is what I know deep in my bones: he didn't do it. I can tell because I've seen the different sides of him—the regret, the love, the fear, and the anger. I do know the sides of Caleb now. I know what a lie looks like, and he's not lying.

"If you told the police it was self-defense, Caleb, your mom would've confirmed it. You didn't have to disappear."

He laughs then, and it's pained. "Oh, no, Jessa, she would not. I wanted to tell. The guilt was too much. I thought we had done the wrong thing, and I couldn't live with it, not in that house, in that room. And you know what she said?

'All·the evidence points to you, Caleb.' She said she kept his pocket watch and wedding band, that they would have my blood. And we used my car to move him. Then we took his car when we left that week and sold it for cheap. I only realized after why she made us use my car, and not his. She said it was because we were selling it, but come on. It was to make sure I never said anything. And if Sean had helped set up my dad back then, then so did my mom, right? Jessa, who had I been living with?"

His voice drops, and he's asking. He's really asking.

"You could've left . . . ," I begin, but Caleb's already shaking his head.

"She would've never given me permission to leave. Not even for college. She's the guardian of my account, and as long as I was there, she could use part of the money to maintain our quality of life. But I have to *be there. Leaving* was not part of the picture for her. You know why she's so determined to find me? It's not because of *me*. It's because the money is no longer hers. It goes to my dad, if I'm dead. It should've been his from the start. My grandparents left the money to me because my dad was in jail. This was the only way."

"It's not," I say. "There are still other options. It's not too late. You have to tell the police."

He shakes his head. "It's my blood on his things. His DNA in my car. He was in my trunk. We were fighting. Mia knows it, everyone knows it. We'd fought before, even you would say that, if asked. I was the one driving Sean's car when we went to sell it. When I told her the evidence could point to her instead, she said there were cameras on the gas stations we passed, the storefronts, every place I drove by, with her following. Evidence that it was me. She had me completely under her thumb. My money was in her hands until I turned twenty-five. Everything went through her."

The cameras that he used, later, to fake his disappearance. This must've been how his mother was so sure he had done it. Destroying the car, a piece of evidence. Using the cameras, to prove it. Leaving.

"You put him in the river?" I ask, my hand on my stomach, the thought unbearable.

"No, not the river," he says. "Not near us. Drove down at night, to the Pine Barrens." He chokes on the horror of what he's done, shakes his head, turns away, as if he can't bear me looking at him, either. Endless miles of untouched forest area, where he might be. "I wouldn't do it. Got sick on the side of the road at the entrance. She left me there. Came back an hour later. So, I don't know exactly. It would be my word against hers."

"How is this life any better? You still lose," I say. We've all lost.

"The trust. On my death, it goes to my dad. We're just waiting for the paperwork to clear. I've been staying in the tent, in case someone comes looking for him. But after that, then we can leave, and we'll be fine. We'll be gone. I'll be someone new."

"You won't be fine. You won't have college. Or family." *Or any of the people you've left behind*, I think.

"She took years from my father. She took years away

from me, too. It's all I want now, to make up that time with my dad, to have the future years with him now."

Of course Caleb had a plan. He always had a plan.

I believe Caleb is telling the truth, that he didn't do it. But I also know I won't trust him again, not in the same way, not ever. I step back.

"You left us all behind. Mia too."

His face falls, and I know I've struck a nerve.

"I've been taking care of all of them for years. My mom can figure it out now."

"Your mother had a plan, too. She was tracking my phone. I didn't know. Until just before. Until it was too late. She's coming, Caleb. She must be."

His father barges through the trailer door, and I jump. He has returned with the tent, and his gear. "Caleb," his father says, "we really need to move."

"You led her here?" he asks. He's angry, but I'm angrier.

"You don't get to blame me for this. Did you know that everyone blames me for your death, Caleb?" He jerks back, and I see he didn't expect that. I know he thought of no one but himself. "She's been using me to find you, because you disappeared. I've been"—*empty, guilty, no one*—"grieving for you, for months." I choke out the last word. Does he not realize the impact his actions have had on everyone?

He's already backing inside the trailer. Throwing the rest of their things in a bag. "She has to find me before the money transfers. Before the bank releases the funds to my father. She needs proof I'm alive, and then she can claim I was kidnapped or something. Either way, I'm alive, and she'll hold on to the funds again."

I am nothing but a pawn. An ex-girlfriend. Just a person in relation to someone else. This cannot all be for nothing. Going through his life, piecing together the story, *finding* him—not just what happened, an absolution, but *him*. All the parts of me he took with him when he left, and I need them to be mine again. For this to *mean* something.

"Where will you go?" I ask.

"It's better if you don't know, Jessa."

"Caleb, I can fix this."

"This isn't your life," he says. "How could you possibly understand? You have the perfect life, with the perfect family. You don't have to worry about anything."

And I think: *He doesn't know me at all.* It makes me immeasurably sad, that he doesn't even notice my own journey—all I've done to make it here. I'm standing right in front of him, and he doesn't even see. How little each of us really knew about each other, underneath the facade.

"Let's move," his dad says. "Now."

Caleb turns to me. "Come on. We'll lead you out to the road this way. You can call for a ride from a restaurant or something."

I look down at myself, wondering if he's really serious. I'm freezing. I'm soaked. He wants to leave me at a restaurant. But I can't go out with them, back to some access road in Pennsylvania. Not right now.

"Max is coming," I say, and Caleb freezes. "I called him. He's coming."

"We'll be gone by then," he says, hauling his backpack onto his back. "We're not waiting."

I shake my head. "My things are on the other side of the

river. If he finds them there, without me . . ." I try to imagine what Max might think. The raging river. The text, that I had tried to cross it. My phone and the backpack left behind. No sign of me.

"He'll be fine, Jessa."

But I jerk back. Is that what he really thought? That we had all been fine when we thought he died? And that we would all be fine without him again?

That's when I realize, I am not who he thought, and he is not who I thought, and we are not alike in the ways that count. There are things I know about Max in my bones, too. That he is coming, and that he wouldn't leave me—and you have to be willing to do the same for each other.

Caleb never seemed to realize the things we had to do for each other, to pull each other up.

"No," I say. "I'm not going with you."

He pauses for a moment, and I think he's going to argue. But he doesn't. There's nothing left to say.

Dragonfly Necklace, Part 2

He has left me once more. I watch his back as he goes, walking down the steps of the trailer.

And then he pauses, turns around. "Did you find the necklace, Jessa?"

"What?"

"Your necklace. You asked me to keep it safe."

And suddenly I can't breathe.

"I left it for you," he says. "On the floor, in my jeans. I hoped you would find it."

"Yes," I say. "I found it."

He left me the necklace. On purpose. Because it was mine, and good luck, and he knew I had trouble doing anything other than the way I'd always done things.

"I tried to make things easier," he says, and he turns, one last time.

The way we broke up, so public that it would leave no doubt. His expression that day on the steps outside his room. Impassive. Stone-faced.

An ugly, cruel breakup that crushed all hope of any reconciliation.

A gift, to soften the blow.

All these things he hoped would remain hidden.

The necklace hangs, twisted on the broken chain, from my dresser necklace holder. It should be at the bottom of the river. It should have been in his pants pocket, when he drove off the road.

The last piece of the puzzle slides into focus, the thing I've been chasing since that very first day. Why go home first?

He came back two days later for the camping gear. Let himself in with a house key. So why did he need to go home first before driving to that bridge, to leave his clothes on the floor, change—change everything?

It was supposed to be the start of his story. *Going to Jessa's race.* Witnesses to see him there, who would notice he left, driving home in the rain. His car on the storefront cameras. An accident. But instead my eyes found his on the starting line, and there he was, a familiar face. *Please hold this for me. Please be careful.*

I had altered his plan, with a necklace in his pocket.

Could it be that simple, then? He went home to leave this behind for me? In a way that wouldn't make anyone suspicious. He didn't hand it to someone else to give back to me, or leave it in my room for me to find. He dropped it on his floor, where it could be found, should I come looking for it. Not in the hamper. On the floor.

I wish that was enough to cancel out all the rest. "Why come to my race that day? Why not something else, another story? Didn't you realize people would think it was because of me? That everything happened because of me?"

He cringes. "I wasn't thinking that, Jessa. I was thinking I just wanted to see you, one last time. That's all."

My stomach aches. My heart aches. He loved me once, too.

"Caleb?" I say. I want to tell him it mattered. It's over, but I cared.

In the silence that follows, when I'm trying to find the words, the rain sounds relentless on the metal roof. "Jessa, I know."

Swiss Army Knife, Part 2

And then I am alone again.

I found him, and lost him again, but things are not the same.

I'm alone in the dark, but I feel the shape of his Swiss Army knife in my pocket, and it gives me comfort. I keep it in my hand as I walk; as I run.

I arrive back at the river. The light still shines, faintly in the distance. I'm almost numbed now, and I remember how I felt that day in the subway, at the ball game. I feel like that again. Like I am alone.

And, like then, I also know that someone is coming. Max will be here soon. And I can't leave him alone, to find a backpack and a flashlight and my phone and a raging river. With no one showing up but Eve, to ask what he's doing there. Eve, who might think he's somehow involved in Caleb's disappearance, if he suddenly shows up here looking for me.

I make it halfway across the river by momentum alone,

my feet grappling below. And I'm just finding my footing on the other side of Nowhere, when I see her.

She's standing beside the light, watching me.

She's in jeans, a raincoat, sneakers. She must've found my car, and followed her gut, if nothing more. And now, she's watching me. I stop moving for a moment, but the water keeps moving past me, and I have to keep going one way or the other, or it will eventually push me over. I keep walking toward her. What are my other options—swim away and run blind through the forest?

"So, you found him," she says, when I am firmly on solid ground. She doesn't hand me my coat. She doesn't come any closer. She has my phone in her hand, but she's locked out. I wonder what she was looking for.

"I didn't," I say, coughing into my fist. I am shaking so hard I can't feel my toes. Everything numbs. *But*, I think, *shaking is good*. I remember this from science—if you're still shivering, you're fine. Maybe not fine. Maybe just okay. Still, I'm okay.

"You're a terrible liar," she says.

The rain has let up to a drizzle, but it coats everything, and I'm soaked through anyway, and the river continues to rage behind me.

Finally, her voice tears through the silence. "Caleb!" she yells.

But only the river answers.

"Is he over there, then?"

I want to tell her she's too late, that he's gone, that she's lost her hold on him, but I also want to give him time. I don't know whether she'll call the police, set up a roadblock. I don't know what she really wants, underneath it all.

"I've done everything for you," she calls, but there's no one to hear. "And you would just leave us?"

"I know what you did," I say, stepping closer, taking my jacket from the ground. "It wasn't for him."

"You don't know what you're talking about," she says.

I think of what I told Caleb earlier, that there was another way, if only he would risk it. "I know that perjury is a crime," I say. "I know that lying under oath, and sending an innocent person to jail, is punishable with jail time."

She stares at me, her eyes wide. She does not know her son discovered this. She doesn't realize the field is even now.

Her eyes drift behind her, to everything circling around us. I know what she sees. Slippery rocks, a raging river, a girl reeking of desperation. "You look so cold," she says. "You shouldn't be in that water, Jessa." Except her words carry the weight of a threat.

But I stare into her eyes, hold her gaze. We are almost exactly the same size. "This time," I say, "it wouldn't be an accident."

And I see the coiled anger come to the surface and then sink back down. I don't believe she's evil. I want to believe she is not a psychopath, or a killer of teenagers. She is, however, protecting something. Her son, yes, but also herself. And if I threaten that, really threaten it, I'm not entirely certain what she'll do.

But neither of us will get the chance to find out. Because

I hear my name. I hear him yelling it. And my heart flips, my body turns to the sound.

But at the last minute, just as I'm opening my mouth to call back—*Max, I'm here*—I feel the world begin to tip. As if I'm leaning too far, because she's got me in a grip, and she's pushing me back, holding me so I'm practically leaning over the river, close to the waterfall. "You let him leave," she says, and the loss is agony, written across her face. And I think that maybe I am wrong, after all. That there is nothing more potent than the power to grasp for something just as you feel it slipping away from your grip. That it's an impulse in all of us, to fight for the thing that we are losing, even if we've already lost.

She lets go.

And I fall.

It only takes me a moment to get my bearings, to think *Just plant your feet down, like you did before.* Except something's wrong. The current keeps forcing me down. This is not just a moving current, but a violent one. The current from the waterfall churns the water around me, and though I poke my head through the surface, I cannot catch my breath.

I picture her on the shoreline, saying, as Max comes into view:

I got here, and she was gone.

I found her things.

Too long in the water.

She's gone.

So I stop fighting so hard against what the current is trying to do. I let go. I let it take me. And after some time, I find my footing downstream, and am able to push my head above water, suck in a breath, just as the current knocks my feet out from under me again. I try once more, standing, and reaching the blade of Caleb's knife to the shore, wedging it into the surrounding roots before I lose my balance. Locking myself in place as I grip onto a low branch with my other hand. I suck in a gulp of air, then turn to see the light in the corner of my eye.

It's not only Max on the shore, now, beside Eve. He's led some people my way. A few rangers, with radios, one lowering himself into the water already upstream, while Eve looks on.

I call Max's name. Everyone freezes. And when the world starts up again, he's running.

The first thing I feel, when I'm capable of feeling again, is the warmth of another, sitting beside me in the back of an ambulance. The first words I process, from the person sitting beside me, with his arms around me, trying to transfer more heat: "Somehow," he says, "I knew you wouldn't wait."

They're telling Max he has to leave the ambulance, but he isn't having it, and eventually, they relent. The doors close.

When I'm sure no one is listening, I press my face close to his, and I tell him the secret. "I found him," I say.

PART THREE

The Future

Contents of a Box

It's the first Monday of winter break, and the doorbell rings. My parents are picking up Julian from the train station again, and I'm almost as excited to see him as they are.

But this doorbell is not them. I walk evenly down the steps, and peer through the peephole of the front door, and I'm not surprised to see him there.

I've left him a letter.

Rather, I've left Carlton Evers a letter, delivered through the lawyer of the trust.

I knew it would get to Caleb, eventually, when he came back for the money.

And so I'm not surprised when he shows back up, after weeks of rumors, standing on my front porch.

He looks, suddenly, like an adult. I see Mia in the car behind him. I'd heard he came back to his house, when his mother got arrested for the concealment of a body. Caleb said there were no other options, and maybe he thought that was true, but I saw another way. I took action.

I couldn't live with someone else's secrets like that. And I don't think Eve would have let me live, knowing I held her secrets in my hands.

Caleb had told me about the cameras. About the fact that he was driving, yes, but I knew where they were heading. I knew they'd taken Sean's car to sell, too, and that the cameras would show his mother following behind him. A sliver of evidence, to get the investigation moving. I didn't know what would happen next. He said it was self-defense, but she still covered up a death.

I didn't go to see him, when I heard he was back. I had said what needed to be said, done what needed to be done. I had already found what I'd been looking for.

So now he stands here, the car full of luggage, and I know he's leaving for good this time.

"I came to apologize," he says.

I run through the list of things he could apologize for: lying to me, leaving me—twice—letting me believe he was dead. "And to thank you. You were right. There was another way."

"I told you there was. You needed to trust me."

"You're right," he says. "I did. I do. I don't know if you can understand this, but I had been betrayed by everyone who I trusted, and it spilled over to you. You didn't deserve that. Or the things I said to you."

I accept his apology, but his words linger. This lack of trust, filtering to the rest of his life. And look where it got us.

"What's going to happen? To you?" I ask.

He shrugs. "I don't know yet. But I've been talking to

the lawyers about testifying. About deals. There are different possibilities." They haven't charged him with anything yet, so I had to hope there was a chance they would not.

I nod. There's unfinished business, and my dad had told me this could take months, years, to play out. I heard, through my parents, that, since Caleb's return with his father, they were adding to the list of his mother's charges— charges of perjury, at the very least, from the case years ago. It would take time to resolve, I knew.

Police had been searching for Sean's body in the Pine Barrens, but they'd yet to find anything, and his mother wasn't talking.

For Caleb, it was just beginning. But this part wasn't my story, anymore.

"Where are you going?" I ask, looking at the car beyond.

"With my dad," he says.

I had heard, through school, through rumors and the spin everyone put on the story, that Caleb, now officially an adult, would be granted temporary custody of Mia. That the money would still be his, but that there was a death certificate to undo, a mess of paperwork to sort through. And so Caleb is, in a sense, still a ghost. Existing neither here nor there.

But the person on my porch is real. And I remember, again, that I loved him once.

"Come in," I say. "I have some of your things."

I lead him upstairs, where I've kept the fragments that led me to him. The shoebox, with the *D* on it, the photos of him and his father, from years earlier. The Swiss Army knife, found in his attic, that I kept as I swam through the river. The seashell. His house key. And last, the pictures of us.

"Jessa," he starts, and how can anyone begin to even say it? To sum it all up, in a box? In a sentence?

How can I absolve him, and myself, for all of it?

"I know," I say.

The Birds

You know you're near when you can hear them.

The gulls.

They call loudly, from the distance, in the summer.

In the winter, there are fewer of them, and the sound is fainter, but they're still there. Coming in from the north, to replace the ones who fly south. A permanent fixture.

I crack the car window, out of habit, like I'm waiting for them. And when I hear the first call, I know I'm there.

I'm at the beach, and I'm alone, because it's still cold. It's just me and the birds, and I don't mind it.

I wrap my jacket tighter around myself as the wind blows up off the ocean, the sand getting caught in my hair.

In the distance, I see a single shape, running from the direction of the pink hotel. He's not the most graceful, and he looks like he's about to keel over, but he keeps a steady, even pace. He slows when he approaches, the sound of his steps growing louder, along with his breathing.

"I thought I broke you of beach runs," I call over my shoulder.

He holds up his finger, bends over, rests his hands on his thighs to catch his breath. "I'm determined not to lose next time," he says.

I laugh. "Lose to who?" Because Caleb is leaving. I know they've seen each other, because they live back to back. I'm sure they had their own things to work out.

"To you, Jessa," he says. "What, you scared to race again next summer?"

"No, I'm not scared," I say.

"Anyway," he says, "baseball season starts soon. And I really do need to stay in shape." He looks back down the beach. "God, that run really is the devil."

"I know it is," I say, "and it doesn't really get any easier, for the record."

"Noted, and noticed. What are you doing today?" he asks, changing the subject, but I'm not ready for it. Not for this question. Not for an answer.

"My big plan is to do this," I say, gesturing to the beach. "Oh, and Julian's coming home tonight. So we'll probably have family time."

He waits for a few minutes, then says, "I'd join you in the whole watching-the-ocean-and-thinking-about-life thing, but I'm kind of gross right now. So, I'll see you?"

I smile over my shoulder. "See you," I say.

I watch him walk back over the dunes, to the wooden steps.

In the next few months, he'll be hearing from colleges. In less than a year, he'll be gone. I don't know how much time we have. I don't know what will happen between then and now. I don't know whether it's worth the risk.

I don't know whether I can ever trust myself with some-one again, whether I'll feel the need to hold back, pull back, always wondering if I'm getting the truth.

But I do know certain things about Max. And I know things about myself now, too.

He looks back once, and I wave, caught, not bothering to hide it. He laughs as he walks away.

It feels like the start of something here. Still, I worry we're already too close to an end.

Except maybe it goes farther back, our beginning. Maybe it was a month ago, on the side of the river, hidden by the trees. Or maybe the start was that day over the summer in a field, looking for Saturn. Or the moment on the bridge back in the spring, when he held me, and I fell. Maybe it's even earlier. Him in my kitchen, with my brother, when I gave him a drink.

No, my brother said, in warning.

Yes, I think.

A Blue Sky

It's three days after Christmas, and the sky is a clear, deceptive blue. There's no snow on the ground. It could be spring, if not for the trees missing the leaves. It could be summer, if I lie on my back, looking straight up.

Which I'm now doing.

Julian looks at me funny from the sliding glass doors to the kitchen, but he doesn't say anything. He knocks on the window, holds up a mug of hot chocolate, offering. But I shake my head and go back to the sky.

My phone dings beside me. It's an email from a store, no signed name. But I feel the smile growing. I can't stop it.

It's a gift for an app that's less than two dollars. It's the perfect gift.

It's a night sky app. I download it onto my phone and hold it toward the daytime sky, scanning it across the horizon. And my screen lights up with all the things I can't see, that are there anyway.

"What are you doing?" Julian asks.

"Look," I say, and he tips his head to the sky. "Perseus."

"Um," he says.

"You can't see it," I say. "But it's there. It's still there."

"If you say so, Jessa," he says.

I catch Julian staring up at the sky, his eyes squinting, and I say, "Hey, Julian, was it worth it? All the years of baseball games and practices and clinics?"

He tilts his head, confused.

"I mean, are you happy?"

He grins. "Well, I do hate it when I lose. Or when I have a crappy outing. But yeah, Jessa, I love the game. Being on a team. The good days. Yes, it was worth it." Then he laughs. "You know, no one's ever asked me that before."

"Huh," I say.

"Don't stay out too long," he says. "It's colder than it seems."

Julian closes the door, but he leaves me the hot chocolate. I sigh, and I take it.

Then I sit up and send Max a message: *I hear you can see Saturn tonight.*

This is a lie. I don't know whether you can see Saturn tonight. But I've made up my mind, and I hope this means that he has, too.

He writes back: *I know just the place.*

I don't even wait for dusk. I know it's coming, but I'm too early. Still, I bundle up in layers. A jacket, a scarf, a hat, gloves. "I'm taking the car," I call to Julian, and I don't give him a chance to complain.

I pull into the parking lot, empty except for one other

car—old, broken in, familiar. I have to go through a group of trees before the field, and at first I don't see him.

But then I do. He's lying on his back between the goalposts, holding his phone to the sky, just as I was doing earlier.

He sits up when he hears my footsteps, and the look on his face almost kills me. The unrestrained smile, holding back nothing.

"You're here early," he says.

"So are you," I say.

I'm all nervous, anxious, contained energy, and it has nowhere to go. And so I don't wait, not any longer. I'm sure this time. It's not the moment, or the setting, or the fact that we are missing someone else. It's him. It's Max.

I close the gap between us, and I kiss him. I feel him smiling in the second before he kisses me back. His hand at the side of my face, his fingers in my hair. Everything that makes Max *Max*.

When I pull back, I feel like the world should be changed somehow, but it's eerily the same. The world is silent. Max is silent. Even the wind has died down.

"Everything is so still," I say, feeling the calm settle through me as well, now that I'm here, sitting beside him—decided on something.

He looks off into the distance. "Right now we're hurtling through space at sixty-seven thousand miles an hour. We're practically flying."

I turn my head to face him, scrunch up my nose, laugh. "Why do you know that?"

He grins, cuts his eyes to me, to see my reaction. "I have a thing about space. I'm thinking about studying astronomy."

I can't stop the smile that spreads across my face. I lean closer. "What else don't I know about you, Max?"

"Wait and see."

Acknowledgments

Thank you to everyone who helped take this project from idea to finished book:

My agent, Sarah Davies, for all the guidance and support on each and every project.

My editor, Emily Easton, whom I've had the privilege of working with on six books now!

Phoebe Yeh, Samantha Gentry, and the entire team at Crown Books for Young Readers/Random House. I'm so fortunate to work with you all.

My critique partners, who are always willing to brainstorm ideas and talk through plots. Thank you to Megan Shepherd, Ashley Elston, Elle Cosimano, and Romily Bernard for the insightful feedback, support, and friendship.

And last, as always, thank you to my family.

About the Author

Megan Miranda is the acclaimed author of *The Safest Lies* and the adult national bestseller *All the Missing Girls*. She has also written several other young adult and adult novels, including *Fracture, Vengeance, Hysteria, Soulprint*, and *The Perfect Stranger*. She lives in North Carolina with her husband and two children. You can follow Megan on Facebook at @AuthorMeganMiranda, or on Instagram and Twitter at @MeganLMiranda.

Read on for an extract from

THE SAFEST LIES

MEGAN MIRANDA

Kelsey has lived most of her life in a shadow of suspicion, raised to see danger everywhere. Her mother hasn't set foot outside their front door in seventeen years, since she escaped from her kidnappers.

Kelsey knows she's supposed to keep a low profile and stay off the grid for their protection, but that plan is shattered when her dramatic car accident and rescue by classmate Ryan Baker sparks media coverage.

A few days later, she arrives home to find her mother missing. And now someone is coming for her. The truth about the past may end up being the most dangerous thing of all . . .

CHAPTER 1

The black iron gates used to be my favorite thing about the house.

Back when I was younger, they reminded me of secret gardens and hidden treasures, all the great mysteries I had read about in children's books.

This was the setting of fairy tales. The vegetation creeping upward in places, ivy and weeds tangling with the bars, and the way they'd light up in a storm, encircling the house—a stark surprise against the darkness.

And we were on the inside.

It was better to see it from this direction, on the way out. It looked different as I grew older. From the other side, through a different filter. A glance over my shoulder as I walked away, and all I could see were the cameras over the entrances. The sterile, boxed walls of the house beyond. The shadow behind the tinted window.

I didn't realize, for a long time, that *this* was the secret.

Still, there was a familiarity to the iron gates, and I couldn't help tapping them as I passed each morning, a routine goodbye as I left for the day. In the summer, the bars would be hot from the sun. And in the winter, when I was bundled up in wool, sometimes I'd feel a spark underneath the cold, like I could sense the current of electricity that was running through the top.

Mostly, though, they felt like home.

Today, my palm came away damp, coated with morning dew. Everything glistened in the mountain sunrise.

Now that I was beyond the gates, and because I saw my mother's shadow, there was a routine I was supposed to stick to:

Check the backseat through the windows before unlocking the car door.

Start the car and count to twenty so the engine had time to settle.

Wave to my mother, watching from the front window.

Two hands on the wheel as I navigated the unpaved driveway made of gravel, and then the winding mountain roads on the way to school.

The rest of the day was a tally of hours, a routine I knew by heart. Swap this Wednesday for any other Wednesday and nobody would notice. My mother said there's a safety to routine, but I didn't exactly agree. Routines could be learned. Routines could be *predicted*. But it would be a mistake to say that. Honestly, it was a mistake to even *think* that.

Here was the rest of my Wednesday routine:

Arrive at school early enough to get a parking spot near a streetlight, since I'd be leaving late. Avoid the crowded hallway, hope Mr. Graham opened his classroom early. Claim my seat in the back of math class, and coast through the day, mostly unnoticed.

Mostly.

My books were already out and I'd just about finished the morning problems when Ryan Baker swept into class.

"Hey, Kelsey," he said as he slid into his seat, just as the bell rang.

"Hi, Ryan," I said. This was also part of the routine. Ryan looked the way Ryan always looked, which was: brown hair that never fell the same way twice; legs too long for the desk beneath him, so they stretched under the seat in front or to the aisle between us (today: aisle); jeans, brown lace-up boots, T-shirt. Autumn in Vermont meant a sweatshirt for me, but apparently Ryan hadn't gotten there yet.

Today he was wearing a dark blue shirt that said VOLUNTEER, and he caught me staring. I didn't know if it was supposed to be ironic or not.

His fingers drummed on the desk. His knee bounced in the aisle.

I almost asked him, on impulse, but then Mr. Graham called me up to the board for a problem, and Ryan started drawing on his wrist with blue ink, and by the time I returned to my seat, the moment had passed.

First period was mostly quiet and mostly still. People yawned, people stretched, occasionally someone rested their head on their desk and hoped Mr. Graham didn't notice. Everyone slowly came to life over the span of ninety minutes.

But Ryan always seemed the opposite—all coiled energy, even at eight a.m. Rushing into class, his leg bouncing under his desk, his hands continually drawing patterns. His energy was contagious. So by the time the bell rang, I was the one coiled to jump. I'd spring from my seat, wave goodbye, head down the hall toward English, and pretend we hadn't once shared the most embarrassing conversation of my life.

The rest of the daily routine: English, lunch, science, history. Faces I'd grown accustomed to seeing over the last two years. Names I knew well, people I knew casually. The day passing by in a comfortable string of sameness. Blink too long and you might miss it.

Wednesday also meant tutoring after school to meet the volunteer component for graduation. Since I was a year ahead of most everyone in my grade, taking mostly senior classes, this was the easiest way to fulfill it.

Today I was scheduled to start with Leo Johnson, a senior taking sophomore science who I kind of knew from the Lodge. *Kind of knew* because (a) Leo was the type of person that everyone kind of knew, and (b) Ryan and I shared a shift at the Lodge twice a week over the summer, and they were friends. Which meant when Leo came in, he would occasionally nod at me, and even less occasionally mention me by name.

He dropped his notebook on the table across from me. "Hi, my name is Leo, and I'm failing." He flashed me a smile.

"Yeah, hi, we know each other already."

He slouched, narrowing his eyes. "Yes, but did you also know I was failing?"

"Seeing as you're assigned to be here after school on a Wednesday, I kind of assumed. Even more telling that you didn't bring any books."

He tipped his head to the side and scrunched up his mouth like he was thinking something through.

I looked at the clock. Only two minutes had passed. He didn't even have a pencil. "Look, I get credit whether I help you or we just sit here staring at each other. Just let me know which you prefer."

He stifled a laugh. "Okay, Kelsey Thomas," he said. "I get it now." He gestured to my stack of textbooks. "Let's do this. I'm told I do need to pass this class for graduation."

Leo turned out not to be the worst student in the world, though he was possibly the most easily distracted. He paused to talk to any person walking by the library entrance, and he checked the clock every five minutes or so.

His head shot up again an hour into our session when he heard footsteps in the hall, and he called, "Hey, Baker!" even though it was the library and he echoed. Leo was the type who didn't mind the attention—good or bad.

Ryan slowed at the library entrance but didn't quite stop. "Gotta run. Later, man." Then his eye caught mine, and he lifted his hand in a half wave. "Bye, Kelsey."

I half raised my hand in response.

Leo laughed under his breath. When I looked back at him, he was still grinning.

"What?"

"Nothing."

I felt my face heating up. I gripped the pencil harder and jabbed it at the paper, waiting for Leo to refocus on the problem.

Thanks to my mother, I was way ahead in terms of school material. But I was too far behind in everything else. I assumed this was how Leo must've felt, staring at these problems like they were written in a code he'd never seen before.

This was the code of high school. I had yet to crack it.

* * *

Leo and I both got our credit forms signed by the librarian, who took off just as fast as we did, locking up behind us.

"Been a pleasure, Kelsey," Leo said as he flew by, a gust of wind as I rifled through my purse for my phone.

The evening routine: call my mom, grab a soda, drive straight home.

"On my way," I said when she picked up.

"See you soon," she said. Her voice was like music. A homing device. I heard dishes in the background and knew she had already started dinner. This was her routine, too.

I hung up, and Leo was gone. The librarian was gone. The halls were silent and empty, except for the hum of the vending machines tucked into the corner. I slid a crisp dollar from my wallet, fed it to the machine. The gears churned, and in the emptiness, I started imagining all the things I could not see.

I felt myself taking note of the exits, an old habit: the front double doors through the lobby, the fire exits at the end of each hall, the windows off any classroom that had been left unlocked. . . .

I shook the thought, grabbed the soda, and jogged out the double front doors, my steps echoing, my keys jangling in my purse. I kept jogging until I made it to the ring of light around my car in the nearly empty lot.

It was twilight, and there was a breeze kicking in

through the mountains, and the shadows of the surrounding trees within the overhead lights looked a
lot like the shadows of the black metal gates at home,
when they were lit up in a thunderstorm.

I ran through the morning routine again, in reverse:
check the backseat, start the engine, let it warm up.
My phone in my bag, my bag beside me, nothing but
gnats and mist caught in the headlights.

This was a good day. This was a normal day. A blur
in a string of others, passing in typical fashion.

The reflectors on the double yellow line caught my
headlights on the drive with a predictable regularity,
almost hypnotic.

October came with a chill at night, and I wished I'd
brought my coat. I leaned forward, turned the dial to
hot, pressed the on button, and listened to the rush
of air surging toward the vents as I leaned back in
my seat.

A burst of heat.
A flash of light.
The world in motion.

I didn't know the air could scream.

CHAPTER 2

*D*on't *be afraid.*

The voice sounded far away, like it had to travel through water, or glass, before it reached me. And then there was that static—a radio? White noise, crackling like electricity, singeing my nerves.

You're okay.

Warm fingers at my neck, and the voice, getting sharper. My limbs were too heavy, like I'd fallen asleep with an arm and a leg hanging off the edge of my bed, and now everything tingled with pins and needles— sluggish and removed—as I tried to shift positions. My eyelids fluttered as I searched for the muted walls of my room.

"Can you hear me?" A voice that was not mine, not my mother's, not Jan's—but familiar nonetheless. A guy's voice. *Not my bedroom.*

I opened my eyes, and nothing made sense—not the feeling of blood rushing in the wrong direction, or the lack of gravity where it should've been, or my dark hair, falling in a cascade across my face. Not the sound of my own breathing echoing inside my head, or the scent of burning rubber, or the dull thudding behind my eyelids, which I'd opted to close again.

But.

Don't be afraid. You're okay.

Okay.

"Hey, I'm going to get you out of here. Everything's fine."

Everything's fine. I repeated it to myself, like my mother would do. But even as I let the words roll through my mind, like soft blankets tucked up to my chin, I felt the fear starting up, creeping slowly inside.

"Where am I?" I asked. There was a pressure in my head, a stiffness through my neck and shoulders, a subtle throbbing in my joints as my limbs were coming back to life.

"Thank God." The voice was coming from behind me somewhere. Vaguely familiar. But before I could latch on to it, something mechanical and high-pitched started whirring in the distance. The static—sharper now, and clearer.

"What's that?" I asked.

"You're okay. Don't panic."

Which meant that (a) I probably was not okay, and (b) I probably had reason to panic.

I attempted to twist around, but a strap cut across my lap and my chest, and metal pressed painfully up against my side, and when I attempted to push my hair out of my face, I could only see white billowing in front of my face, like a sheet. I was trapped.

Not okay.

Reason to panic.

Out. Get out.

I pushed against the metal for leverage as my breath started coming too fast.

The other person sucked in a breath, wrapped an arm around the seat to still me. "Also," he said, "don't move."

His arm was shaking. *I* was shaking.

There were other voices now, farther away, and the humming of the equipment grew louder. "Coming down," someone called.

"Okay," the voice called back. And then to me, "Listen, you're okay, you've been in an accident, but we're going to get you out now. It'll be a little loud is all."

I was in an accident? *The bend of the road and the reflectors in the double yellow line. Headlights, and I cut the wheel, and the sound of metal—*

Oh God, how long had I been here? Had my mom tried to call? Was she panicking already, unable to reach me? I pushed my hair aside again, tucking it into my collar. I moved my arms around, feeling for my bag. Best I could tell, I was hanging—kind of diagonally and forward, and my purse had been on the seat beside me. So that would mean . . .

I reached my arms over my head, but the metal was

too close, warped and bent, and I couldn't feel any bag. "Really," he said. "Don't. Move."

"I need my purse. I need my phone. I need to call my mom." My breath hitched. He didn't understand. I had to tell her I was okay. *You're okay.*

"We'll call her in a few minutes. But you need to keep still for now. What's your name?"

"Kelsey," I said.

A pause, and then, "Kelsey Thomas?"

"Yes." Someone who knew me, then. Must be someone from school. Or the Lodge, or the neighborhood, maybe. I strained to look in the rearview mirror, which was closer to me than it should've been. The world appeared disjointed.

The mirror was cracked and askew—I could see branches, the rock making up the wall in the side of the mountain, but not my rescuer's face. "Ryan," he said, as if he understood I was grasping for something. "Baker," he added.

"Ryan from my math class?" I asked, which was only one of the many things I could've said, but it was the first in my head, and the first out of my mouth.

A slow, steady breath. "Yeah. Ryan from your math class."

I was surrounded by metal and white pillows, and I was presumably upside down, but I could wiggle my toes, and I could breathe, and I could think, and I was having a conversation with Ryan Baker from my math class, so I tallied off the things I was not: paralyzed;

suffocating; unconscious; dead. My mother said it made her feel better to list the things she *was*—always starting with *safe*—but I preferred to carve out my safety with a process of elimination.

"The other car?" I asked.

He sucked in a breath. "Kelsey, I'm going to cut you out of your seat belt, but not until they remove the back panel. It'll just take a minute."

A minute. The air bags were in my face, and I felt the first pinprick of panic—that I would suffocate here, or that the car would explode between this moment and the next. I grasped for the reassurance of Ryan's words—*you're okay*—but it was too late. The thought had already planted itself in my head. An explosion. A fire. All the ways I could die, flipping through my mind in rapid succession.

"Cut me out *now*."

"No, that's not a good idea."

Illogical fears, that's what my mother's therapist, Jan, would say. Not something that would actually happen. Remember the difference. I could move the air bags aside and I'd be fine. Ryan from my math class would cut my seat belt and I'd be out, and then I'd find my phone and call my mother and she'd list off the things that were okay before she got to the fact that I'd ruined the car.

I pressed down on the inflated air bags, pushing them lower, away from my face, to prove it to myself.

"Wait, Kelsey. Don't."

But his words were too late—I'd already gotten a glimpse of precisely what he didn't want me seeing, and all the air drained from my body.

There was absolutely nothing *fine* about it.

The windshield was gone. And there was nothing below me. No pavement, no rocks, no grass or tilted view down the road. There was *nothing*. I was hanging toward air. Air and distant rock and fog—

"Oh my God," I said. And suddenly, I was perfectly, completely oriented.

Behind me were rocks. To my side, I could just make out the rough thick bark of a branch. There was a leaf resting on the air bag, the tips browned and starting to curl with the changing weather. I heard something creak.

"Are we over the cliff? We are, aren't we? We're in a tree over the goddamn cliff!" My shaking hands fumbled for the buckle as the pinpoint of panic crossed over into full-out hyperventilation.

"I told you not to panic!"

"Get me out!"

His hands gripped my arms from behind. He was pressed up against the seat, and I heard his voice through the fabric in a low plea. "Please stop moving. *Please*. Do not do *anything* to move the car."

And if I wasn't panicking before—I certainly was *now*.

I let the hair fall over my face again, and I closed my eyes, and I gritted my teeth, and I tried to think of anything, *anything*, other than the fact that I was hanging, suspended from a branch, over the edge of a cliff.

Jan would call this a legitimate fear. Not like a meteor crashing into our house, or getting trapped inside the freezer in the basement, or being forced to talk to Cole—all of which were so unlikely as to never happen, and were therefore irrational. But *this*, this was a legitimate fear: a thing that might happen. I was hanging upside down from a car stuck in the branches of a tree hanging over the edge of a cliff. The only thing holding me in was the thin strip of cloth from a seat belt.

"How do I get out?" I shouted over the whirring behind us. "How the hell am I getting out of here?"

"They're cutting out the back windshield. Then I'll cut the seat belt and take you with me. I have a harness."

A harness. Oh God, we needed a harness.

"It's just you?" I asked.

"It's the safest plan," he mumbled.

Ryan from my math class was possibly the last person in the world I'd want in charge of this plan. Ryan Baker, who could not remember the difference between sine and cosine. Who tattooed meaningless, intricate patterns on the inside of his forearm with pen instead of taking notes each class. My future was in the hands of someone who didn't understand basic trigonometry. What if he got the angle wrong? Misjudged the timing? How could I trust someone who didn't understand the geometry of a right triangle?

This seat belt was strapped across my chest at a right angle. The branches and the car and the cliff—all angles. This was a goddamn real-world application.

Fear: I might die today. I might die a minute from now.

Worse: if I moved, I'd also potentially kill Ryan Baker.

"What the hell are you doing here?" I asked.

"I'm a volunteer firefighter."

"I want a real one," I said, my voice high and tight.

"I *am* a real one."

"A different one!"

"Trust me, I would not object. But I'm the lightest one. Least chance of making the car fall out of the tree."

And there it was: the car could fall. They knew it, too. They had to make a *plan* for it. Falling, dying, was a real thing that could really happen, right now.

"You're not even that *light*," I said. He was decidedly taller than me, broad-shouldered, more lean-muscled than bulky—but definitely not *light*. I felt tears forming at the corners of my eyes, and I tried to pray. *Please please please.* But the branch still creaked below us.

"We're going to be fine," he said. But he sounded like he was trying to convince himself, too.

I settled on the deep breathing that Jan taught my mom, and my mom taught me.

The car lurched, and I braced my hands on the steering wheel, my stomach settling as the car stilled, and then lurching again as it tilted, dangling precipitously.

Also from Penguin Books

'Do yourself a huge favour and grab this atmospheric, unique mystery' – *Bustle*

'An icily atmospheric story with a captivating hook . . . A pacy page-turner that packs a significant emotional punch' – *Guardian*

HOW DO YOU KNOW WHO TO TRUST WHEN YOU CAN'T EVEN TRUST YOURSELF?

I look at my hands. One of them says FLORA BE BRAVE.

Flora has anterograde amnesia. She can't remember anything day-to-day: the joke her friend made, the instructions her parents gave her, how old she is.

Then she kisses someone she shouldn't, and the next day she remembers it. It's the first time she's remembered anything since she was ten.

But the boy is gone. She thinks he's moved to the Arctic.

Will following him be the key to unlocking her memory? Who can she trust?